The Naive Wife

Rachel's Diary

UFUOMAEE

THE NAÏVE WIFE: RACHEL'S DIARY

Copyright © 2020 Ufuomaee

All rights reserved.

ISBN: 9798695344455

This novel is a work of fiction. The names, characters and incidents portrayed in it are the work of the author's imagination. Any resemblance to actual persons, living or dead, events or localities is entirely coincidental.

Photo credit: www.canva.com
Unless otherwise stated, all Scriptures referenced are from www.blueletterbible.org.

AUTHOR REVIEWS

"You constantly allow God use you to correct the misinformation and vices in our world today and you do it in such a way that everyone gets the point. You really are amazing!"
- Ifeoluwapo Alatishe -

"Ufuomaee is a realist (I love the fact that she includes happenings in the society in her stories, sensitive topics we don't like to talk about. For instance, of sexual abuse in the Church and home as portrayed in The Church Girl and Broken respectively). Ufuomaee has that magical power to keep her readers spellbound. I also love the fact that she writes from a Christian perspective."
- Jesutomilola Lasehinde -

"Truly, you are one of the few people I delight in reading their posts. You make the book so real, I sometimes see myself as one of the characters. And I've been blessed by your books. You have a unique style of portraying your characters. You give them life."
- Folashade Oguntoyinbo -

"Ufuomaee is an author that writes fiction as though it is real. A Christian not ashamed to put her values into writing and I find myself reading the Bible passages she puts at the beginning of her stories. A great author whom everyone needs to read from."
- Jimi Kate Darasimi -

DEDICATION

"And the Lord said, Simon, Simon, behold, Satan hath desired to have you, that he may sift you as wheat: But I have prayed for thee, that thy faith fail not: and when thou art converted, strengthen thy brethren" (Luke 22:31-32).

To all the Simons, who are anointed for ministry but are fallen and do bitterly weep; You shall rise again by the grace of God. Amen.

THE PROLOGUE

October 1st, 2014.

Dear Diary,

It's been a while since I wrote to you. I've just never been good at journaling, but I'm going to try because I feel I need someone to talk to and somewhere I can pour out all the emotion I'm feeling.

I met a man last year who I felt I really connected with. He was rather persistent and seemed to really get me. We started dating about a year ago actually, just days after my 32nd birthday, and by Christmas, he proposed. Honestly, I thought it was all moving too fast and wanted a long engagement so that I could get to know him more and really feel that we were in love.

Well, with the advice of my parents, we had a short engagement and got married on June 21st. So, I've been married to Doug, that's his name, for three and a half months now, and I suppose we're happy. But I still don't really think that we are in love, the way I always wanted to be with my husband. I don't want to say I made a mistake, because I really thought I was being led by God, but something does not seem right...

I've seen things, I've heard things, and I feel like I can't trust my husband. The other day, a friend of mine told me that she saw another woman in his car and they looked 'chummy', and she was very sure it's him. I didn't want to believe her, but when we were home watching TV last night, someone kept sending him messages, and I got curious and checked them. It was a girl or young lady, who had taken pictures of herself in his car and was sending them to him.

Of course, I confronted him about it, and he assured me that it was completely innocent. I had to tell him that I didn't like it at all, and he needs to keep boundaries to protect our marriage. I don't know if I got through to him. Honestly, he didn't seem moved, but I don't want to worry about that now...

The thing is, I'm pregnant. I suspected I was a few days ago and confirmed today at the clinic. I'm happy about it. I want this baby, but I can't help feeling like I'm not in the marriage I thought I was. We're just not the way we used to be. We don't really talk like that, and he definitely doesn't show the same interest in me nor give his attention like he used to. I'm sure it's not uncommon, so I don't want to say he's changed, but...

Anyway, I'm an aunty now. Rochelle got married last August and had a baby girl two months ago in America. They are still there and doing really well. They're supposed to be coming back this weekend.

Well, I just thought I should get my thoughts down, and maybe I'll get a better understanding and feel better about the things going on in my life. I hope to write soon. Later!

***

Rachel bites her lower lip, as she puts aside her pen. She'd hoped to write more, but a part of her is anxious about Doug stumbling on her diary and reading it. She closes the book, ignoring the itch to tear out the paper and burn it. She decides to hide the diary in an old suitcase and put it out of her mind.

After securing it away, she steps off the stool and takes a deep breath, exhaling slowly. She should pray, but that's something she's been doing less of these days. She can't help but feel let down by God. She had been expecting to feel ecstatically happy in her marriage, especially at this early stage. Didn't she seek His will? Didn't she pray? Didn't she obey?

Rachel's shoulders heave with another sigh. Where did she miss it? She shouldn't be having these feelings and doubts about someone she's supposed to spend the rest of her life with. *God, I think I made a mistake. What am I going to do? I feel so unhappy…*

She gives in to her need and cries out to God. It's all she can do. Going unto her knees, she prays that He will guide her and enlighten her path and give her the grace to do His will in her marriage. Through this brief fellowship, she remembers that, with Him, nothing is impossible. Rachel takes comfort in the scriptures, specifically 2 Corinthians chapter 12, verse 9, where He told Paul, *"My grace is sufficient for you, for My strength is made perfect in weakness…"*

CHAPTER ONE

"Do you take this man to be your lawfully wedded husband, to have and to hold, for better or worse, so help you, God?" the minister asks.

Rachel's beaming, looking at the handsome man before her. Her heart is racing with excitement at the prospect of becoming his wife. His dark eyes are piercing into hers and making her weak at the knees. How did she get so lucky?

With joy, she responds, "I do."

"With the powers vested in me, I now pronounce you, husband and wife! You may kiss your bride."

Rachel's lips long for the taste of his. They'd waited for this moment to seal their love with a kiss. He removes the veil from her face and leans in to plant a titillating kiss on her pink, puckered lips.

Their mouths connect, and she receives him. His tongue awakens her body, sending shivers down her spine and tingles to her tips... She always knew Ejike would be an amazing kisser.

As he pulls away to take a breath, she beholds the man she has married. He has a sweet smile on his face. But something isn't right. He looks different... *This is not Ejike.*

He looks concerned, as she seems to have gone rigid and pale. "Are you okay?" Doug asks.

Rachel wakes with a start, her heart racing over her weird

dream. *Where did that come from?* Feelings of guilt arise in her as she realises the meaning. A deep sense of loss and foreboding lingers at the revelation that she married the wrong man. She turns her head to observe Doug snoring loudly beside her. Turning her gaze up at the ceiling, she lets the salty tears fall from her eyes. Her dream was not the nightmare; her life is. *When will the nightmare end?*

***

"Rachel, did you hear what I said?"

Rachel looks at her husband, trying to process his request. She swallows and nods.

"So, what do you think?"

"I think it's too risky now. We have a baby coming, and I'd rather we save the money."

"But this is better, don't you see? It's an investment, which will provide for the child, and us, later."

She slowly shakes her head. "Setting up a studio will cost much more than that. It's not just about the rent. What about the equipment and all? You can't use all the money from our wedding to set this up. Before we see the returns…"

"Look, I'm not the only one bringing money. Nike has small money saved up, and we're going to get an investor too. But if we don't put something down now, we'll lose the space."

"Please, Doug. I don't like it. You'd be tying up our money when we really need the cash… I think after the baby --"

"You're not listening, Rachel. We still have six months until the baby comes. If there's a time to invest, it's now."

Rachel rubs her head, exasperated. "It's a lot of money. What if it doesn't work out?"

"I knew it. You don't believe in me. That's what this is all about. I'm your husband. Why don't you trust me for once?!"

Trust is earned! Rachel resists the urge to shout out her thoughts. She rather looks at the frustrated man before her.

"Look, it's my decision to make, and I'm making it for the family!"

"You dare not! That's *our* money! And we have a baby coming! We're not even the ones paying my medical fees…"

"I'm just trying to make a little more money for us…and we won't have to rely on your family so much."

"You have a job… If…"

"What useless job?! You don't even have a clue!"

Rachel takes some breaths. The conversation has quickly taken a turn for the worse, the way most of their conversations go these days. They can't ever seem to see eye to eye.

"Like I said, I don't need your permission."

His eyes are daring, and hers burn with anger. He will do what he wants. She couldn't stop him before, when he decided to quit at the radio station, putting her name to shame. Angry tears burn at her eyes, fighting for release. She turns away from him.

"Do what you feel is best," she mutters as she walks away.

***

"Hey, y'all! How's it going? Are you getting in the spirit of the season? Anything getting you down? Don't worry… Call in and **Ask Rachel**! I'm with you for the next hour, as we talk life, relationships, family, and faith," Rachel speaks into the microphone, adjusting her headset as she settles into her programme.

She hopes it will be a slow day today, so she can play more love songs, instead of answering lots of questions from her listeners. She has been getting quite a few of those days lately. And more and more, with the challenges in her marriage, she's feeling inadequate to advise anyone on their relationship. She closes her eyes and prays that God will give her renewed passion for this ministry and her marriage.

"There's this song that's been on my heart lately... I have a feeling someone out there needs to hear it, so let me kick off today with Yolanda Adams, as she sings "This Too Shall Pass...""

Rachel takes off her headset as the music plays. Dongjap is looking at her, the care in his face unmistakable.

"Are you okay, Rache?" he asks.

She forces a smile as she looks up at him. "I'm fine, thanks. Sorry, just a bit tired."

"You know, you can take some time off... Until you feel more like yourself again."

She shakes her head. "I don't want that... It will pass," she beams up at him. "How are you?"

"I'm good," he responds with a casual nod.

She puts on her headset again and tries to get back in the mood. She begins to talk over the gospel track, encouraging her listeners, and herself, that there's no trial they are going through that is unique to them, and that God's grace is always sufficient to see them through any storm.

The phone lights up with a call, and she picks it. "Hey, caller! Where you calling from?"

"Hi, Rachel. I'm Abiola from Lagos Island."

"Nice to have you on the show, Abiola. Do you have a question for me?"

"Yes, I do. I really needed to hear that song today. I've been going through so much in my marriage...and I need some advice."

"I'm here to help... What's the problem?"

"My husband doesn't have a job. He has been out of work for almost two years now. He was actually sacked for embezzlement, and it has been hard for him to get work anywhere else. It's my small business that has been keeping us afloat and paying for our children's fees..."

"I'm so sorry to hear that."

"That wouldn't even be so bad if he didn't keep trying to

control how I run my business and taking money from it to invest in small projects he wants to do. He feels like, because I'm his wife, he has as much, if not more say, in my business, and it is affecting me seriously! I want to honour him as my husband, but he is making it very hard to respect him. I am so afraid that we will lose everything."

"Wow! That's a tough problem to have, Abiola. I thank God for the wisdom He has given to you to manage your business and support your family. I can also tell that you love and respect your husband very much, which is why you have borne with him for so long. I pray He will give you more grace."

"Amen! But please, what can I do? I really need some advice."

"I think you need to take Jesus' advice to be wise as a serpent and gentle as a dove. In regard to your business, you must be very wise and vigilant. Handle it like a business woman, and let your husband know, in no uncertain terms, that you are the CEO, and he is not even an employee. Unless he wants you to hand over the business to him, knowing that it is what has kept your family surviving, then he better let you handle it the way you deem fit."

"Okay..."

"But you are still his wife, so as much as you can, you need to show gentleness and respect for him. Do not neglect to honour your duty to him as a wife, which includes giving him unconditional respect and support. Even if he isn't pulling his weight at home, respect and help him because where he is down, you need to cover for him. Tables have a way of turning, so don't let the fact that you are prospering in your business give you occasion to disrespect him."

"I understand."

"You will need prayer and wisdom to know when to be hard and when to be soft. He won't always understand, especially if he has a very misogynist mind that makes him feel superior for being the man. But if you continue to show him love and respect, while standing your ground where your business is concerned, he will soon come to respect you for it. If he is so unreasonable, though, you may need to call in your elders to help resolve the situation. I hope you understand me."

"Yeah…"

"It's not everything you can handle by yourself. Knowing when you need help and outside intervention is very important. The main thing is that everything is done with wisdom, grace, and love. May God help you, sister."

"Thank you, Rachel. I actually feel a bit better. I'll pray on how to deal with him and love him. God bless you."

"Amen, and you! Thanks for calling."

***

The television is on, and the moving pictures are acting out a drama, but Rachel isn't listening nor watching. The volume is on low, as she tries to gather her thoughts.

It's 9pm, and she has not heard from Doug since he left home for work in the morning. She'd sent him a message in the afternoon, asking what he would like for dinner, but the message, though delivered, still appears unread. He also didn't pick up when she tried calling twice in the evening.

Rachel sighs, wondering when her husband will get home. She'd prepared a native soup for him and packaged and kept it in the fridge. Wraps of poundo yam laid in a cooler, waiting for when he would return. Her own plates have been washed and put away already, so all she can do now is wait.

She thinks back to her show earlier today and the advice she'd given her caller, Abiola. She'd felt, at the time, that their situations, though quite different, were relatable. She did feel anxious at the prospect of Doug managing their finances. He had not proven himself to be reliable nor trustworthy. But she realises now that unless she allows him the opportunity to fail, he would never really be able to show himself as capable.

She needs to exercise more trust and faith in him, as the head of their home, she concedes. Even if she doesn't agree with his decisions. At least, her family are happy to support them, as needed. They are luckier than most.

Feeling repentant, she picks up her phone to send her husband a message via WhatsApp.

"*Hey, babe. When you coming home? I made efo riro soup with poundo yam.*"

The message is delivered, and moments later, the blue ticks, which indicate that it has been read, appear. Soon after, Rachel can see that Doug is typing a response.

"*I'm fine. I ate out. Still busy. Will be back later.*"

"*Okay, dear. I also wanted to let you know that I'm sorry for my attitude earlier. If you really believe the studio would be a good investment for us now, I support you. Love you.*"

The message delivers, but the blue ticks don't appear. Rachel sighs, as she drops her phone on the coffee table. She picks up the remote control and increases the volume on the television.

CHAPTER TWO

At just over three months pregnant, Rachel's clothes are starting to feel too snug and tight, telling of her expectancy. She smiles at the little bump she sees in the mirror, as she dresses to go to the radio station. It's taking her longer to get ready each morning, due to the struggle to find something to wear.

She settles on a floral print, cocktail dress she hasn't worn in years. With the accompanying belt, she looks cute and not obviously pregnant. She's only told Dongjap of her expectancy, anticipating that, soon, her undeniable baby bump would make the announcement for her at the studio. After applying some light make-up, she slips into a comfortable pair of sandals and makes her way downstairs.

Upon sighting her husband on the sofa, eyes transfixed on a TV programme, she asks the obvious, "You haven't gone yet?"

Doug shakes his head in response, not regarding her nor her question. She sees that the lunch she'd packed for him is already consumed, with the container uncovered on the centre table.

Rachel heads into the kitchen, where she toasts egg and bread for a quick breakfast. She settles down at the dining table with a mug of tea, catching a glimpse of the programme on Africa Magic that's captured her husband's attention.

She's a little concerned as to why he hasn't gone to work yet, seeing as his usual hours are 9 to 5pm.

"I hope no problem," she mutters, hoping he would clue her in.

"I'm going soon. Just want to finish this."

An unsatisfactory response, but making a deal about it would only cause an argument. She decides to drop the matter. Her eyes fall on the wall clock, which reads 10:05am. She needs to leave soon to make the Monday morning meeting at 11am. She finishes her breakfast and takes her prenatal vitamins with a glass of water.

"Alright, dear. I'll see you later," she says, going to kiss him goodbye. He raises his head briefly for the kiss, before returning his attention to his show.

Rachel can't but look back at the TV screen, wondering of what importance the programme is.

***

The 9am alarm sounds again, stirring Rachel from her sleep. She reaches out to switch it off at last, feeling a resolve to get out of bed. It's her day off, and she can afford to sleep in longer, but the alarm reminds her that she needs to have breakfast so she can take her prenatal vitamins. Lazily, she rises from bed and stretches.

She can hear the TV going downstairs, a not too strange occurrence lately, as Doug has taken to leaving for work at random times of the day. She can't help but feel concerned about his commitment and performance at the firm her father connected him to. As a Development Officer, he's charged with meeting clients and securing contracts, so perhaps he doesn't need to be at the office at 9am every day. But, at home watching TV hardly sounds productive either, she thinks.

She slips on a robe and goes downstairs. At the bottom of the stairs, she greets him, "Good morning."

He turns to look at her and mutters, "Good morning,

dear."

He's in a good mood today. Best not to spoil it with criticism or too much enquiry. "I'm making plantain and egg for breakfast. You want some?"

"Sure."

In the kitchen, she starts making the meal. She's surprised when she feels his arms around her waist and a soft kiss on her cheek. She smiles.

"How's baby?" he asks.

She nods. "Baby's fine, thanks. How are you?"

"I'm fine."

She turns to get four eggs from the fridge. "Cool. What about your studio? Did you get the property you wanted?"

"Not yet."

"Oh… No problem, I hope."

"Nike pulled out on the deal. He thinks it might be 419… We're still looking, though."

"Okay… Well, better to be sure," Rachel smiles, her eyes betraying her relief.

"I'm thinking of asking your dad to join as an investor. We will definitely need more capital. Can you talk to him for me?"

That explains his pleasant and affectionate tones… Rachel swallows. "Why don't you email him and copy me? I think it's best you approach him yourself, and I can just put in a supportive word."

"Okay. We're still working on the proposal. Thanks, babe."

As he heads back to the living room, she feels the need to ask, "No work, today?"

"I have a client I'm seeing on the island this morning. From there, I'll go to the office."

Rachel nods in understanding. "Okay. Food will be ready soon."

***

"Mrs Olumide," the gynaecologists says. "How are you doing today?"

Rachel smiles contentedly. "I'm fine, thanks."

"Any complaints since we last saw you?"

She shakes her head. "No... Well, I've been experiencing some sensitivity with my teeth. I don't know if it's related."

The doctor nods. "Yes, some women experience dental problems during their maternity period. Now would be a good time to visit your dentist, or I can refer you to one if you want."

"Okay, thanks. I'd appreciate the referral."

"Sure," Dr Sangosanya replies. "Alright, why don't you lie down, let me listen to your baby's heartbeat? Then we can go over the results from your previous screening."

"Okay, ma. Thanks," Rachel says, taking position on the examination bed in her gynae's office.

"A good strong heartbeat," the gynaecologist says, smiling at Rachel. "Next time you come, we will perform an ultrasound to examine the baby's development and organs. You'll also be able to see the sex of your baby."

"Oh, great."

"I know it's hard for men to attend all the appointments, but it would be good if your husband can accompany you for this one."

"Yeah. I'll schedule it with him."

"Perfect," the gynaecologist beams.

Rachel sighs as she walks out of her doctor's appointment. All her tests came out well. The only thing is that she would need to take extra iron, to compensate for anaemia. Dr Sangosanya also gave her some dietary recommendations so that her prenatal vitamins will be more effective.

***

Lying alone on her sofa, the lights dimmed, and the stereo playing some Norah Jones, Rachel rubs her rounding stomach and muses on her life. It's 8:30pm, but Doug hasn't returned from work. Neither has he sent her a message asking how she's doing, though she'd informed him of her doctor's appointment in the afternoon.

She really shouldn't let it get to her. He's obviously busy. At least they enjoyed a lovely breakfast together in the morning.

The only thing is that she's feeling lonely. But that will soon change when the baby comes. She will have someone to shower with so much love and attention. She can't wait, she thinks, as a smile spreads across her face.

Her phone rings with a call, and she stretches her hand to retrieve it from the centre table. It's Doug. She smiles, encouraged that he called.

"Hey, babe…" she greets.

"Hi, dear. How are you?"

"I'm fine. How are you?"

"I'm good. I'm out with Nike. We're checking out a few places for the studio. I'll be back later. Just wanted you to know."

"Okay, hon. Stay safe. See you later."

"Okay, dear. Bye."

Rachel feels better after Doug's call. Now she knows she'll be home alone for longer, she wants to make a few calls. She decides to call Rochelle first.

"Hi, Rache," Rochelle answers, sounding jolly.

"Hey, how are you?"

"I'm good. How are you and the baby?"

"We're good too. Thanks!"

"What's up?"

"Ummm… Nothing much. Just chilling. Thought I should holla."

"Awww…thanks. We're good. Still trying to get into a new routine with Jen. At least, we're able to sleep at night now."

"Yeah… That's good. How's Ekene coping?"

"Oh, he's awesome. He's so hands on, I've actually suggested to him to stay home and watch Jen, and I can go out and get the bacon," Rochelle giggles, and Rachel joins in.

"That's great! I'll come over this weekend and see you guys."

"Sure. Thanks, Rachel. I'll chat you up later."

"Aight, bye."

Rachel cuts the call and ponders on her brief conversation with her half-sister. Rochelle sounded so happy, and Ekene is so supportive. They are indeed a good couple, she surmises.

She looks through her phone contacts, wondering who else to catch up with. Rachel comes across an old message from Bose, planning a meet up after her return from her honeymoon. Unfortunately, life got too busy, and they never did get together. She decides to call her.

"Hey, girl… How *nau?*" Rachel says cheerfully when Bose picks the call.

"*I dey, oh.* How are you, Mrs Olumide?" Bose teases.

Rachel laughs aloud. "I'm good, oh. We thank God. It's been too long. How you doing?"

"I'm fine, dear. Just been hustling and looking for Mr Right…"

"*Eh*, what about Nonye?"

"*Mtcheew*," Bose hisses. "That one? Forget him, *jo!*"

"Really? You guys broke up? What happened *nau?*"

"What did I do? I just suggested that maybe we take things to the next level. I mean, we've been dating for almost two years…"

"Hmmm…"

"See how the guy just ghosted me! Just like that. He can't pick his call or return my calls or messages. I even went to his house, and I know he was at home, 'cause his car was in the driveway, but the security said he wasn't home. *Mtcheew! Abeg, I don fashi his side.*"

16

"So sorry, dear. I didn't know…"

"*I for tell you*… I just didn't want to believe it at first. You know, we were supposed to hang out. It was about that time."

"I think maybe he was feeling pressured, since Doug and I just got married."

"Yeah, whatever… Anyway, what's new with you?"

"Well, Doug and I are expecting…" Rachel says.

"Haaaa!!! Congratulations, Rachel! When did you find out?"

"Ummm… It's been a couple of months actually. I'm sorry, I didn't tell you earlier."

"Oh, it's okay. I understand how sensitive these things are. Thank God, *sha*."

"Yes, oh. Thank God."

"*Shey* you're strong? Do you know the sex yet?"

"No, not yet. We'll find out next week. Sometimes, I can't believe it, y'know?" Rachel lets out a sigh. "Another human being is growing inside me."

"It's wonderful! I'm really happy for you, Rache. How's Doug?"

"He's fine."

"Okay, hon. Thanks for calling. I have to go and do something. I'll talk to you later."

"Okay, dear. Later."

***

The waiting room of the Maternity Ward at the Oakland Specialist Hospital is buzzing with vibrant young kids, playing with each other and the toys provided for them by the facility, as they wait for their mothers to be seen by the gynaecologists. Rachel is enjoying watching them play, imagining her own child among them. Three other expectant mothers are waiting to be seen, and she's the only first timer. Two women are accompanied by their partners; one couple looking particularly cosy. Rachel tears her gaze away.

She flicks through a magazine on the coffee table, and looks occasionally at the door, whenever it opens. She'd informed Doug of this appointment, and he'd assured her that he'd try his best to make it. But even though they were running late to see her, he was yet to show up. She heaves a sigh and flicks another page.

When she's tired of the magazine, she puts it down and picks up her phone instead. Visiting their chat on WhatsApp, she confirms that, not only has the reminder she sent this afternoon delivered, it has also been read. But there's no reply from Doug.

"Mrs Olumide," the nurse calls. "Dr Sangosanya will see you now."

Quickly, she types a message. *"Where are you? I'm going in now."*

When she's done with her appointment and the scan, she retrieves her phone from her handbag. There's a new message from Doug.

"Sorry, I couldn't make it. I got held up. How did it go?"

"It was fine. Baby's fine."

"Boy? Girl?"

"It's a boy 😊"

"Oh, wow! Great! See you later, babe."

"Yeah. Later."

Rachel puts her phone away and heads out to the parking lot. She spots the happy couple leaving with their two boisterous boys, and waves back at the beautiful woman, who waved in recognition. She fights a bout of jealousy and pity, as she unlocks her car and gets in.

CHAPTER THREE

Pulling into her parents' home at Osborne estate, Rachel feels nostalgia. Even in February, the lights from the Christmas before still hang on the pine trees that surround the compound. The grandiose, white building stands glorious with a new coat of paint. She can't help but feel a measure of pride as she drives into the driveway and parks her car among the other prestigious vehicles that adorn the space.

"Good afternoon, ma," she is greeted by the security men on duty.

"Good afternoon, Felix. Good afternoon, Akeem," she greets them by their names, waving as she makes her way to the front door of the mansion.

From an appraisal of the other cars in the driveway, she can see that Rochelle is also around. There are a couple other cars that she's unable to identify who owns, but she assumes that they belong to the wedding planner and one of Mrs Eden's close friends. Her assumption is confirmed when she enters the house, which is lively with servants working and laughter from the dining area where a meeting is being held with the wedding planner.

"So, what do you think of the selection?" the wedding planner asks, spreading her hand across the dining table where a spread of assorted cakes lay.

As Rachel approaches, she sees that the cakes are arranged

according to their bakeries, with four different options available. They all look so delicious and irresistible. As she draws nearer, a few eyes turn to acknowledge her presence.

"Hi, Rachel," the wedding planner greets, cheerfully. "Come and help us decide on the cakes for the traditional wedding and reception."

"Good afternoon, Funto," Rachel smiles and greets her. Going to Mrs Eden, she bends to kiss her cheek. "Good afternoon, mom." To the others, she beams, waves, and greets, "Good afternoon."

"I think the cakes from Aisha's Secrets are the best, but I particularly like the fruitcake from The Royal Bakery. It will be perfect for the traditional wedding," Mrs Eden says, ignoring the brief interruption, caused by Rachel and her entrance at the meeting.

"I agree," Rochelle seconds.

"Hmmm… I actually like the fondant cake by Burgeon. It's very rich!" Mrs Abimbola, a long-time friend of Mrs Eden, contributes.

Rachel fills a plate with a selection of cakes from each bakery and takes a seat next to Rochelle. She swoons quietly as she takes a bite of a red velvet sponge cake. She notes that the bakery responsible for the delicious cake hasn't yet been acknowledged. Before making a comment, she decides to try the other cakes first.

"Yes, they are all really great cakes," Funto says. "If only the bride was around to taste. When is she due to arrive, again?"

"Ryan and Cassie will be coming in a fortnight, two weeks before the trad wedding," Rochelle answers.

Rachel takes note of that information that she wasn't formerly privy to. She and Ryan are not particularly close, and if not for a message the wedding planner sent about the cake tasting, she wouldn't have been aware of this meeting. Though she'd tried to keep in the loop of plans, she seems to always be the last to know what's happening.

As the meeting goes on, Rachel makes minimal contributions. She spends more time listening and observing, hoping for an opportunity to participate in her half-brother's wedding, though most of the details have already been ironed out. They eventually settle on the cakes by Aisha's Secrets and The Royal Bakery for the reception and traditional wedding, respectively, a decision with which Rachel is pleased.

After the meeting, Rachel goes upstairs to greet her father, who's in his quarters, probably watching sports. She knocks and hears his response to "Enter."

"Hi, Daddy," she beams, and he smiles back.

"Hi, Rachel! How are you?"

She goes over to hug him. "I'm fine, Dad."

"Wow, you're very big now. How many months?"

"I'm 24 weeks plus, so about six months now."

"Wonderful! You look beautiful."

"Thanks, Dad!" Rachel takes a seat beside him on the sofa. "How are you?"

He sighs as he responds, "I'm fine. What about Doug?"

"He's okay..."

"He didn't come with you?"

"No, he had to work."

"Hmmm..." Chief Eden mutters. "I've been meaning to talk to you about that. Is everything okay with Doug?"

"I don't know what you mean..."

"Well, Henry called me the other day complaining about him. He said he has not been meeting targets and is constantly giving excuses. He feels like no one can talk to him, because he carries himself like the boss, even talking back to Henry. I'm quite surprised."

"Oh, wow... I did notice his attitude towards work slipping, but I just wanted to believe he was still on top of things."

Chief Eden shakes his head. "Henry is a very patient man, so I know he must really have been frustrated to come back to me with that report. I don't think Doug can continue working there... I just don't understand what is happening with him."

"I'm so sorry, Dad. Please, let me talk to him. I'm sure he'll apologise and change."

"Hmmm..." was all Chief Eden could utter.

***

Rachel returns home from her visit feeling anxious about her imminent conversation with Doug. She's surprised to find that he is at home and asleep on the sofa, with the TV blaring. She immediately moves to turn it down, before switching it off.

"Hey, I was watching that," Doug mumbles, stirring from sleep.

Rachel doesn't switch it back on but decides to put aside the remote control. "Doug, we need to talk."

"Please, give me the remote."

She hands it to him and watches as he puts the TV back on. The commentary on the ongoing football match continues.

"I met with my dad today..." Rachel begins, hoping that would grab his attention.

"Oh..." And it does. Doug looks at her expectantly.

"Mr Henry called him to talk about your performance at work..."

"Oh..." His expression changes. "What did he say?"

"Not good things... That you've been rude and not taking the work seriously."

"Hmmm... He said I've been rude?"

"Yeah, that you don't listen and even talk back to him. Why would you do that?"

Doug hisses. "Please... I'm tired of that place, *jo*! They don't even appreciate what I do. *Abeg*, leave it..."

Rachel's surprised by his dismissive attitude. "Doug, my dad went out on a limb for you, getting you that job! Why are you behaving like this?"

"Are you the one driving hours every day to work and chasing clients up and down?! And for what? The job doesn't even pay *sef*... I bring ideas about how they can be more effective, but it's only to be delivering proposals that they know. It's okay. I'll just quit."

"*What?!*"

"It's okay, Rachel. Just leave it. I'll set up my own studio, and we'll be fine. This 9 to 5 is not my thing, *abeg*."

Rachel is dumbstruck, not even knowing how to respond to Doug. But he doesn't give her the opportunity as he increases the volume of the TV set. She marvels, *what kind of ungrateful, irresponsible human being is this?*

✱✱✱

"Jesus told the Parable of the Talents to let us know that, though we all have different giftings and abilities, one thing is demanded of us..." The preacher pauses and looks about the hall. "We must bear fruit. We must bring back a profit to our master. Whatever our talent is, wastefulness of it could be our biggest sin! When we compare ourselves to others and get depressed or complacent because of how bad or well we think we are doing compared to others, we also commit a big sin against ourselves. Children of God, our competition is with ourselves. It is important for us to know our talents and the will for God in our lives so we can use them to His glory! I pray that none of us shall hear those dreaded words, "*cast ye the unprofitable servant into outer darkness.*" Let's pray!"

Rachel and Doug bow their heads as the preacher leads the congregation in a prayer. The lesson is profound, and all are considering their lives, whether they have discovered their talents and are using them profitably to God's glory or whether they are still ignorant of God's will in that regard. It is something Rachel has pondered on many times before, and she felt she'd discovered her talent when she'd discovered her love for teaching and counselling. She'd been even more sure of it when she'd gotten the coveted job at Urban Fm, and was convinced all the more when the relationship counselling show she'd pitched to the MD had been approved, following her qualification as a marriage counsellor.

But now, she is not so sure. She is newly married, yet she feels miserable half the time. All the advice she'd dished out to others while single seem to be mocking her in her own marriage. But her marriage is still young, and she'd been warned that it wouldn't be easy. Maybe this *is* her talent, and her current trial is just a test of faith. Afterall, isn't marriage ministry? No, she's not going to despair. She would just have to work on herself and keep building her home in love.

On the drive back home, Doug seems to be lost in thought. The silence in the car, though common, feels unusual today. Rachel feels the need to break it, to work on their communication and relationship.

"You okay, babe?" she asks.

Doug turns and looks at her, before he sighs. "Yeah," he says, with a nod.

"I thought it was a good service today," she continues, trying on a smile.

"Hm hmm," he mutters. "Me too. It's making me think about my talent."

"Oh, yeah… How so?"

"Well, my job at the firm was definitely not it, for one. I really believe my calling is in producing, like I was doing at Urban Fm."

"Oh," Rachel sighs.

"I shouldn't have accepted the job and quit at the radio."

"So, why did you?"

Doug turns and eyes Rachel, shaking his head as he turns back to face the road. "Why are you acting clueless? Was I supposed to say no to your dad when he was offering me a job that paid more? Chief Henry even promised I'd be earning double after six months…"

Rachel looks out of the window, hurt by Doug's accusatory tone. She'd been in favour of the job offer at the time, but she remembered leaving the decision up to him. And she'd definitely not expected him to leave the station without serving out his notice! Her boss had been quite pissed off about that.

She turns back to look at Doug. "So, what do you want to do now?"

Doug shrugs. "Can you have a word with them at the studio?" He turns to look at Rachel, the resemblance of a smile on his face. Rachel's shock is almost tangible. "I mean, ultimately, I'd like to run my own studio. But in the meantime, I'd appreciate the job experience and exposure. Plus, it's more income for us…"

Rachel swallows, struggling to form the right words to express her disagreement. "I don't think that's going to happen, Doug…"

Doug rolls his eyes and sighs deeply. "Here we go again…"

"You can't expect them to just give you your job back!" Rachel retorts, unable to keep the annoyance from her voice.

"I'm sure they'll understand, once you let them know you're pregnant, and we need the extra money…"

"Doug, you didn't even serve out your notice! You left them hanging, and Dongjap had to cover for you!"

"All I'm saying is ask. Will it hurt?" Doug looks at her pointedly.

Rachel heaves a sigh and shrugs. "Okay," she says, turning to look out of the window.

She can't help feeling bad as she realises that she really doesn't want Doug to get his job back at the radio station. Even though she doubts the possibility, it still fills her with dread and embarrassment, thinking about them working in the same environment and potentially having to make excuses for him. No, Doug working at Urban Fm would be a really bad idea!

CHAPTER FOUR

"Hi Rachel, this is Ngozi from Ojota."

"Hi Ngozi, thanks for calling into the show. What would you like to **Ask Rachel**?"

"What is a woman to do when her husband doesn't love her?"

"Hmmm… Are you asking because you feel unloved in your marriage?"

"Yes. I am convinced my husband doesn't love me. In fact, he told me so."

Rachel holds back a gasp. "Oh, my dear. That must have been painful for you. But, are you sure he wasn't joking?"

"I'm sure. He says it often. He said that he only married me because of my wide hips because he thought it meant that I would give him lots of babies. We've been married for five years now, and we've tried everything, but still no baby. He said that he doesn't want to be married to me anymore."

"Oh, my God! That is awful. I'm so sorry about your situation."

"I don't know what to do. I've prayed and fasted. I've begged and cried. He doesn't even care. And he just told me that his girlfriend is pregnant. I guess I have to let him go… But I wanted to ask you. Is there anything more I can do?"

"Oh, no. Ngozi, you have really put up with a lot. What your husband has done is really terrible. And yes, unfortunately, it seems clear that he doesn't love you. How do you feel about yourself, though?"

"How do you mean?"

"I mean, are you happy with yourself, as a person? Do you care for and love yourself?"

"I don't know... I think so. I mean, I feel inadequate, especially about not being able to get pregnant."

"I really think loving yourself should be your focus right now. The Bible says we should love our neighbour as we love ourselves, and that assumes we already have a healthy love and respect for ourselves. We cannot give what we do not have. And with your husband shirking his responsibility and duty of love to you, you really need to make sure that YOU are fine, as an individual and a person."

"Okay. Are you saying I shouldn't worry about what my husband is doing?"

"Ummm... Yes...yes. I'm not saying it's not important, and you shouldn't pay attention and respond. I'm simply saying you need to take care of yourself *first*. You've suffered a lot, and you are worried about your marriage. But you're one-half of that equation. If you're unwell, mentally or spiritually, your marriage cannot be well. But if you are well, and loving yourself, then you're in a better position to do the needful, whatever it is, for your marriage."

"Hmmm... Like when they say "put on your mask first"?"

"Exactly! Just like that. I suspect you've been neglecting yourself, and you're probably stressed out about how to make your husband love you. Sincerely, there's nothing like desperation to kill romantic feelings. As absurd as it may sound, loving yourself and looking after yourself is a surer way to attract a man and keep him interested."

"Hmmm... Okay."

"But the truth is, you can't make anyone love you if they don't. No amount of manipulation nor scheming nor magic will work. But I just need you to realise that YOU are important and worth loving too. I'm sure when you remember that, you will know what to do about your husband. But first things first."

"Okay. Thanks, Rachel. I guess I wanted to know if I can leave him… I know God hates divorce."

"I really wish you'd focus on that good part first, which is loving yourself, and remembering how much you're loved by God. If your husband wants to leave, he is free to, as it is clear that he is an unbeliever. And if he leaves, you, my sister, are free, as the scripture tells us. Because we are called to peace, 1 Corinthians chapter seven, verse fifteen."

"Oh, okay. I'll check out the scripture. Thanks, Rachel. Can I call back if I have questions?"

"Anytime, Ngozi. I wish you well, sister. You are loved!"

✳✳✳

"Hmmm, that was one of your better shows," Dongjap says, when Rachel's show comes to an end.

Rachel takes off her headphones and smiles at him. She thinks so too. She's particularly pleased about the advice she gave Ngozi. It was a good reminder for her too, to remember that she's worthy of love and to rest in God's peace. "Thank you," she mutters.

As she gathers her things to leave, she remembers her husband's request. She hesitates and looks at Dongjap, who's sorting through some discs.

"Hey, Dj…" she stutters. He looks up at her, arching a brow. "Ummm… I want to ask you something."

He shrugs. "Sure, what is it?"

"Ummm, well, it's about…Doug."

Dongjap stops what he's doing to pay attention to Rachel. "Okay…?"

"He…he… Well, we were wondering if there's a chance for…"

"Not a chance in hell!" Dongjap interrupts.

29

"Let me finish, *nau*…"

"You want to know if he can come back to the station?" Rachel nods. "Not happening! But I have to hand it to the guy, he has some nerve!"

Rachel bows her head. "I know he left things in a bit of a mess, but… There's no but. I'm sorry. We kind of need the job, with me being pregnant and all…"

"Look, Rache… I'm doing all I can to keep your showtime. I mean, you haven't really been yourself, and your ratings have been low lately. The station manager has been gunning for your time slot! I'm not about to put my neck on the line for Doug too! I know you're pregnant, and I'm happy for you guys, but there are no free meals here. I'm sorry."

Rachel swallows. She's shocked about Dongjap's revelation about her show. She knew her ratings were down, but she never imagined that her show would be threatened. She nods her head. "I understand. Thanks for all you're doing for me. I'll try to do better myself. I'll let Doug know there's no vacancy."

Dongjap sighs and resumes his previous activity, while Rachel quietly leaves the studio. He looks at the door as it shuts behind her, unable to understand the sadness he feels for her. She'd lost her joy and vibrancy, and though many speculated why, he was sure the answer was the loser masquerading as her husband.

***

"Rachel!"

Rachel turns to see who is calling her name. She sees her Aunty Pat heading towards her, a big smile on her face. She pauses until the older woman gets to where she's standing with Doug. He throws on a smile when he recognises the elderly woman.

"Haaa… Rachel, see how you fine! Marriage suits you, oh…" Aunty Pat beams at the couple. "My in-law, how *nau?"*

Doug bows in greeting. *"Migwor,* Aunty!"

"Vrendoh!" she responds, and then winks at him. "You have done well, oh…" she chuckles as she rubs Rachel's protruding stomach. "I am seated over there. Make sure you come and greet me before you go."

"Yes, Aunty," they both respond, looking in the direction Aunty Pat pointed out; outside, under the canopies, close to the buffet area. The meaning is not lost on them that she is expecting something from them, especially as Doug had failed to seek her out first before making his marriage proposal, as she'd requested.

It's Ryan's traditional wedding day, and the whole compound is jampacked with wedding guests. The traditional ceremony is still ongoing inside the Eden mansion, and television screens stationed all around the compound ensure that every eye is able to witness the ceremony. All eyes are on the bride as she makes her way down the glorious stairway to the living area, where her husband, his family, and her relatives are already convened.

"Wow," Doug gasps and gawks. "So beautiful!"

Rachel nods, knowing how right he is. She remembers the first time she met Cassie on her own wedding day. She'd been taken aback by her stunning looks. But today, dressed in the Urhogbo native attire, made up like a queen, her long, blonde locks pinned back with jewels, she looks like a goddess.

Rachel looks over at the groom, and his eyes are transfixed on his bride. Sitting nearby, she observes Ekene and feels a wave of jealousy wash over her seeing how, at this very moment, his eyes and attention are on his own wife, making her feel like the most beautiful woman in the room. Rachel returns her gaze to look at Doug, but he has already left her side to get a better view of the bride and the ceremony. She sighs.

✳✳✳

"Wow! This is…incredible!" Bose marvels when she finally meets Rachel inside the grand wedding hall. "Your parents pulled out all the stops for this, oh…"

"Well, he is their first son!" Rachel laughs. The wedding is the biggest the Edens have thrown to date, and she knows it's partly due to Mrs Eden's effort to show off to their American in-laws, who flew over for the festivities. "Did you finally get a good parking spot?"

"Yes, I was lucky. Someone was driving out. Where's Doug?"

Rachel looks over at their special table, where he'd just been, expecting to see him. "I think he's probably rustling drinks for his friends. Come, we're seated over here."

Bose follows Rachel to their table and places her purse down on an unoccupied seat. She admires Rachel in her wedding attire, a special gold and blue fabric for the sisters of the groom. Her chosen design does well to accentuate all her curves.

"Pregnancy really looks good on you, Rache!"

Rachel beams. "Thank you!"

"Hey, Bose!" Doug greets fondly, arriving with a couple of new friends.

"Hey, Doug! Been a while… How *nau*?"

"*I dey oh*… You're looking sweet, *sha*."

Bose beams and strikes a pose. "When I never marry…"

Rachel looks between them, observing the rapport they share. Doug is back to his old charming self, and he introduces Bose to his friends seated at the table. Soon, they are all giggling.

Rachel's gaze wanders about the room, looking at the many guests that have turned up to celebrate with her family. In her heart, she knows she's looking out for a familiar face. She's not sure if he would have travelled for the wedding, and she'd never gathered the courage to ask about him. She'd hoped to see him at the traditional wedding, and when she didn't, she figured he might only show up for the white wedding and reception. Sadness fills her heart as she wonders if she'll ever see him again.

"Hey, sis…" Richard says, settling into the seat next to hers. He places two bottles of *Dom Perignon* on the table and smiles at her and Doug. "I thought you guys might need a top up."

"Aw, thanks, bro!" Doug says, grabbing a bottle.

Rachel smiles at her brother. "Thank you."

"What's up, sis? Can I get you anything?" Richard asks, looking her over. They haven't had much time to catch up since his return to the country about a week ago. Fortunately, he has plans to stick around after the wedding and set up a business in Lagos.

"I'm fine," Rachel says.

"When are you due?"

"Baby's due in May."

"Cool… So, another three months? Cool."

"Yeah, it's exciting," Rachel beams.

"You're delivering in the States, right?"

She nods. "Yeah… By God's grace."

"Is Rochelle travelling with you?"

"I doubt it. She has her hands full with Jennifer. Mom said she'll join me before I deliver, though."

"Oh, that's cool. I know Ryan plans to move back after his honeymoon. But, Ejike is still there, and I'm sure he'll be happy to help too."

Rachel feels butterflies at the mention of his name. She swallows. "Oh, how's he?"

"He's good. Very good, actually. He just got engaged over Valentine's. I hear they are planning to marry at Christmas."

"Oh…" Rachel's smile wanes, and she struggles to restore it. "I'm happy for him."

"Who are you talking about?" Doug turns and asks.

"Ejike… He's getting married," Richard replies.

"Oh, wow! How about that?" Doug chuckles. "Isn't it great news, Rache?"

"Yeah, I said so," she answers uneasily.

"Aight… Let me leave you guys! Chat later, Rache!"

After a brief hug, Richard leaves Rachel with her guests and an excited Doug.

"Hmmm… So, the player's finally settling down," Doug laughs, giving Rachel a side glance.

She says nothing but grabs a bottle of water to wash her parched throat.

CHAPTER FIVE

She's had this dream before. Even realising this, Rachel can't seem to break away from it. In fact, her anxiety increases at the prospect of the dream ending pre-maturely again.

His lips feel so soft and taste so sweet on hers. She parts hers wider for his tongue to penetrate deep. A thick hand falls over her waist before slowly caressing her stomach.

Rachel's eyes open as she realises that she's already awake, and her dream has become a daydream, though it's still dark out. She tries to fall asleep again, but the lingering hand won't let her.

Doug rubs his body against Rachel's, desirous to enjoy his wife. He nibbles on her neck, stimulating her from sleep. She'd gone to bed early last night, and he'd been randy. Something about weddings always seemed to make him horny.

"I'm sleeping…" Rachel grumbles. But it's far from the truth. She's aroused, but her desire is not for the man in her bed. Still, her hunger must be quenched. If not by her fantasy reaching its climatic conclusion, by her husband satisfying his desire and ultimately leaving her dissatisfied and sexually frustrated.

"You don't have to do anything…" he mumbles. "I'll be quick."

Rachel sighs as she turns to him. There's less disappointment when she doesn't try, but she's actually quite horny this morning, thanks to her dream. Maybe she will enjoy it, and maybe she too will come this time.

***

It was a good effort, but no luck on the climax. Doug has entered the bathroom, and she can hear the shower going. She decides to go to the spare bedroom across the hall to have her bath, as she often does after they've had sex. It's hard to call what they do 'making love'. So much is missing from the act, particularly the love part. But what can she do about it?

After their honeymoon, she'd expected that they would resume their counselling sessions with the pre-marital counsellor at her church, as they'd agreed to, but Doug had blatantly refused. And when she'd suggested continuing their counselling at his church instead, which they had chosen to attend as their family church, he'd also rejected that option. In his words, "*We don't need counselling. We're fine.*"

But now, as they dressed up to go to church for Ryan and Cassie's thanksgiving, she knew he couldn't be more wrong. There was definitely something unnatural about the way they related to each other. Sometimes, she wondered if it was just her, but it was getting harder to believe that he didn't feel it too. *This isn't normal.*

As they journey to the church, Rachel checks her phone for messages. She has a couple on WhatsApp and a few notifications on Facebook too. She smiles as she goes through them. She'd received quite a few likes and comments on the pictures she posted of the wedding yesterday.

A particular comment grabs her eye. It isn't so much the comment but the profile picture accompanying it. The name of the commentator is quite obscure, but something tells her that she knows exactly who C.N. Fury is. Instinctively, she clicks on his name to visit his profile.

The bigger view of his profile picture makes his handsome features more visible and confirms the owner of the account to be none other than Ejike Okafor. But why the obscure name?

His profile does not reveal much, owing to the fact that they are not Facebook friends. But, with 28 mutual friends, that just seems wrong. Plus, they are family, after all, Rachel appeases her conscience, as she does what she'd been desirous to do for a long time, and sends Ejike a friend request.

Returning to his original comment on her post, she likes it and responds with "*LOL!*" It feels so good to finally be in touch after such a long time.

***

Rachel's phone vibrates with a new notification, as the pastor delivers his inspirational message. She resists the urge to check it until it beeps again. Now, she's too curious and distracted, she decides she has to check it and respond to the enquirer.

"*Hey, Rache! How are you? It's been ages…*"

Rachel can't help the smile that spreads on her face nor her racing heart in her chest. She notices Doug turn to observe her and immediately mutes her phone, before putting it away in her handbag. She'll respond to Ejike later.

Later doesn't come soon enough. It feels like the longest day ever, as Rachel's mind keeps returning to her muted phone all day, distracting her from the post-nuptial ceremonies the Edens had planned. Finally, back in her bedroom, with Doug safely confined to the couch in the living room, where a football match is showing re-runs, she brings out of her phone to check her messages.

Apart from a couple of new comments on her pictures, she hasn't received any other message from Ejike. Disappointed, she takes the time to go through his Facebook timeline and albums. His relationship status reveals that he is 'Engaged to Ifeoma Eke'. Naturally, or foolishly, Rachel follows the link to learn more about Ejike's chosen bride.

Ifeoma is indeed beautiful, but her profile doesn't reveal much. Rachel is not bold enough to add her as a friend, thereby revealing to Ejike that she'd been snooping on his profile. With a sigh, she opens their chat and reads his message again. There's nothing to be read into it. He's certainly no longer in love with her, as he'd expressed the last time she'd seen him... And that should mean it's now safe for them to reconnect.

"*Hi, Ejike. Yeah, it's been a while* 😊 *I'm good. How are you?*"

A few minutes pass, and then a beep.

"*I'm doing fine, Rachel. Happy to hear from you. And congrats to Ryan!*"

Rachel smiles as she reads his response. An old but good feeling fills her heart. "*Thank you. I hear congrats are in order for you too!*"

"😊 *thank you.*"

What more to say? It seems there's nothing more, so Rachel puts her phone away. Some minutes later, it beeps again. She brings it out to check.

"*Congratulations to you and Doug. Ekene said you guys are pregnant.*"

"*Yeah, we are. Thanks.*"

"*You excited?*"

"*Of course* 😊"

"*Cool.*"

A brief pause.

"*So, how's America? Which state are you in?*"

"*Chicago. It's pretty cool. Ever visited?*"

"*Yeah, well, our holiday home is in Cook County.*"

"*Oh, of course! So, are you planning on coming over to have your baby?*"

"Yup, that's the plan…"

"Nice one! I'll probably see you when you're in town…"

"Yeah, probably…"

"Well, it was nice catching up with you, Rache."

"Yep. And you."

"Don't be a stranger…"

"Okay :). Bye."

Rachel looks over her conversation with Ejike, wondering at the apprehension she's feeling. He'd suggested that they might see each other while she's in the States. Well, obviously, he can't have any romantic expectations, being engaged, and with her carrying Doug's baby. But still, the thought of seeing him again, and the knowledge that he's betrothed to another, hurts so much, she's scared to think about what that means.

***

Time is fast approaching for Rachel to travel to America for her baby's birth. Her visa is still valid from her last travel, but Doug is waiting to hear about his application. She has booked her ticket for the end of March, when she'll be 31 weeks, and Doug plans to join her in May, closer to her delivery date.

Today's her last show before her maternal leave starts, and Rachel's having mixed feelings about leaving the radio station for the next four months. Though she'll miss the work, her colleagues, and her listeners, she's excited about the break, the time to rest and shop in Chicago and prepare for her baby's arrival. However, she has a feeling that, even if her job is still available after her leave, she won't want to return. But she doesn't want to submit her notice now, not until she understands what she's feeling and knows what she's going to do.

Everyone's smiling at her, hugging and kissing her goodbye. A few people even bought her parting and congratulatory gifts, which take her by surprise. It's almost as though they also know that she won't be coming back. Few presenters who become mothers ever return to their employment at the studio. Yewande, however, is among the exception.

"Hey, kiddo!" the cheerful British-born and trained presenter, and the station's women's rights advocate, says, pulling Rachel in for a hug. "Take care of yourself, okay? Take as long as you need, and trust God to direct your steps."

It is as though she knows Rachel's inner plight. Tears break free from Rachel's eyes as she hugs her friend. "Thanks, Yewande."

"Motherhood is wonderful, so enjoy it. Don't ever let anyone make you feel bad for doing what you think is best for your kids and family. Just because they won't, doesn't mean you can't or shouldn't," Yewande adds with a wink.

And Rachel realises that her colleague is also an expectant mother, again. She can feel the slight bump against her protruding one. She beams at her and whispers, "Congratulations!"

Yewande beams. "You've got this!"

Rachel watches as Yewande walks away, feeling somehow strengthened. There's no need to worry, but there's every reason to be joyful. And with a smile on her face, she enters her studio to start her last show.

"Hey," Dongjap greets when she walks in.

"Hey," she replies, fighting off the emotions that are rising to the fore again. Of all the things and people to miss at the studio, she will miss him the most.

"You're ready for your show?"

"As ready as I'm going to be," Rachel sighs.

***

"That was a good show, Rache," Dongjap says after Rachel takes her headpiece off.

"Thanks! It got a bit emotional, though."

"It's understandable. Your listeners love you! You're

going to be missed."

"Awww, thanks," she beams, going to hug him.

Dongjap hugs Rachel tight. The one that got away from him... He closes his eyes and gives her a quick kiss on her forehead before releasing her.

Rachel looks at him, understanding his feeling and feeling a bit sad herself. "I will miss you," she says, truthfully.

Dongjap swallows and nods. Clearing his throat, he says, "I got you something..."

"You too?!" she frets.

He laughs. "I know you have everything you need, but it's the least I can do..."

"Aww, thanks, Dj. I wasn't expecting anything," she says, as she collects the wrapped gift.

"I'll miss you," he says, and they hug again. Pushing her away with a giggle, "Now, get out of here!"

Rachel giggles as she collects her things and scampers out of the studio. Closing the door behind her, she rubs her stomach and heaves a sigh. *God, I'm in Your hands...*

***

With only a day to go before her travel to the States, Rachel's all packed and ready. She collected a note from her doctor at her appointment this week, in case the airline has any concerns about her transatlantic travel, seeing as she has passed the 28 weeks recommended threshold for flying while pregnant. They have also received the feedback about Doug's application for a US visa. Though obviously disappointed, he didn't seem so bothered about the fact that he won't be able to join his wife as she delivers their baby.

"I'm working on a few things anyway, and I need to be around. It's no big deal. I'll get the house ready for you both," he'd said with a cheerful smile.

Today, as they drive out of their home, there's a certain peace in the air. Doug's taking his wife for a romantic dinner, their last chance before she travels out of the country for the next three months. He's excited at the freedom the next few months promise. This will be the peace before the chaos of parenthood and family life really begins when Rachel returns. His last *hurrah*, and he's not one to let opportunities go to waste...

Rachel's watching the cars as they race down the expressway, turn into busy streets and slow down at traffic lights. The air is light and breezy, as the sun sets on the horizon. She breathes in deeply, feeling relaxed all over.

She looks at Doug as he drives and observes that they are driving in the direction of her favourite Chinese restaurant. She'd been hoping for somewhere new, but when in doubt, Chinese food is always best, so she's pleased all the same. But they pass the restaurant and continue down the road.

"Oh," she mutters. "I thought we were going to Pearl Garden?"

"Nah... I want to try this new place," Doug replies with a smile.

Rache smiles back, relaxes in her seat, and watches as he drives and comes to a stop at a seafood restaurant/bar. She makes to come out, but he says, "Don't worry, I'll get it." She beams happily. This feels good, like the Doug she knew.

He leads her to the restaurant and opens the door. Rachel steps in and sees a banner across the room, bearing CONGRATULATIONS!!! The blue and yellow balloons and ribbons, and other smaller banners indicate that it's indeed a baby shower. In the same second, her friends and family arise to shout, "SURPRISE!!!"

"Oh my God!" Rachel turns to Doug, obviously astonished. "Wow! I had no idea!"

Doug hugs her and kisses her in the presence of their family. And Rachel hears the crowd swoon, "Awww..."

It's indeed a lovely surprise. Rachel has forgotten how thoughtful her husband can be. Today, she smiles and laughs and feels like a happily married, expectant mother. And

Doug is at his best, as the devoted husband who is in love with his wife.

CHAPTER SIX

Rachel hopes she looks fat, and not pregnant, in the navy-blue boubou she's wearing, as she stands in line at the immigration checking point at O'Hare International Airport. She's a bit nervous about being asked about her reason for travel to the States. She's heard too many stories of people being turned away at the US Borders. As she watches the immigration officers at work, she spots a lady that she thinks looks rather pleasant and hopes that her lot falls with her, as the line continues to move.

It's been a long night's journey, but with almost 18 hours and only one changeover at Frankfurt, it was one of the shortest routes to America she could have taken. Nevertheless, her feet are bearing the effects of the transatlantic flight, and she can't wait to get home and soak them in some warm water. She looks down and adjusts her gown, before returning her gaze to the family of three in front of her. She has been watching them since they got onto her connecting flight in Germany, some seven hours ago. She found their accent fascinating and admired their rapport.

The immigration officer she had her eyes on is suddenly free, and the young family heads over to be attended by her. Rachel sighs and looks anxiously at the older, Caucasian man who is now available to attend to her. She carries her hand luggage and strolls casually to his kiosk.

"Good morning, Sir," she greets cheerfully.

He gives her a small, strained smile, sticks his hand out, and says, "Your passport and boarding pass, please."

Rachel retrieves her passport, which also holds her boarding pass, from her handbag and slides it across the counter to the officer. She watches as he flips through the pages, obviously noting that she's made several trips to the US in the past, though none in recent years. A couple of times, he looks up at her face and back down at her passport, and she wonders how old her passport photo must be. She braces herself for a barrage of questions.

However, she's elated when, instead, he stamps her passport and pushes it across to her, before signalling for the next person to come forward. She beams with relief, collecting the document and putting it in her handbag. "Thanks," she mutters, as she walks quickly away.

***

Whenever she arrives at a foreign international airport, Rachel can't help but compare how advanced and well maintained they are compared to her home country's. She looks about in awe at the interior design of the O'Hare International Airport, which has had a make-over since her last visit to America a few years ago. The signs to the baggage claim area are clear, and she follows them, rolling her hand luggage on the moving walkway, rather than enjoying the leisurely ride.

At the conveyor belts, where the luggage from her flight is to arrive, she stands ready, with a trolley, to collect her baggage. The young, German family are across at the other end, and the little girl is hanging on to her mother's leg. The sight makes Rachel's heart flip. She'd really hoped to have a daughter first, but she's sure a little boy will be just as wonderful as a first child.

Rachel turns her gaze to the conveyor belt and searches for her suitcase. She'd packed a small one inside a big suitcase, as she expected to return with a lot of baggage, baby's things, and a few nice things for herself and her loved ones back home. Within minutes, she spots her bright pink suitcase and walks to meet it on its journey, reaching out to grab it from the conveyor belt.

"Please, let me," she hears and turns to see a handsome, Black American man pull at the handle of her suitcase with a little too much effort than was needed. He seems to notice and gently places the luggage aside, before lifting it unto her trolley. "It's lighter than it looks!"

Rachel beams, "Yeah, I know. I packed light. But thanks!"

"No problem, ma'am. My wife is also pregnant, and I hate to see a lady struggle."

"Awww, that's nice of you. Congrats to you both!"

"Thank you. Have a nice day, ma'am."

Rachel smiles as she pushes her trolley towards customs. So far so good. She'd prayed for favour on this trip, seeing as she would be travelling on her own, and so far, God has been awesome. She sighs as she continues to pray for a safe transit home.

After clearing customs, she will buy a sim pack and call home to let them know she got in safe. Then it's just a 20 minutes cab ride to her family townhouse at Lincoln Park. Happily, she pushes her trolley on, paying no mind to the police dogs and the custom officials that line her exit from the airport terminal.

***

Rachel walks through the doors at customs to enter the arrival lounge, where family and friends stand expectantly to welcome their loved ones. Some people are bearing signs with names for the passengers they are expecting, while a couple others are advertising their cab services. Rachel heads over to the kiosk where they are selling sim packs and calling cards and asks about their various prices. She feels a tap on her shoulder and instinctively holds her handbag tighter, while turning to look at the stranger seeking her attention.

"Hello, stranger," he says.

Rachel's eyes are wide with shock, and it seems as if her jaw has smacked the floor. She pulls it shut and swallows.

"Ejike?! What are you doing here?"

"Picking you up, of course! Surprised?" he asks, a grin adorning his face.

Rachel's still trying to get her heart to stop racing. She opens her mouth to breathe. "Yeah... How did you know...?"

Ejike slips his hands into the pockets of his black, cargo pants as he observes her reaction to him. "Richard told me you were coming alone and thought it would be good if I could meet you at the airport. I thought it was a great idea too, especially in your condition."

Rachel looks down at her bump, her hand following her eyes to caress it instinctively. She blushes and looks back up at Ejike. "Thank you. I told them I would take a cab. I'm quite used to travelling alone..."

Ejike raises a brow, his eyes moving from her bump to her eyes. Instead of arguing, he says, "You must be exhausted. Let me help you with your luggage."

"Ye...yeah," Rachel stutters, releasing her hold of the trolley so Ejike can push it. "But I need to get a sim pack."

"No problem. I'm waiting," he responds with a smile.

Ejike waits for her to complete her transaction and put the sim pack in her purse before he begins to push the trolley towards the elevators. She's one of those fortunate women who only carries her pregnancy on her stomach. If anything, she looks more beautiful to him in full bloom than she did when she was not pregnant. Well, she does walk a little awkwardly, no doubt because of the ball-like nature of her tummy, he thinks with a smile.

At the elevators, he pushes the button to go down to the

parking lot, while continuing to observe her from the corner of his eye. She's clearly nervous, as he is, but for the life of him, he can't figure out why. Maybe she's still sporting over his proclamation of love. He knew it might be a problem, but he hoped that since they had both evidently moved on, it wouldn't.

Clearing his throat, he says, "So, how was your flight?"

Rachel's relieved that Ejike has broken the silence. She'd been thinking of different things to say or ask to get them talking, but each time, she thinks better of it. She sighs and smiles at him. "It was great!"

He smiles at her. "That's good."

The elevator opens, and they enter to go down to the parking lot. The doors close, and the lift makes its way down.

"Thanks again for picking me up," she says nervously.

He chuckles and shakes his head. "You need to stop thanking me. We are family." His gaze is intent all of a sudden, as if he'd just spoken a revelation. But it was a realisation he had to come to terms with, one of the things that had made it easier for him to walk away from her. "You are family."

Rachel looks at him, their eyes meet, and there seems to be an unspoken understanding as they connect. She looks away, just as the elevator doors open at the underground parking garage. She swallows and nods. "Cool."

***

"Do you mind if I put the radio on?" Ejike asks as he drives out of his parking space.

Rachel shrugs, her eyes still admiring the interior of his Range Rover Sport. "No, I don't," she confirms.

Ejike selects one of his favourite stations that plays the latest pop tunes. They soon burst out of the parking garage and are greeted by a hot sun, high at noon. Rachel smiles as its heat and the sweet melody of John Legend's "All of Me" warm her body and soul. Even though the atmosphere is still cool, being the last Sunday in March, the brightness of the sun gives the feel of a hot summer's day. She looks about as Ejike drives on the expressway, enjoying the view, the music, and the company.

After a while, Rachel leans her head back hoping to sleep, but it evades her. She finds herself watching Ejike as he drives. He is clean shaven, as usual, and she admires the hard lines of his jaw. As he whistles to the music, she notices again what deep dimples he has. And as he swallows, her eyes are drawn to his Adam's apple. She breathes in, thinking what a beautiful man he is. With that thought established, she looks away, back at the road.

"You okay?" Ejike turns and asks.

"Yeah, I'm fine."

Then she remembers that she has forgotten to call home and alert her family of her safe arrival. She brings out her purse and gets the sim pack, opening it to retrieve her new sim. After inserting it into her phone, and adding her credit voucher, she looks up Doug's number and calls him. With Lagos ahead by six hours, it would be about 6:30pm there, which should be a good time to connect.

"Hello," his voice comes through.

"Hey, babe, it's me. I just got in."

"Oh, Rache! Thank God for journey mercies. How was your flight?"

"It was good, thanks. How are you?"

"I'm great, dear. This is your number, right?"

"Yeah, it is…"

"Okay, I'll buzz you later so we can chat. In the middle of something now. Okay?"

"No problem," Rachel says. Hesitantly, she adds, "Love you."

"Yeah, babe. Talk to you later!"

The line cuts, and she takes the phone from her ear. She decides to call her dad next. He's much more cheerful when he picks up. She tells him that Ejike picked her up, and they are on their way to the house. He's happy to hear it, and when she says, "I love you," he says it back.

Satisfied, Rachel puts her phone away. A look at the road ahead reveals that they are almost home. She can't wait to get in and take a nap. The foot treatment will have to wait till the evening.

Ejike helps her offload her luggage and carry them to the townhouse. He uses a key to open the door, much to Rachel's surprise. Silently, she follows him into the lavishly furnished abode, noting how fresh and clean it feels. Someone has cleaned this place up, she surmises. She'd planned to get a cleaning service to do that after she arrived.

After dropping her suitcase in the downstairs bedroom, Ejike returns to meet Rachel in the family lounge. She's admiring the new furniture Mrs Eden has chosen for the living area, and the new 55inch, ultra slim, curved TV. She turns to Ejike when he enters the room.

"Did you clean up?" she asks.

"I hired a company," he admits, sheepishly. "There's also food in the fridge. I did some shopping yesterday. I figured you'd be tired. There are enough native dishes in the freezer to last you three days, but I'll be back tomorrow morning to check on you."

Rachel swallows. "Oh, okay. You're leaving?" *What am I saying? Of course he's leaving.* She just didn't realise how much she would miss him. He nods. "Thank you! I mean it. Thanks! I didn't expect this."

Ejike beams. "No problem, Rache. Any time. Let me get your number so I can call you, and you can reach me any time, day or night, okay?"

Rachel nods and hands him her sim pack displaying her US number. She watches as he punches it into his phone, until hers rings with a call. He cuts it and pockets the phone.

"So, I'll see you later," he says, as he heads towards the

front door.

She follows after him. At the door, he turns, looks at her, and wraps his arms around her in a brotherly embrace. Rachel closes her eyes as she hugs him back, his cologne wafting to her nose. He soon releases her and backs away.

"Welcome to America, Rache," he mutters, before turning and walking to his car.

After watching him drive away, Rachel leans back on the door and lets out a really deep breath.

CHAPTER SEVEN

At the time Rachel called that evening, Doug had just received a call from Chief Eden to pay him a visit at the mansion that night. He was not prepared for that and sought to make himself ready to present his case for support. He was also a little anxious of what Chief might have to say. He could think of a few things he'd done recently that his in-law might have an issue with, so his anxiety was not for nothing.

Arriving at the mansion at about 7:30pm, he parks his 2011 Toyota FJ Cruiser, which Chief Eden had given him last year, next to the new midnight blue, Lexus SUV, Chief was now sporting. The older man's love for cars and expensive jeeps was as famous as his prowess in industry. Doug had his eye on the black Ford Mustang, parked in the shaded area, to one day inherit. He smiles as he walks past it to knock on the front door.

The house-help opens the door just as he gets to it, and Doug straightens his shoulders as he walks in. He heads towards the grand lounge the Edens use to entertain their guests and settles into one of the exquisite Italian sofas. While waiting, he decides to take some selfies in the decorated parlour.

On seeing Chief Eden climbing down the stairs to the lounge, he rises to his feet. "Good evening, sir."

"Hi, Doug," Chief replies and indicates for him to sit

down. He goes to settle next to Doug on the settee, placing his phone on the coffee table. He leans back and draws in a breath before looking at Doug. "How are you?"

"I'm very good, sir. How are you?"

"I'm okay. So, Rachel's gone to America…"

Doug sighs. "Yes, sir. I'm missing her already."

Chief smiles. "She'll be back soon. You'll be fine."

He nods and smiles. "Yes, sir."

Chief sighs. "So, I saw the email you sent me. I've been meaning to respond, but it's been a busy period for me."

"I understand, sir."

"I thought it would be good for us to talk now, especially as Rachel's away, and you have time to get a few things in order before she returns."

"Yeah, I was thinking the same thing…"

"Good. However, I feel we need to address what happened with Ogwo Petroleum… I was surprised when Henry called to tell me you'd quit," Chief says, observing Doug's reaction keenly.

"I'm sorry, sir. I know I should have come to you first. I just didn't feel like I was at my best there. I didn't feel challenged, and I didn't feel appreciated." He pauses, and Chief continues to wait patiently. Doug swallows. "Recently, I feel led by God to follow my passion. I want to produce music and shows. That's where my passion is. That's why I sent you that email to help us start up a studio. As you probably know, the entertainment industry is very lucrative, and I believe it would be a worthy investment." He sighs, believing he has delivered a good pitch.

Chief exhales. "The studio idea isn't bad. But I feel like you didn't appreciate why I placed you with Henry. Henry has many years' experience in starting up and sustaining businesses, and he is a very intelligent man. I thought you'd learn a lot from him and also prove your strengths too. I was really quite disappointed when he told me you were not taking his direction."

Doug looks down. "I'm sorry. It wasn't like that. I... I... I'm sorry."

"It's a bit hard for me now, because you haven't really shown that you are competent, so starting up a new enterprise with you is a great risk. You know, the Bible says that *"if you are faithful with the little things, you will be entrusted with much. But if you're not, no one will trust you with more."* Can you see my dilemma?"

"I can, sir," Doug swallows. "But I promise you, you will get the best of me. I'm about to become a father. I'm just thinking about my children. This means everything to me. And being my own boss will allow me to be more present with my family, which is very important to me."

Chief nods his head. "Okay..."

"I won't let you down, sir!"

"It's alright, Doug. I'll give you another chance to prove yourself. I looked through your proposal, and I have a few issues with it. I'll send you my feedback so you can work on it and come back to me with something more realistic."

Doug nods excitedly. "No problem, sir. Thank you."

"In the meantime, I have this property at Obalende that will be available from next month. Why don't you check it out, and see if it would be suitable for your studio?"

"Oh, wow! Thank you, sir! It will, I'm sure."

"Okay. Just check it out. Contact Gerald so he can take you there and give you access."

"Okay, sir. God bless you so much!"

Chief smiles. His phone rings, and he picks it up to look at the caller. "I have to take this."

Doug rises up. "No problem, sir. Thank you," he says, as he bows and exits the lounge, resisting the urge to jump and punch the air.

***

Ejike is still reeling from seeing Rachel again. He'd

convinced himself that he could do it, that he no longer had feelings for her, but today had proved him wrong. He would have to do his best to stay away, just so that his feelings do not deepen, not that he's afraid of doing something they would both regret. He is sure that he has enough self-control for such not to happen. And he cares too deeply for his fiancée to let it…

He looks at a photo of him with Ifeoma, framed on his desk, that they had taken on Valentine's Day. Her wide, white smile and the puppy dog look on his face as he beholds her, reminds him that they are meant to be, and he and Rachel were definitely not, and will never be. Picking it up for a closer look, he decides to call her.

"Hi, darling!" Ifeoma greets him with her usual feminine drawl.

"Hey, babe… Was just thinking of you. How are you?"

"Missing you!"

He chuckles. "I really needed to hear your voice right now… How soon can you come home?"

Ifeoma giggles. "Awww…poor baby! I should be back by tomorrow evening. I hate leaving you."

"Okay… No problem. I'll call you later. I have to get back to work."

"Okay, dear. I love you."

"I love you, too." Ejike cuts the call. He has nothing to worry about. What he has with Ifeoma is real… He's a very lucky man, and he is not about to ruin a good thing.

Placing the phone down on his desk, he returns his gaze to his desktop computer. Now, if he can just concentrate on the work to be done.

***

The three long beeps from the kitchen indicate that the microwave is done, and his dinner is warm. Doug rises up to collect his meal and a cold beer to wash it down.

As he eats, he remembers that he's supposed to call his

wife back. He checks his phone, and it's now 9:10pm, meaning it's ten past three in the afternoon in Chicago. He'll finish his meal and call her later.

About an hour later, when his tv programme finishes, he remembers that he still hasn't called Rachel. He picks up his phone and sees some notifications on his WhatsApp. A few of his contacts have commented on his new display picture, one of the photos he had taken at the Eden mansion that evening. He smiles as he reads and responds to the messages.

One of them is from a girl called Trisha that he had met a while back. They'd spoken for a while but nothing really came out of it, and it had just fizzled out. Maybe she's interested now.

"*Nice pad,*" she'd written.

He sends her a wide grin in response, followed by, "*Been a while. How are you?*"

***

Ejike looks at the silver standing clock on his desk, which tells him that it's five minutes to closing time. He runs his hand through his low-cut hair and wonders where the time has gone. Quickly, he completes the report he has been working on and saves it to read over and send in the morning. It was hard to get back into it, but he's glad he was finally able to focus on his work and tick something off on his to-do-list.

He'd normally have stayed later to continue working, especially as he has no plans with Ifeoma tonight, but his mind still feels heavy and tired. He wants to unwind and have a relaxing evening, so he packs up for the day and heads out of his office. He greets some colleagues on the way to the parking lot. They chit chat about some office gossip, but he really can't wait to be alone with his thoughts. Maybe he'd read a book or continue with his Bible study on the first book of Corinthians.

"You're okay, man?"

Ejike turns his attention to his friend and colleague, Matthew. "Uh? Yeah, yeah... Sorry, got things on my mind."

"Want to go for drinks and talk?"

"Nah, I'm good. I just need to catch up on some rest, I think."

"Sure, no probs. Later, man!"

Ejike waves goodnight as he turns in the direction of his parked car. As he gets into his car, his phone rings. He fumbles in his pocket and picks it up.

"Hi, Ejike. I hope this isn't a bad time."

"Oh, no. What's up, Rache?"

"I'm sorry. I feel real silly to call you about this, but I'm having a problem turning on this TV!" She giggles nervously and laughs when she hears him giggling too. "I don't suppose you know how...?"

Ejike laughs at the situation, feeling silly too. It was one of the things he'd planned to show her when he drove her home. However, he'd felt the need to leave her alone almost as soon as they'd arrived at the house that he'd rushed out without doing so. "No problem, Rache. I'll come over and talk you through."

"Do you live that close? Or is your office nearby? I don't mean to disturb you... In fact, you can actually just..."

"Will you relax, Rache? I'll be over in a minute. Have you eaten yet? Should I bring you something?"

Rachel beams, especially at the prospect of his company. "Actually, I am craving some peppersoup. I didn't see any in the freezer."

"No problem. I'll see you soon."

Ejike wonders about his changed mood, as he drives out of the parking lot. He suddenly feels light, happy, and excited. And something tells him that *this* is exactly what he wanted to do tonight...

***

Doug wakes up to the sound of a jingle playing as another show concludes on television. Checking the info, he realises that it's already after midnight. He had shut his eyes for just a while, hoping to get some rest before going out to meet Nike at the club. It is not too late to go out and meet him. But he has to do something now, so he's not bothered later.

The phone rings only twice before Rachel picks up.

"Hi, dear," she greets casually.

"Hey, babe. How are you doing?"

"I'm good. How are you?"

"I'm cool. I had some of the jollof rice. Quite tasty!"

"Thanks! You're welcome."

"Have you eaten?"

"Yeah, I had some toasted sandwiches for lunch. I haven't had dinner yet, though."

"Okay…" Some pause. "How's our boy kicking?"

Rachel smiles, and it carries into her voice. "Like a champ!"

Doug giggles. "Nice one! I wish I was there with you…"

"Yeah… It would have been nice."

"I hope you're not too lonely. When's your mom coming?"

"Next month, but I'll be fine until then."

"I don't think it's safe, dear. Can't you hire a live-in maid?"

"I guess… I planned on hiring a cleaner, but I'll see about a maid instead. She can help with cooking too."

"Good. I feel better." He yawns. "I'm so tired. You know it's late here…"

"Yeah, no problem. We'll talk tomorrow."

"Ok, dear. Love you!"

"Love you too," Rachel replies with a small smile.

Doug smiles as he puts his phone down. He hurries upstairs to take a quick shower before he heads out again. Nike said some Nollywood big names loved to frequent their chosen club, so he hoped to make some business connections tonight. Actually, he wouldn't mind making some personal ones too…

CHAPTER EIGHT

Rachel's a little apprehensive about Ejike coming over tonight. She feels some odd excitement down in her belly but tells herself it's because she likes his company, and she doesn't want to be all by herself on her first night in America. She is fine doing things for herself, but she can't deny the wisdom that she needs some taking care of in her condition.

Lying on the L-shaped sofa in the lounge, she looks out at the veranda, watching the tranquil neighbourhood. It's so still and peaceful out, with only a quiet motor cruising by every now and then. A low fence surrounds their own property amidst the affluent homes that share their street. In the distance, she sees the moon rising as the sun descends into the night.

From the headlights that appear on the road, she can tell that a vehicle is driving past her house. Except it doesn't, and the lights go out, and she hears the click sound of a car locking with an electronic key. Footsteps follow, and then her doorbell rings. It must be Ejike.

Rachel arises, slips on her house robe, and heads to the door. She puts on the light in the hallway and catches a glimpse of her reflection in the mirror. Her hair is looking a little rough, so she takes some time to smoothen the edges with her hands before opening the door to him.

He is tall and handsome, regal in his dark suit. She's taken back to the first moment she laid eyes on him in her father's house. His slow smile wakes her up to the realisation that she's been staring and blocking his access into her abode. Blushing, she moves aside.

"Sorry… I just wasn't expecting you to be looking so…so dressed up."

"Yeah, I came straight from work. And it's still a little nippy out, so I wore my jacket. It's nice and warm in here though," he says as he slips out of it, revealing firm abs and broad shoulders that strain at his white office shirt. Rachel now wishes he'd kept his jacket on. She swallows. "Here, I brought this for you."

Rachel collects the nylon bag from him and mutters, "Thanks." She opens it to see three containers of food, the fresh smell of tilapia peppersoup rising to her nose and stirring her hungry stomach. "Wow, smells good. Where did you get this?"

"There's this African Restaurant downtown. They do all sorts of native dishes. That's where I get most of my meals. It's not too far from my office, which is convenient."

"Cool!" Getting to the lounge, she places the nylon on the centre table and removes the three containers. "I see you also got goat meat peppersoup."

"Yeah, I wasn't sure which you'd prefer. I also thought you might like the other for breakfast with yam in the morning."

Hmmm… How thoughtful! "Nah! I don't want to eat alone. You came all this way. Won't you join me?" she asks, looking up at him and hoping he would say yes.

He beams. "Sure."

"Great! I'll get the plates," she says as she heads to the kitchen.

When she returns to the lounge, the television is already on, and Ejike is flicking through the stations. She dishes the soups into bowls and serves the yam slices into two plates, with some palm oil and sprinkles of salt, as is her native tradition for eating yam and peppersoup. When she's done, Ejike is still browsing the channels.

"Ummm… What do you want to watch?"

"Ummm… I don't really know. I like sitcoms and comedy shows."

"Okay, cool. There are a few on BET, so I'll just leave it here. By the way, this is how you switch the TV on and off," he says as he goes closer to show her on the remote control. The sweet fragrance of her Flowerbomb by Viktor & Rolf perfume tickles his nostrils and causes him to pause in appreciation. "This remote controls the decoder, the television, and the DVD player. All you have to do is power them at the wall, and press this button, and then this one."

"Oh, okay. Thanks! It looks so easy now."

Ejike smiles at her and settles down on a sofa perpendicular to her, to the left of the television. "Thanks for the food," he says, picking up the plate closest to him.

Rachel turns to him sharply, giving him a strange look. "Are you okay?! It is I who is thankful."

He laughs and shakes his head. "If you say so…"

She too giggles as she settles down to eat her meal.

"Hmmm… This is delicious!" Rachel moans. "I think I want this every day."

Ejike smiles. "*Afrikan Star* will do that to you. But there's nothing like eating at the restaurant. It almost feels like you're back home, in your mama's house."

"Really?! I'd love to go. I mean, if you don't mind, and you have the time. Just once would be nice."

Ejike looks at her and feels a little caution in his spirit. He wants that too, but is it really wise for them to be spending so much time together? And at a restaurant? He swallows and is taken in by her childish pleading eyes. "No problem."

"Yeah!!!" she rejoices playfully. "I'd like to try the catfish. *Hmmm…* This is so good!"

Ejike looks at her and back at his food. He never knew she was so vibrant and playful. He likes it, and it makes him want to stick around longer.

As they eat, a Black American sitcom plays on the TV, with occasional laughter from the audience. Rachel chuckles along, and Ejike smiles. He also loves the show, although the humour is not exactly 'Christian'. But what are the Christian alternatives? He'd learnt overtime to watch such programmes with a spiritual sieve. It's not everything he will agree with, but the realness of what they depict is, to him, the funniest element.

Rachel thinks Ejike is being a little quiet. But she has noticed that he's generally pensive, at least around her. He's one of those people who are hard to read, and while it can be very sexy, it's also a bit unnerving for her. But she's trying to relax in his company because he said they are family. And that they are. There's no need for there to be any weirdness between them, especially when she enjoys his company and is without an alternative.

Thinking of what to talk about, she remembers something that had caused her some pause earlier. "Why do you go by C.N. Fury on Facebook?"

Ejike turns to Rachel, a sheepish look on his face. He shrugs. "I love The Avengers."

Rachel raises a brow. *"Huh?"*

"Yeah, I'm a big fan of Marvel comics, and of Samuel L. Jackson too."

"Oh," she swallows. "I actually thought it might be something…else. It's a little *razz*, isn't it?" She stifles a giggle as she beholds the man before her. She'd never have pegged him for a fanatic.

Ejike giggles. "Actually, I decided not to use my real name because I had an issue with an obsessive ex… I changed it for a while, and it kinda stuck."

Rather than reply, Rachel nods. She's happy to learn

something new and personal about him. She sighs as she remembers another thing. How can he be here with her when he is engaged to someone else? Does his girlfriend know where he is? And if she does, doesn't she mind? It gives her some pause, and she wonders how to ask him about his relationship.

"Ummm," she mutters. "I hope I'm not keeping you from your fiancée?"

Ejike looks at her and shakes his head. "No, you're not."

"Everything okay, I hope…"

"Yeah, we're cool. She travelled for work."

"Oh, okay. What does she do?"

Ejike clears his throat, evidently nervous about discussing his relationship with Rachel. "She's a flight attendant with United Airlines."

"Oh…"

"Yeah… So, she's away a lot."

"Wow… How are you able to carry on a relationship?"

"We manage. In a way, it's good, because when we are together, we make the most of it… But it can be hard to synchronise sometimes, and we can go long periods without seeing each other."

"Oh, wow. I can't do that. Never been one for long distance relationships."

"Yeah, it's hard, I won't lie. But she's only doing that until we marry. She's eager to come home with me and set up a business in Nigeria."

"Oh, that's cool. At least, you agree and have a plan for the future. What's she into?"

"Fashion. She's also a fashion blogger, but she wants to set up a clothing line."

"That's great! I'm happy for you guys."

"Thank you."

Rachel's done with her soup and notices that Ejike is too. She rises up to carry the dishes to the kitchen.

"Please, let me," Ejike says, taking the plate from her.

"I'm not an invalid you know?!" Rachel objects.

"I know," he smiles but collects the plates with determination. "And we'd like to keep it that way…"

She can't help but smile at his rebuff. She lets out a sigh and leans back on the sofa. She can hear him washing the plates in the kitchen and marvels at what a considerate man he is. There's no sense at all that he is the player everyone makes him out to be. She wonders if she had him all wrong from the beginning.

He soon returns to the lounge, and she admires him as he walks down the hall to the living area, the sleeves of his shirt folded up, revealing thick, slightly hairy, fair arms. His shirt is still tucked into his trousers, and she notices how narrow his waist is. *Damn, he's fine!* She looks away as he draws closer.

"Okay, I guess I should show you how to operate the blinds before I go," he says when he gets to her.

"Oh… Which blinds? Isn't it just to close the curtains?"

"No, your dad installed blinds all over the house last year. They use remote control, and they serve aesthetic and security purposes. Come, let me show you."

Rachel rises up to meet him and looks at the small white remote in his hand, which she'd wrongly assumed was for the air conditioner. After he teaches her how to operate the blinds, he leads her down the hall to teach her how to set the security lights and alarm.

"Okay, thanks. But I'm a bit stumped about how you know so much about the house."

"Well, I spent some time here with Rochelle when she was pregnant last year…"

"Oh, right… I see. Well, it's been years since I visited. Quite a lot has been upgraded. Thanks for putting me through."

"No problem, Rache." Big sigh.

"So, it's been nice. Thanks for everything," Rachel says,

resisting the urge to hug him.

"You're welcome, Rache," Ejike says. He opens his arms ready for an embrace, and Rache happily obliges. When they separate, he adds, "Take care of yourself, okay?"

"I will. Will you still check on me in the morning?"

"If you want me to…"

"Please. Where do you stay?"

"It's just a five minutes' drive. It's no trouble at all."

"Okay, great! I feel better."

He beams. He feels a little hesitant to go, like he's rushing out again when he'd rather stay. But he already said that he's leaving, so he can't take it back. As he walks to the door, he enquires, "When is your doctor's appointment?"

"Tomorrow afternoon."

"Northwestern?"

Rachel nods. "Yes."

"Okay… It's just about 10 minutes from here. I can give you a lift if you want…"

"That would be amazing, but don't you have work?"

"It's lunchtime, right? It'll be fine."

"Thank you. I appreciate it."

"No worries, Rache. Have a good night," he says with a wave goodbye.

"Good night!" Rachel raises her hand for a slight wave back, and then locks up after him. She really wishes he could have stayed longer, but he's not her husband. He has his own life, and he's already gone over and beyond for her. She sighs as she walks back to the living room.

She yawns, feeling sleepy again. The clock on the wall tells her that it is 9pm already. She'd slept almost five hours straight this afternoon, but she's ready to sleep some more, no thanks to jet lag. She switches off the television and heads towards her bedroom.

She decides to have a quick shower before going to bed. The water is refreshingly hot against her tired skin, and she basks in it. After applying her body cream and special oils, she dresses in a slip and climbs into bed.

Oh, Lord! The mattress feels like heaven against her bones. She cuddles inside the soft, duck feather duvet and rests her head in the goose feather pillows. She utters quiet words of appreciation to God for her safe journey and pleasant first day in America. She prays for favour for the rest of her trip and commits her plans and loved ones to the Lord, before giving in to sleep. She's soon sound asleep and snoring like only a tired, heavily pregnant woman is allowed to.

Her night is dreamless, as she gets the best rest she has gotten since she got married. Right now, she has no care in the world nor anxiety about tomorrow. And she's happy.

CHAPTER NINE

Rachel hears the doorbell sound just as the alarm she'd set to wake up goes off at 8am. Turning to slide her finger across her phone screen, she gathers the will to get out from under the covers and rise out of bed. Her body feels so relaxed, and she instinctively yawns. The doorbell rings again, spurring her on.

Lazily, she waddles to the front door, with only her house robe above her bedtime slip, and her hair still contained in a net. She doesn't look her best, she knows, but at least she doesn't look indecent. The house is still dark as the shutters are down, and she's almost blinded when she opens the door to her visitor.

"Good morning, sleepyhead," Ejike teases her at the door.

"Good morning," she mumbles with a big yawn, remembering to cover her mouth, so her voice sounds even more muffled. She stretches as she trods into the living room, leaving Ejike to secure the front door. He goes ahead to disable the security system and open the shutters. Rays of sunshine pour into every room in the house, instantly energising the sleepyhead.

"How was your night?" Ejike asks, standing at the doorway to the lounge and observing Rachel as she makes herself comfortable on the settee.

She nods and smiles. "It was good, thanks. And yours?"

"T'was good." He heads towards the kitchen as he asks, "What are you having for breakfast?"

"I think I'll just take cereal... I saw Coco Pops. I haven't had that in ages!"

She can hear his laughter in the kitchen and his voice as he bellows, "I thought you'd like it."

She's surprised to see him return with a tray bearing semi-skimmed milk, a bowl, spoon, and two boxes of cereal.

"I brought Cheerios too. I thought you might like to combine them..."

"Genius, thanks! By the way, I am quite capable of making my own breakfast, y'know..."

"You've started again!" he retorts, and they both giggle.

Ejike watches as Rachel brings her hands together, over the tray, and mutters a prayer. Her prayer is short and simple, and soon, she's pouring some milk into her bowl.

"Won't you join me?" she asks, looking across at him.

With a shake of his head, he says, "I already had my breakfast, thanks. I'll be leaving soon too. I have to be at work in 20 minutes. I just wanted to make sure your day's off to a good start."

"Thank you. I appreciate it."

"It's no problem."

A short silence. Ejike watches as she begins to spoon cereal to her mouth. "So, ummm, what time should I pick you for your doctor's appointment?"

"I'd like to get there by 1pm, so twelve thirty would be ideal..."

"Okay, cool. Do you have any other plans after?"

"Well, I'd like to hit the shops at some point, but today, I just want to go to the hospital and watch some telly."

"Yeah... You have lots of time." He coughs. "Well, Ifeoma is coming into town tonight, so I won't be able to come over after work, but I'll still check on you in the morning."

Rachel is happy to have cereal in her mouth, which she swallows, and it seems to neutralise her expression. "Sure… If you can't come, I'll understand. I'm actually thinking of hiring a nurse anyway."

"Oh, okay. I'm happy to. Even if you have a nurse. I can take care of those things you need a man to handle. It's no biggie."

Rachel simply nods and continues with her cereal.

Ejike stands up and exhales. "Well, I have to be going. Take care of yourself, okay?" Rachel looks up at him, her lips spread in the slightest of smiles. "I'll see you around noon."

She watches as he turns and heads towards the door, choosing to remain in her seat. The door shuts, and the sound of silence that follows is sickening. The loneliness she felt she'd left back in Lagos creeps on her again…

***

Rachel can hear the long, loud beeps of the microwave, indicating that her dinner is ready. She laughs at one of the characters in the sitcom she's watching, before pausing the television to go to the kitchen. After retrieving her steaming bowl of egusi soup, she unwraps the poundo yam she'd prepared earlier and sets it on a plate, then carries her tray to the living room.

Before unpausing her show, Rachel takes a moment to utter a prayer. She's thankful for a good day and her fruitful visit to the hospital. She was able to meet her gynaecologist and is very happy that she's a woman too, like her gynae back in Nigeria. Dr Linda Harrison was very professional and talked her through everything that would happen, easing away any anxieties she might have had lurking in her subconscious.

Rachel's also grateful that she wasn't alone. Even though she'd told him she'd be fine taking a cab back home, Ejike didn't want to hear any of it. He endured the wait at the hospital for the appointment and different tests, as well as sitting through the session with Dr Harrison. The only awkward moment was when the consultant assumed he was the father of her child and commented that they would be passing some 'beautiful genes' to their son. Rachel smiles as she remembers it, even though she'd been very embarrassed at the time. Ejike had taken it in his stride.

It made her think of her husband and wonder if she would have been happier having him by her side. But the inkling that there would only be a strained silence between them, as they engaged themselves with their mobile phones while waiting to be seen, only made her feel sad. They just didn't seem to have anything to say to each other, and often ended up in arguments on the occasions they attempted to communicate. Truthfully, she hadn't missed him at all, and it seemed the feeling was mutual. Since his call the night before, she hasn't heard from her husband, even though she'd sent a message about her visit to the hospital in the morning.

Rachel draws breath, realising that she has derailed from her prayer. She quickly wraps it up by praying for her food and blessing the hands that prepared it. Smiling, she unpauses the television to continue watching an episode of Friends. No matter how many times she has watched this sitcom, she never stops finding it hilarious, she thinks as she chuckles along with Chandler, who has cracked another dry joke.

She's almost done with her meal when her phone pings with a notification. She's happy, no, more like relieved, when she sees that it's a message from Doug.

"*Hey, dear. How are you?*"

"*Hey… I'm good. How are you?*"

"*Good, too. How's baby kicking?*"

"*He's good. How is your day going?*"

"*It's fine, thanks! I went to see a place in Obalende for the studio this morning. Your dad said I could use it.*"

"*Wow! That's great! I'm happy for you. So, I guess he's onboard with you setting up the studio.*"

"*You didn't think he would be?*"

"*No, I didn't mean it like that. I'm just pleased that things are moving forward.*"

"*Yeah, I'm excited. I'm going to be quite busy setting it up before you guys get back. I need to rewrite the proposal and everything.*"

"*Okay. Cool.*"

"*How was your doctor's visit?*"

"*It was great. She said baby's growing well.*"

"*Nice! Did you take a cab?*"

"*No, Ejike took me and brought me back.*"

"*Really? He doesn't have a job?*"

"*Well, he said it was okay. I told him I'd be fine, but he was eager to help.*"

"*Of course he was. Remember I warned you about him? I don't like you guys spending time together.*"

"*Please, Doug. Even if you don't trust him, trust me. I married you, didn't I? He's just being helpful. And he's the only family I have nearby.*"

"*Hmmm… Just be careful.*"

"*Okay, I will.*"

"*I'll chat you up later.*"

"*Later x*"

Rachel sighs as she closes their chat. She hadn't told him that Ejike was the one who picked her from the airport, nor of all the helpful and thoughtful things he'd done since she'd been in Chicago, but she's glad she was able to mention about his support today. She doesn't want it to look like she is hiding anything, but if he doesn't ask, then he doesn't need to know, especially if it will only compromise her comfort and safety.

But what's to worry about anyway, when Ejike is happily engaged to another? Rachel heaves another sigh, thinking about him with Ifeoma, who is now back in Chicago. She wonders what they will get up to tonight. Are they making love this very minute? Ejike said being separated often means that they "make the most of their time together". *What does that mean?*

Rachel shakes her head as if to erase the thought. She shouldn't be thinking about that. She had had the chance to choose Ejike, and she'd turned him down. She doesn't know him at all, and it appears that their values are very contrary. There's no point wondering "what if…" Even if he's turning out to be a pretty terrific guy from her recent interactions with him, his obsession with The Avengers notwithstanding.

Resolutely, she returns her attention to the sitcom. It's just the distraction she needs to stop thinking about how miserable she feels about her marriage. And it does the trick.

***

May 13th, 2015
Dear Diary,
I am 38 weeks gone and expecting my baby any day now. My step-mom is coming over this weekend so she can help me through the birth and after-birth. I'm quite excited and nervous because this is becoming too real. I'm going to be a mom!

Doug was denied his visa, so he won't be around for the birth. I know he can't help that, but he's been absent in more ways than one. He rarely calls, and when he does, we hardly chat for up to two minutes before he needs to go. I know he's busy setting up his studio, but I don't think I'm asking too much for him to take more of an interest in my care. Sometimes, I wonder if he realises that we are having a baby.

Anyway, I hate to compare, but unlike Doug, Ejike has been so thoughtful and kind since I got here. Even though he's engaged and has a really demanding job, he makes so much time for me. Every morning and every night, even if he can't visit, he calls to check in on me. And whenever he comes, we are so free and comfortable with each other, it's like I've known him all my life. We've grown so close since I arrived in Chicago almost two months ago, and I don't know how I would have coped without him.

And he's not anything like what I imagined! He believes in God and is passionate about the gospel. Sometimes, I am so amazed by the things he says. He's really a great guy, and I keep wondering how I missed it.

His girlfriend is nice, I guess. She is definitely a fashionista. I met her on my first weekend. I'd asked Ejike about going to a restaurant in town, and he decided to bring her along. I'm sure he did it to ease her mind about us spending time together because we haven't all hung out together since. Whenever she is in town, he's unavailable for visits, and when she's not, he's my chaperone, which isn't bad at all. I guess she's not so threatened, since I'm pregnant, married, and somehow related to her fiancé. Well, actually, I'm sure her confidence is more in the fact that he's a good Christian man, and for that, she's very fortunate.

Anyway, I got a live-in nurse through an employment agency a couple of days after arriving. The pressure from family was just too much, with everyone concerned about me having a fall with no one around to help. It has never happened, and it won't, but I knew I had to be careful since regret is a terrible emotion. She helps with cleaning and some simple food preparations, but I still rely on Ejike for getting my groceries to cook Nigerian dishes that I get cravings for. Occasionally, he brings packed dishes from the African restaurant near his office too. My fridge and freezer are always stocked!

I've been doing lots of shopping for baby, but I think I've got everything I need now. I used to go to the stores because I do love walking through the mall, but my gynae says that I can't continue to stress myself like that. I'm already getting Braxton Hicks contractions, which are like practice contractions before the real deal. They are so painful, though!

Anyway, I've started online shopping, and mehn, I didn't know there were so many things to get for babies! Some of the things I got at the mall are really overpriced, but I'll just have to make do. I can't be stressing myself returning items!

Anyway... Two more weeks until DD, but Dr Harrison says it could be any day now. I can't but think my life is about to change in a really big way. I think I'm ready for it, and I need it. I can't wait to see my baby!

CHAPTER TEN

"Otioye otare? Oshare na omuegbe akpo."
Translation: *"That's what he said? That man is not serious at all!"*

Rachel hears her step-mother speaking to her father in his native Urhogbo language and marvels that her parents seem to be constantly in touch. Though of Hausa heritage, having served her NYSC in Delta State, Mrs Eden had learnt to speak the native dialect and perfected it over time, through their relationship and subsequent marriage. Since she arrived yesterday morning, she has spent countless hours on the phone, and the perplexing thing for Rachel is that most of that time has been in conversation with her husband! She can't help but wonder, *what do they talk about all day long?*

Five minutes is her current record with her husband, and even then, she was scratching her brain looking for something interesting to discuss. They'd exhausted the first two minutes talking about baby, and the second two about how they had spent their days. Doug had even thrown in some sweet talk, but like a short match, their fire never stayed ignited for long.

Rachel looks up at the sound of cackling coming from her mother, pushing down the feeling of jealousy. She's reminded of how things had been when she'd been in Dubai preparing for her wedding. It was a taste of what was to come, if only she'd heeded the warning. But now, no amount of nagging got her the attention she desired. They only argued and grew more distant.

Sincerely, Rachel knows that it isn't Doug's fault alone. She has never been much of a talker. He was the one who drew her out in the beginning, when he was making every effort to connect with her and get her. But she never imagined that he would stop so suddenly. Though she's used to being alone, the loneliness she feels in her marriage feels so foreign and painful.

She hears Mrs Eden say, "Talk to you later," before hanging up the phone. They are thrown into silence again. Even though Rachel's grateful that her step-mom came all the way to assist, she also doesn't know how to communicate well with Mrs Eden. The intermittent phone calls that have kept them from engaging are also the only sounds that fill the air when the television is off, as it is now.

Rachel's both disappointed and relieved when Mrs Eden rises up, wordlessly, to go to her bedroom, leaving Rachel alone in the living room. Rachel continues browsing her social media accounts, catching up on what's been happening in Nigeria. Doug has posted a few pictures with some new friends. He seems to be having a good time, she surmises.

She's surprised when her phone suddenly rings and even more so when she sees who's calling.

"Hi, Ejike,"

"Hey, Rache, how are you doing?"

"I'm good, thanks. How are you?"

"I'm fine. I'm sorry I didn't come over this morning. I figured, with your mom around, you wouldn't need me to…"

"Oh, no. It's okay. I understand. Thanks!"

"I guess you wouldn't be needing my company tonight either…" *Is that longing in his voice?*

Rachel smiles. "Why not? You can still come over."

"Really? I don't want to be weird or anything."

"Hmmm… *I guess*. But if you plan on staying away, it's going to be a very boring couple of weeks till my delivery. I don't think I can take it!"

Ejike laughs out loud, and Rachel giggles. "Okay, I'll come by, but not tonight. Let me give your guys some space."

"Sure. Thanks! Maybe we can see a movie this weekend? I still haven't watched the new Avengers movie."

"*What?!* I've watched it twice already! Hmmm, I promised Ifeoma we'd see "Pitch Perfect 2" together on Friday, but I don't mind watching Avengers again with you, maybe on Sunday."

"Oh, really? We can watch something else, though. When's she coming in?"

"She's arriving on Thursday and leaving for New York on Saturday."

"Cool."

"Yeah…" Big sigh. "So, maybe I'll stop by tomorrow evening. I'm craving a game of Chess."

It's Rachel's turn to laugh out loud. She'd introduced Ejike to the strategic game, and he'd become almost as obsessed as she. He was proving to be quite an opponent too, and she found that to be another alluring trait in him. Doug had given up on the game after losing to her three times, and she'd missed it so much.

"You're on!" she chuckles, feeling suddenly excited and happy to be alive.

***

As promised, Ejike visits the next evening. Mrs Eden doesn't seem at all surprised nor bothered to see him and smiles brightly when he walks into the living room. He immediately bows in greeting the elderly lady.

"How are you, Ejike?"

"I'm fine, ma. How are you?"

"I'm okay, can't complain. Did you come to see me?"

"Yes, ma. And also to visit Rachel."

Mrs Eden passes a glance across to Rachel before looking back at Ejike. "Okay. I hear you've been checking up on her."

Ejike nods. He takes a seat on the sofa and glimpses at the television, which is on the Documentary channel, obviously Mrs Eden's choice. "Yes, she's carrying my nephew."

There's a short pause before Mrs Eden speaks again. "How's our wife? Ifeoma, is it?"

"She's fine, ma."

When she says nothing more, Ejike turns to Rachel. "How are you?"

***

It's 3am, and Rachel's still awake. Her soft pillows are now damp from the tears she's shed. Her heart aches with so much sorrow as she thinks about her life and the mistakes she has made.

Tonight was great. Rachel was so happy to have Ejike over, even though they were both conscious of Mrs Eden's observant eyes. They enjoyed three thrilling games of Chess, and Ejike finally won one, which made him laugh and smile brighter than she'd ever seen him do. It was then that Rachel knew, without a doubt, that he'd entered her heart. She loves this man!

She didn't mean to, but she's fallen in love with a man that isn't her husband, a man betrothed to another, who can never be hers. And the realisation that what she has with Doug isn't love makes her feel so dirty, so destitute, so doomed... She and Doug aren't going through a miserable phase, as she'd wanted to believe. She's now certain her whole marriage is destined to misery because she didn't choose the one she loved. *What have I done?!*

Rachel heaves as more tears pour out of her eyes. How could she have been so wrong? What is she going to do now? She knows she has to avoid Ejike, but the thought of pushing him away and never being with him again fills her with a more desperate gloom, where the idea of ending it all sounds like sweet relief.

***

The next few days pass uneventfully. At first, Rachel is relieved that Ejike seems to have chosen to keep away, but by Saturday, the fifth day since his last visit, she finds herself longing to hear from him. At least to know that he's okay and everything's fine between them. It's really unlike him to not have called nor texted for days. And though she should let it go, the silence is getting more agonising with each passing day.

Unable to take the pain, she reaches out with a WhatsApp message.

"Hi, Ejike. How are you doing?"

The message is sent but undelivered, making her wonder if she has been blocked from his phone. Maybe he too realised that she has fallen in love with him. Maybe he's trying to be a good guy and stay away. Her apprehension is soon dampened when a double tick indicates that the message has been received. She breathes a sigh of relief.

The blue ticks indicating that it has been read still refuse to show, and Rachel decides to put her phone away. He will reply when he's ready, she tells herself.

In the evening, when she still hasn't heard from him, she checks their chat. The blue ticks reveal that her message has not only been received, but also read, yet there are no messages from him, though his status bar reveals that he is 'online'. Rachel doesn't know what to make of his silence and rejection but decides to give him the benefit of the doubt.

Later that evening, as she's watching TV, her phone pings with a new message. But it's just Doug sending his mandatory, daily "check-in" message.

"Hi, dear. How are you?" he'd written.

"Fine, thanks. How are you?"

Her response is delivered but unread. He seems to have left their chat. She follows suit.

"Hey… What's up?"

The notification pops up as she's about to put her phone aside. Rachel can't help the feeling of happiness that begins to come over her, like a current, starting from her toes and rising to the crown of her head, spreading a smile across her face, despite being a little worried and a tad bit angry at his silence.

"Hey," she types back.

"How are you?"

"I'm fine. You?"

"Yeah, me too. It's been a busy week."

"Ok."

"I'm sorry I haven't been in touch."

"It's no problem," she lies.

"You still want to catch a movie this weekend?"

Rachel's heart leaps and begins to race. She should blow him off. End this crazy thing between them. But like a drug addict, she can't resist the opportunity of spending more time with him. *"Yeah, if you're free."*

"Cool. I'll pick you up for the 4pm showing tomorrow, aight?"

"Thanks 😊"

She leans her head back after sending the message, letting the excitement wash over her like a flood. *If this is wrong, why does it feel so right? God help me!*

***

Rachel's gone back and forth about her decision to go to the cinema with Ejike so much that she's now absolutely confused and dizzy. It's not like it's their first time going to the movies together. She supposes that things are different now because she has finally admitted to herself that she's in love with him. She used to say they were just feelings, which could be controlled, but what this week has proven is her inability to wilfully stay away from him.

But there's no saying that he feels the same way… And just because they have feelings for each other doesn't mean that they will do anything. After all, they are both morally-strong people, with personal convictions, who are in committed relationships. Just the notion that she could cheat while pregnant causes laughter to bubble in her throat at the ludicrousness. *Seriously, who wants to kiss someone else's pregnant wife?*

No, she's overthinking this. They are family. He doesn't feel the same way anymore. Her emotions will pass, especially if they can just be cordial and not make a big deal out of a cinema date! *There, it's settled. This is perfectly innocent.*

"You okay?" Ejike asks, snapping her out of her mental ordeal.

She turns to him and smiles. "Fine, thanks."

He returns his attention to the road as he continues their drive to the cinema. She watches him, noticing more things about him that she finds appealing. *You are lusting over this man*; she rebukes herself and turns away.

Clearing her throat, she decides to initiate conversation. "So, how was "Pitch Perfect 2"?"

Ejike looks confused until what she's asking registers. "Oh, it was okay. Not really my kind of movie."

"Oh…"

"Ifeoma really enjoyed it, though. But nah, can't sit through it again."

Rachel nods, thinking it's a shame. She'd been interested in watching it with him too. "Thanks for watching Avengers with me."

He beams. "No problem! I love it! I hope we can catch it in 3-D."

Rachel returns his smile and looks ahead at the road, admiring the cinema complex as they approach it and park outside. The complex also houses a bowling alley. They'd been once before, and she's keen to go again after their movie.

Hours later, as she steps out of the cinema, her mind still aroused by all the audio-visual stimuli she'd been exposed to in the theatre, Rachel understands why the "Avengers: Age of Ultron" is such as box office hit, and why Ejike has now watched it three times! Smiling and giggling, she says, "I want to watch it again!"

"*As in?!*" Ejike replies, smiling like the cat that got the cream. "Now, that's my kinda movie!"

Rachel laughs out loud and pees a little. Only that the pee doesn't want to stop. She's shocked as she looks down to see that she's wet herself. She looks up at Ejike, mortified, but he doesn't appear grossed out in the least.

"Wow! I think you're having your baby!"

And that's when Rachel realises what has happened. She begins to giggle, but it's interrupted by a painful contraction.

"Hey, let me get you to the hospital!" Ejike says, pulling her closer to hold her, comfort her, and lead her safely to his car.

CHAPTER ELEVEN

"*Omote na ovwere. Atare no avware sa kpo ode…*"

Translation: "*She's still sleeping. They said we can leave tomorrow…*"

Rachel opens her eyes slightly as her sleep-inducing medication wears off. She can hear Mrs Eden on the phone and turns her head in the direction of her voice. Mrs Eden rises upon seeing her movement and walks to her bedside.

She smiles as she says, "Congratulations on your bouncy baby boy!"

Rachel beams. "Thanks, mom! Where's he?"

"They took him to change his diaper. How are you feeling?"

"Tired…"

"Get your rest."

"Thanks, mom."

Rachel wants to ask after Ejike, but thinks better of it. He would have returned home and should be at work now. The clock on the wall says it's 3pm. He'd stayed at the hospital until she put to birth in the early hours of Monday morning, even though he was not permitted to enter her delivery room. Her step-mom had arrived in time to offer that support, and it appears that she'd chosen to stay the whole night.

Rachel leans back on her reclined bed and shuts her eyes again. She'd been having an interesting dream, but can't seem to recall what it was about. Rather, she recalls last night's ordeal. Though she had known what to expect, nothing could have prepared her for the pain of vaginal birth. However, the feeling she'd felt on hearing her baby's cries made it all worth it. They had spent only two minutes together before he was whisked off to be washed, tested, and fed.

"Hi, Rachel."

Rachel opens her eyes to see an attractive doctor standing over her bed. She looks at him wearily as he performs some vital checks, while asking her questions to gauge her physical and mental agility. He changes one of Rachel's drips, before stopping and smiling at her.

"Are you ready to try breastfeeding your baby?" the doctor asks.

Rachel nods eagerly.

"Great! I'll ask the nurses to bring him over, shortly. You delivered a very healthy, young boy. If he's feeding well by tomorrow morning, I see no reason why you can't return home tomorrow. We would just like to keep you overnight to make sure you're strong enough to look after your baby yourself, okay?"

Rachel nods. "Thank you, Doctor."

"You're welcome, ma'am. Congratulations again!"

***

Rachel's breastfeeding when Ejike visits in the evening. By then, she's had her bath and has been up for several hours watching television. Mrs Eden has been a quiet companion, reading a novel, and occasionally making and taking calls.

Rachel smiles at Ejike when she sees him walking in with a bouquet of flowers and a small teddy bear for the baby. After greeting Mrs Eden and placing his gifts on a shelf, he goes to stand beside Rachel, glad that her baby's head is blocking his view of her working breast.

"Congratulations, Rachel!"

She beams up at him. "Thanks, Ejike."

"How's Junior? What are we calling him?"

"Ezekiel. That's what Doug and I agreed on, but we haven't chosen his native names yet."

"Ezekiel is a lovely name. A name of purpose. I like it."

"Thanks! And he's doing fine. I was nervous about breastfeeding, but he's taking it so well."

"That's great! You're going to be an amazing mother."

"Thanks, Ejike. How was your day?"

"It was good, thanks. Busy. I had a few meetings, but nothing out of the ordinary."

Rachel just nods, turning her attention to Ezekiel who has detached from her breast. She successfully gets him to latch on again and continue sucking. It feels a little tender and occasionally painful, but for the most part, she's enjoying this connection she has with her baby. And he looks so adorable. *I can't believe I'm a mommy!*

***

After Ejike leaves, Rachel finally feels energized enough to check her phone. It has been buzzing with messages and calls since morning, but she's been too tired to read, let alone respond to any of them. Mrs Eden had shared info and pictures to her family via their group on WhatsApp, and from there, word reached their extended families, friends, and acquaintances.

She tries her best to respond to all the well-wishers, sending smiley faces to most of them. However, she's still not up for returning phone calls, apart from that of her husband, the father of her child. Doug has called twice, and he left a wordy message in their chat.

"Hey darling, congratulations on the delivery of our amazing son. Mom posted the pictures in the chat group, and they are so beautiful. Thank you for giving me such a wonderful treasure. I love you so much, and I can't wait for you guys to come home. Rest well, dear. I'll call you later 😊😊😊*"*

Rachel's amazed at his emotional and expressive message. Though Doug is sometimes affectionate and expressive, she feels that he does so erratically, and he often comes off over the top, like now. He seems to be compensating for all the times he should have been emotional and romantic in a single dramatic gesture. It makes her wonder about his true feelings. Maybe he really does love her and just doesn't know how to communicate his feelings or show his passion.

Rachel takes a deep breath and replies him with a brief text. "*Thanks, babe. Congratulations to you too xoxo*"

Moments later, he calls.

"Hey, darling! You're finally awake. I've been calling you. How are you, and how's Ezekiel?"

Rachel thinks he sounds overly exuberant, almost like he's high on something, but she's sure it's only his joy at being a father. "Hi dear. We're fine. How are you?"

"I'm fine. Have you spoken to my mom? She said she's been calling you."

"No, not yet. Still catching up on rest."

"No problem. Maybe you can call her tonight. Everyone is so happy, I had them all praying for your safe delivery."

"Thanks."

"Ezekiel is really beautiful. Well done, baby. Please, don't stress yourself out, just relax and let Mommy help. That's what she's there for."

"I won't."

"Okay, let me let you rest. I love you, baby!"

"I love you, too."

As she hangs up the phone, Rachel feels sad because she knows that's not the truth, and she hates lying, but what else would have been an appropriate response? She reckons it's the same way saying "I'm fine," is the socially accepted and *expected* response to "How are you?". But at those times she says she's fine when she doesn't feel so, she never feels like a liar the way she does now. Perhaps it's because the meaning of "feeling fine" is broad. However, Rachel's coming to understand how the definition of love is not so narrow either. In a way, she does love Doug, but not in the way he thinks or she ought.

✳✳✳

"I love you," Rachel mutters to her infant, wrapped in a blanket and cradled in her arms. She knows it's the truth because she feels it in her heart, a sort of sweet pain and joy all at once, accompanied with the conviction that she'd do anything, even put her life at risk, to save him. She bends her head to his forehead and plants a soft kiss.

God sent you to save me, she thinks as she beholds her son. She had been feeling like she had nothing to live for. But now, she wants to, and needs to, live for Ezekiel, to give him a life worth living. She wants to fight for him, be there for him, and discover the other treasures and possibilities life – *God* – has in store for her. "I love you, Ezekiel!" It feels so good to say it and mean it with all her heart.

The unmistakable sound of Ezekiel's bowel movement makes Rachel smile. "Oh my, have you done a stinky doo-dah?" she teases.

Rachel brings his changing bag out to change his diaper. She lays him on the mat, and he has another poo. "Maybe I should let you finish."

"We might as well bath him now," Mrs Eden says. "Go and boil the water."

Rachel makes sure Ezekiel is safe before leaving him to go to the kitchen. It's 6:30pm and almost his bath time. While the kettle is boiling, her phone rings. She returns to the living room to get it.

"Hey, dear," she greets cheerfully.

"Happy Anniversary, babe!"

With the time difference, it's already the 21st of June in Nigeria. Rachel smiles, happy that Doug remembered their first anniversary.

"Happy Anniversary, Doug!"

"How are you and Ezekiel?"

"We're good, dear. I'm just preparing his water for his bath."

"Okay, cool. Let me leave you to do that. I'll call you later in the day. I just thought I should call now, so I don't forget."

"Thanks, babe. Talk to you later!"

Later, he chats her up on WhatsApp, with emojis to express his thoughts and feelings. She sends him pictures and videos of Ezekiel, and he marvels again at what they created. And they express their affections for each other once more.

***

Ejike doesn't come around nor call as much these days. Rachel knows it's because she is no longer pregnant and has her stepmother around to help, but she can't help thinking he might also be creating distance between them. But it's just as well. She misses him, but this is for the best.

Mrs Eden has been an invaluable support, bringing her years of experience raising children to the table, and helping Rachel with cooking delicious meals, bathing Ezekiel, and babysitting, so Rachel can nap. They decided to relieve the live-in nurse and get a part-time cleaner to come instead, and they have been coping fine for weeks. Over time, the initial unease between step-mom and step-daughter had diminished, leaving a friendly atmosphere in the home.

Rachel still marvels at Chief and Mrs Eden's constant communication. In the first week of baby's birth, Doug had made more of an effort with communicating, often choosing to call rather than send messages. Rachel sent him pictures every day, which she often later found on his social media pages, as he wrote about how proud he was to be a father. However, the calls soon reduced, replaced by irregular messaging. But Rachel has been too pre-occupied with looking after herself and her baby to be worried about

Doug's attention or lack of.

Ezekiel had his six weeks check-up and immunizations yesterday, so they are all set to return home this weekend. Rachel's already sorted out his passports, US and Nigerian, and is almost completely packed to go. Mrs Eden will be travelling back with them, and Ejike has offered to drive them to the airport.

Rachel zips her last suitcase and smiles, feeling happy at the success of her travel. Three big cartons are in the corner of the room, waiting to be collected and shipped to Nigeria ahead of them. She wonders what else needs doing and remembers that she has some clothes in the laundry. They will fit in her hand luggage, she decides.

The smell of freshly boiled rice wafts in her nostrils, and her stomach growls in response. Lunch is ready, and her guess is that it will be delicious. Mrs Eden cooked a pot of spicy fish stew yesterday that would taste amazing with the Basmati rice.

"Come and eat!"

When Mrs Eden calls, she's more than ready.

***

It's a beautiful day to travel. The sun is high in the sky, and there's not a grey cloud in sight. Rachel looks out of the window as they drive along the Kennedy expressway. Ezekiel's in his car seat, and Mrs Eden is sitting with him at the back. The radio is the only sound they hear until they arrive at their destination. Today, maybe for Mrs Eden's benefit, the dial is on a smooth jazz station.

Rachel's transported to the high heavens when Sade's "By Your Side" comes on. She closes her eyes in sweet bliss and hums along to the soulful tune. She doesn't notice Ejike turn to steal a look at her, lost in her world for a minute. But she does notice when he turns the volume up slightly, and she turns and beams at him. She loves that they seem to have a similar taste in music. Actually, they seem to have a lot in common.

Ejike stops at the departure terminal, where Rachel, Mrs Eden, and Ezekiel alight with their luggage. After parking, he returns to assist with loading the suitcases unto two trolleys and pushes the heavier one to the check-in desks. Rachel pushes the other, while Mrs Eden carries Ezekiel. Ejike stays with them until all their luggage is scanned, weighed, and tagged, and they have collected their boarding passes. They are now ready to go to their departure lounge.

"Thank you," Rachel says, damning what anyone might think and pulling him in for a fond hug. "Thank you for all you did for me."

"You're welcome, Rachel. I'm really going to miss you."

"Yeah, who will beat your ass at Chess?!"

Ejike laughs out loud. "Keep talking. I'll be practicing, and I'll kick your butt next time!"

Rachel laughs and then looks shyly at her step-mom. Ejike embraces Mrs Eden too. "Safe journey, ma!"

"Take care of yourself, Ejike."

Rachel looks back, one more time, as they walk away and waves goodbye. She's going to miss him so much! In fact, she's missing him already.

"Now, that one is special," she hears Mrs Eden say, but she can't be sure she heard right. However, she doesn't dare ask her meaning. Only a fool could miss what a great catch Ejike is. Only a fool!

CHAPTER TWELVE

December 5th, 2015

Dear Diary,

I'm really not good with this journaling thing. The last time I wrote in here, I was still expecting my baby. Well, life has been busy ever since I gave birth to Ezekiel. In fact, I don't know where the time has gone.

Five months ago, I returned home with my baby, after three months in the States. I was very fortunate to have had Ejike around to support me while I was pregnant, and my step-mom came in time to help with Ezekiel's birth and postnatal care. Unfortunately, Doug couldn't join us, but he was at the airport to pick us up when we arrived in Lagos.

Doug had lost a bit of weight but looked fit and happy. He gathered me in his arms when we met and greeted me with a brief kiss before greeting my mom and helping her with Ezekiel's buggy. I have to say, I was quite surprised considering our general lack of intimacy, but it was nice. It made me feel like maybe it had all been in my head... Lol! I guess I still want to believe that he cares for me, and with effort, our marriage could work. Do I have a choice?

The house was no different from how I'd left it months ago, which made me wonder what exactly Doug had done to prepare for our return. Apart from a Ben 10 wallpaper in Ezekiel's room, there was nothing to show that a baby was on the way. Doug said he hadn't had the money needed to do what he wanted because of all the money he'd sent for Ezekiel's delivery.

Having made no prior financial contribution to my care during pregnancy, I guess it must have come as a bit of a shock to him when I'd asked him to transfer the money we'd received from our wedding (basically all our savings) to settle my hospital bill. I'd also been surprised at the request from my parents, but it made sense for us to take some financial responsibility for our child. They'd helped with my flights, accommodation, shopping, and even contributed significantly towards the settlement of our bill. It really wasn't too much to expect that we'd share the burden.

However, what it meant was that I returned home broke, with a new baby, to a stressed-out husband. Our safety cushion was gone, and I was resolved to stop presuming on my parents' support, but rely on my husband and manage whatever income we could earn together. They've done so much for us, and it was high time we learnt to fend for ourselves.

Still, my dad continues to send me money monthly, as he did while I was single. Considering our financial struggles, I decided to keep the money in a trust for Ezekiel and save towards his education, so that we don't end up spending it on our living and have to run to my parents later for help. I also hoped my decision would deter Doug from presuming on that money, as he had been doing, and motivate him to work to provide for us.

I guess it did because he threw himself into his new career as a music producer, such that he is hardly ever around. He often comes home very late and occasional sleeps at his studio, two things I'm not happy with. It hasn't helped to build trust or love, which were already lacking in our relationship. Though I haven't heard anything new about him, I really wouldn't be surprised if I found out that there's somebody else. But I don't know what to do about it...

Well, I resumed work at Urban Fm in August, seeing as we could really do with the extra income. I proposed a new idea for my show, a 26-part series on marriage, called The Marriage ABCs. Every week, I focus on a letter of the alphabet and share important lessons for married couples. It's been my way of counselling myself and thinking positively about my marriage, and it's been well received by my listeners since we started in September.

Though it has been challenging, I feel a renewed energy for my work. I've been able to draw on my new experience in motherhood also. And even though I hate being away from my baby, I love the time I spend with other grownups and the satisfaction I get from interacting with my audience.

Ezekiel was three months old at the end of August, and we did thanksgiving at Church. We also had a small gathering at the house to celebrate. Bose and Dongjap both came unaccompanied, and I introduced them, hoping they would hit it off.

I hadn't seen much of Bose since I got back, as she has been busy with work, but it was nice to see her at the party. She looked really good, and I could tell Dj was into her. We've spoken only once since, but it seems my match-making effort was futile. She said he's not her type. Oh, well...

Okay, I think I'll leave it there. Ezekiel just woke up, and I need to attend to him.

Oh, I almost forgot... Ejike is coming into town tomorrow! Actually, we've kept in touch...and he's coming to prepare for his wedding in two weeks. Yeah... It's really happening. I guess I feel the way he must have felt when I was about to get married. Like, if only I could stop it and turn back time so that it would be us standing at the altar, professing to love each other forever.

***

Rachel closes her journal and puts it back in its secret place before hastening to go to her child, whose whimperings have turned to loud cries.

"Shhh, shhh, ohh baby," she soothes as she carries him from his rocker. "It's alright. Mommy's here. Shhh, shhh... I got you!" She decorates his face with her kisses until he quietens down, then she returns to the sofa, where she cradles him.

As Rachel breastfeeds Ezekiel, her thoughts return to the last entry in her diary. So, Ejike is coming home tomorrow and getting married before Christmas. She's still processing her thoughts and feelings about it and trying not to feel like it affects her in any way. Ejike's a friend, not an ex. They never had a relationship, and there's no way to know that if they'd had one, they'd have lasted.

She knows they share a special connection, but does that damn Ejike from marrying someone for the rest of his life? *No...* He has moved on, and it's not her place to question his decision...just as she had told him when he had tried to disrupt her engagement. But if only she had known then what she knows now... *If only*, she heaves a sigh.

The notifications on her phone draw her attention back to the present. Unlocking it, she opens her WhatsApp chat with Doug.

"*Hey, Babe,*" he'd written. "*How are you and Ezi? I'm having a few friends over for games night next Saturday. I'll send some money so you can prepare your special fried rice. I'll be home late tonight. So don't wait up.*"

Rachel sighs and responds, "*Hi, Doug. We're fine. Okay. Stay safe.*"

She returns her attention to her baby and hums an old melancholy tune.

***

Rachel thinks it's strange how staying out late the night before never seems to hinder Doug from making it to Church in the morning. Sometimes, he wouldn't even come home first, like he did today, but head over straight from wherever he spent the night. When she'd called him this morning, he said he had a leaders' meeting, which would start much too early for her to accompany him with Ezekiel in tow. She said she'd meet him at their fellowship.

Arriving at the church by 10:30am, in time for the second service, Rachel notices Doug, who is stationed along the aisle, where he serves as an usher. He is dressed in matching attire with the other ushers, a new fabric they had been given to sew specially for today's service. Rachel is directed by another usher to a seat at the far-right corner of the hall. From there, the altar looks like a concert stage, all lit up with spotlights. She settles down, using her handbag to reserve her husband's seat. Sometimes, he makes a point of coming to sit with her, and other times, he lingers with the other ushers and/or leaders, for the duration of the service.

Rachel looks up at the large screen ahead, which announces the theme of today's ministration – 'Love is an Action Word'. She's thrilled to see that Haley Banks, a well-known Black-American preacher, will be ministering today. Haley usually addresses women's issues, marriage, and singleness, and Rachel finds her teaching insightful and inspiring. Rachel bows her head in prayer to prepare to receive a word from the Lord.

"When Jesus said *"if you love Me, you will obey Me,"* he was making the point that love is an action word. It's not what you say, it's what you do. In our lives as Christians, this is extremely important for people to believe our witness and come into fellowship. Our brother, James, said much about this, especially when he said *"faith without works is dead."* People will never take us at our word unless it agrees with our actions.

"In his letter to the Ephesians, Paul addressed marriage and taught that husbands ought to love their wives as Christ loves His Church. And we know it was not in word alone that Christ loved us, but in *deed*…in blood, sweat, and tears. In service and total surrender. This is what the Church needed, and it is also what every wife needs to feel safe enough to trust and submit to her husband, as she ought.

"It is a shame that while there are many classes for women, before and during marriage, on how to be trusting, submissive wives, there are very few teaching men how to be loving, thoughtful husbands. Men need to be taught that the love that is necessary is beyond words… It may be hard, but if you truly love someone, it will and must show in what you do…"

Rachel wipes tears from her watery eyes at the preacher's words. She looks about for her husband and spots him laughing with another usher at the other end of the church hall. The lady's ankara ribbon, which matches her mid-length, fitted dress, wraps her hair in a neat bun. Doug isn't listening, but Rachel knows it's a message he must have heard many times before. It's nothing new, but a reminder could have helped their marriage. Rachel looks away and returns her attention to the preacher.

***

"Hey, Babe," Doug says as he approaches Rachel after the service.

"Hey," she replies. He comes close and pecks her lips. An unusual action, probably owing to the fact that they are in public, and in Church.

As they walk out of the building together, he stops to greet several of his friends, workers, and leaders at the church. They '*ooh and ahh*' over Ezekiel, and Rachel maintains a smile until they get to her parking spot. As they arrived in separate cars at different times, so they will be leaving. Doug still has things to do at Church and may not come home straight away. He gives her another kiss, this time on the cheek, as she enters her car to drive home.

He mutters an awkward "Love you," and she smiles,

thinking about today's ministration. He's gone before she has the chance to say it back, and she sighs. *It's just as well.*

The house is quiet and lonely. After feeding Ezekiel and putting him down for his nap, Rachel brings out a book to read. It's one she hopes will aid her communication in marriage. "Avoiding the Trap of Being Offended" by Kenneth W. Hagin. She started it a couple of days ago. So far, it's been a blessing.

Her phone vibrates on the centre table, and she stretches to pick it up. A smile forms on her face upon seeing his message. She almost forgot that he would be arriving today. It feels like a pleasant surprise to hear from him so soon after his arrival too.

Ejike had written: *"Hey, you. Just got in. Home now. How are you and Ezi?"*

"Hi, Ejike 😊 *Thank God for journey mercies! We're fine. How are you?"*

"Great. Me too. Just wanted to let you know I'm in town. I also brought a couple of things for Ezi. Let me know when and where to bring them."

"Oh, you shouldn't have! Thank you 😊 *Anytime you're free. I'm usually home. We're in Lekki."*

"Okay, cool. I'll reach out during the week."

"Thanks, dear. Have a good night."

Realising that she is smiling from ear to ear, Rachel pulls herself together. Why doesn't she feel this way when her husband sends her messages?

Pondering on it, she supposes that since he rarely sends messages, whenever he remembered to, there would be a mountain of resentment at the unmet expectation of his attention. But there's no such expectation and corresponding resentment with Ejike. *Maybe the secret to happiness and satisfaction in marriage is no expectations,* Rachel speculates. In any case, offence is a choice she keeps making with Doug, and she really needs to get over it, she concludes as she resumes her reading with a sigh.

CHAPTER THIRTEEN

"The issue of money must be raised from the moment someone is talking about marriage in a relationship," Rachel speaks into her microphone at the start of her show, the 13th episode of The Marriage ABCs, themed "Money Matters in Marriage." "It shouldn't be postponed until later because it might seem unromantic, or greedy, or even unholy. Let's face it, marriage is of the world… And money is of the world too. The two have relations – a practical relationship. When two people come together, it is not simply their bodies or their hearts that are united, but their finances and assets too."

After the first couple of episodes, Dongjap advised Rachel to get experts to share their thoughts so that she could have informed discussions on air. It had really helped to improve her ratings, and she had also learnt a lot more about the diverse issues relating to marriage and how to address them.

"I totally agree," Ruth Ihenacho, today's money expert, contributes. "The problem is, when we leave these discussions until after we have invested ourselves emotionally into each other, one or both partners may be bamboozled by 'love' to enter a marriage that is financially problematic or doomed. It is like driving under the influence. You really don't process the information properly. You take short cuts in your thinking. You assume too much, and your judgement is off. You make hasty decisions, and then you find yourself in a mess. But you still have to get over your hang-over and clean up the mess before you can actually get back on track."

"That's so true!" Rachel smiles, trying not to think about how Ruth has summarised her journey to marriage. She notices Dj nodding along and returns her attention to Ruth. "So, what are the things singles should take note of before deciding to marry their partner?"

"Well, probably the most important is their attitude to money. You would also want to know their spending habits, financial goals, strategy for financial independence and stability, and last but not least, their capital. By that, I mean their assets and what they have in the bank!" Giggling, Ruth adds, "If they have debts, you need to know just how deep before you dive into the hole with them."

"Hmmm… Word." Rachel manages a smile. If only she had considered these things before getting married.

"There's a need for agreement and transparency on these issues…" Ruth continues.

Rachel listens attentively as Ruth expands on the five points she'd highlighted. She takes a couple of calls from her callers, who have questions relating to the topic, and one caller in need of marital advice. Before long, their hour is used up, and Rachel rounds up the discussion.

"It's been great having you with us, Ruth."

"Thanks for inviting me, Rachel."

"So, there you have it, folks. Money matters in marriage. Don't deny it. Don't ignore it. Don't run from it. Don't lie about it. Deal with it. Honestly. Together. In submission to God. Have a great day!"

***

Rachel pauses to examine a stain on Doug's shirt collar. The maroon smear spreads with touch, and she takes a sniff. *Hmmm…* She's not 100% certain, but it smells like make-up. Something like this is easily refuted, explained away, or simply argued about, with no resolution in her mind as to its cause.

She decides it's not an issue to be worried about and throws the shirt in with the pile of whites she's gathered for washing.

Her day off is usually the only time Rachel can catch up on her house chores, as Ezi's nanny is around to mind him. Gloria comes Monday to Friday, leaving Rachel to care for her child without help over the weekend. Rachel was able to negotiate this new schedule with the station, which respects her desire to spend as much time with her baby as she's able.

After a late night yesterday, Doug is still sleeping, a luxury he now enjoys being self-employed. Things seem to be going well with his new studio, and he'd mentioned that he is working on a track with Fatt Boy. Rachel had been surprised because Fatt Boy's music glorifies crime and denigrates women, and partnering with him would take Doug out of the Gospel genre. However, he'd explained his stance by stating that, *"There is no religion when it comes to music. It's art and life, it's real."* She didn't completely agree, but the list of things they disagreed on these days was piling up.

With the laundry sorted, Rachel carries the whites downstairs to wash first in the washing machine. While the first load washes, she tidies the kitchen. She opens the fridge to see what she can prepare. There isn't a lot because Doug is yet to send money for December. She also remembers that he is expecting her to cater to his friends this weekend. She has to remind him to send the money so she can go shopping.

Just then, she hears his footsteps on the staircase. It sounds like he's on his way out. They meet in the living room and greet awkwardly. Doug drops an envelope on the coffee table.

"Please, I need you to sign this," he says, pointing to the document.

"What is it?"

"It's for my CAC registration. Can you just sign?"

"Okay. I'll look it over and sign la—"

"Please, I need it now. I'm in a hurry," Doug responds impatiently.

Rachel picks up the document and quickly flips through. Doug's exaggerated breathing compels her to sign before she's confident about what she's doing. It seems harmless enough, anyway.

"Thanks," he mutters before slipping it inside his bag and heading towards the front door.

Rachel follows him, nervous about how to raise the issue about the monthly household spending allowance. "Ummm… Are you still expecting people this weekend?" she asks instead.

"Yeah…" he says, as he slips into the driver seat of his FJ Cruiser.

"Okay… You promised to send money for it. When will you, 'cause I need to go shopping?"

"I'll send it," he says before pressing the horn and silencing her. The security guard opens the gate for Doug to drive out.

Still, she perseveres. "Okay. I'm still waiting for this month's allowance too…"

"I'll send it," he repeats before driving out of the gate. Rachel lets out a frustrated sigh and returns to her chores.

***

Rachel sees the alert from her bank on Friday afternoon, after her show. It's N10k less than what she was expecting, but it's better than nothing. She decides to branch to the supermarket on her way home.

While at the supermarket checkout, her phone rings. Fumbling through her handbag, she retrieves it and answers the call. "Hey, Ejike… How's it going?"

"It's good. How are you?"

"I'm good. At the supermarket."

"Okay. I'm in Lekki. I wanted to drop the things I brought. Where can we meet?"

"Ummm... Do you know the new Domino's on Admiralty?"

"Hmmm, yeah. I can find it, *sha*."

"Cool! See you soon."

Rachel ends the call and completes her payment. Domino's Pizza is on her way home, which is why she suggested it. She figured it would be easier than trying to describe how to locate her house. Also, it wouldn't be funny if Doug arrived to find Ejike at their home. These days, his movement is hard to predict, and he isn't in the habit of communicating his activities nor whereabouts with her.

Ejike is already there when Rachel arrives. He rises up upon spotting her. She beams at him, and they hug.

"You came alone?"

"Yes, *nau*... I'm coming from the supermarket, remember?"

"Okay. I was hoping to see Ezi. Another time, I guess."

"Yes...another time."

Ejike hands her a big carrier bag. "For Ezi," he says with a shy smile. Rachel thinks he looks devastatingly handsome but distracts herself by opening it. "Please, do that at home."

"Oh, okay." She closes the carrier bag and sighs. "Thanks so much! You really shouldn't have."

"Don't you start again," he giggles, his hands buried in his pockets. "So, you've eaten?"

What she wouldn't give to dine with him... Rachel swallows. "Yes, actually. I also have some frozen food in my car, so I need to get home."

Ejike shrugs. "Sure, no probs. Another time."

As they walk to their cars, Rachel remembers to ask, "So, how far with wedding plans?"

"It's going well, thanks." Their eyes meet, and Rachel tries to hide her feelings. He doesn't do as good a job, and she feels her knees go weak at his gaze. She looks away. "You coming with Doug?"

"Yes, we'll be there…" she breathes.

"Good. Good." Ejike kisses her cheek before he steps back, allowing her to get into her car. He stands in the same position until she has driven out of sight, then exhales.

***

"Hmmm, Rache, you made this?" Nike comments, his eyes sparkling in enjoyment.

Rachel beams at the compliment. "Yes…"

"Really? This is like restaurant quality!" Seto, another one of Doug's friends, says.

"Yeah, my wife makes the best fried rice," Doug replies proudly, wrapping his arm around Rachel's waist and drawing her close. He leans down and pecks her lips, and Rachel smiles at their audience.

"Thanks," she mutters shyly, before returning to the kitchen to check on the chicken.

They are having a games' night, apparently a fortnightly event, and it is Doug's turn to host. She hadn't realised that he would be having such a big get-together. He'd given the impression that it was just a few of his close friends, and she hadn't prepared enough food to go round. Fortunately, a few people had brought snacks to share, and someone came with an extra-large pizza.

"Where can I put this?" Rachel turns to see Nike in the kitchen, holding his plate, with only a chicken bone as evidence of his meal.

"Oh, you can give that to me," she says as she collects it from him.

"Thanks. Aren't you joining us?" Nike asks.

"I will. I just want to tidy up here and check on Ezi first."

"Don't you have help?"

"Not over the weekend. I actually didn't know it would be this big, otherwise I would have had my cleaner come in to help. But it's fine. I'll join you guys soon."

Thirty minutes later, Rachel settles down to join in the

game of Taboo. Doug looks so happy and in his element, surrounded by his friends. *He's like a totally different person*, she marvels. He actually looks at her when he talks tonight that no one would suspect the empty shell that is their relationship. Unfortunately, she doesn't know how to feel and behave differently in front of others and finds herself bothered by his split personality.

After the last of his friends have gone, Doug settles on the sofa to watch some television and invites Rachel to join him instead of tidying up. It seems he's still on his happy high. She goes to sit next to him.

"Thanks for tonight," he says.

Rachel appreciates that, and the words thaw the barrier of resentment she usually feels around him. She smiles warmly, "You're welcome."

The thought has occurred to her that, though several of his friends came with their spouses tonight, she has never been invited to attend these games' nights with him before. Well, maybe it is because she just had a baby, and before that, she was away…and before that, she was pregnant. She probably wouldn't have wanted to go anyway. He says as much when she decides to ask him.

"And actually, it's a new thing. I'm like the third person to host," he adds.

She nods in understanding. Doug leans in to kiss her, and they get intimate on the sofa with no disruption from Ezekiel.

Afterwards, Rachel wants to linger and cuddle, but Doug has lost his emotional high. He wants to watch TV now, and he abruptly ends their romantic time with a peck on the cheek, and a complimentary "I love you." To Rachel, the words feel so empty and devoid of truth.

Rachel swallows, feeling hurt that Doug doesn't want to spend more time with her. She doesn't know how to express her feelings to him, but she knows she has to try. "Why do you say "I love you" when you don't mean it?"

Doug turns to look at her, his expression hard to read.

Realising that it sounded like an accusation, she tries again, "I mean… You say it so flippantly, like you don't really mean it. It makes me feel like you don't love me…" she manages to say.

Rachel looks at him expectantly, hoping he would calm her fears and affirm his love. She's stunned and shattered when all he says in response is, "Okay."

Did he just confirm her darkest fear, she wonders, watching as he returns his attention to the TV set?

CHAPTER FOURTEEN

Ejike stands, staring at his reflection in the mirror, as he fixes on his cuff-links. His steel-grey tuxedo hugs his broad-shouldered frame delectably. He rubs away an imaginary crease and straightens his bow tie. Taking in a deep breath, he checks out his full image. It's time, but he doesn't feel ready.

"Hey, bro," Ekene says, a hand on Ejike's shoulder. "Let's take our photos. You can't beat perfection."

Ejike turns around and laughs. Ekene's in-joke about his vanity comes across as a compliment today. Even he must admit that no one has ever looked so good in a tux. Rather than let his brother see his confliction, Ejike wraps his arm around Ekene's shoulder and smiles into the camera.

They take a few more shots before his groomsmen join them in taking group photos. As the photographer clicks away, he has no more time to think about his decision or indecision. He enjoys the photoshoot and is soon chuckling with his friends and brother about what the future holds for him.

They bundle into the limo to drive to the church. As they ride, Ejike gets lost in his thoughts again, silencing the chatter around him.

This is it! Today, you're marrying Ifeoma, and it will be only her for the rest of your life. Are you sure she's the one? Is there even anything as the one???

No, don't think about her. She can't be the one because she's married. If she was the one, she would have trusted you when you tried to end her engagement. You just have to let it go and see what God has prepared for you.

Ifeoma is right for you. She's Christian, brilliant, creative, sexy... She's all the woman you need. And most of all, she loves you. She's the one.

Ejike is shaken from his thoughts as the limousine parks inside the church parking lot. He steps out confidently. Today's the day he becomes a man. A man that makes his own destiny.

***

He watches as she struggles to pull the skirt over her hips. Not at all an attractive sight. Yes, her hips and ass are a little bigger, and that would be nice if that was all that had changed. It's been seven months since she delivered Ezi, and her stomach still looks like he was born yesterday. *Gross!*

Doug grimaces as he watches his wife get dressed for the wedding of his former best friend. A wicked smile crosses his face as he remembers how and why that friendship ended, and how miserable Rachel would be to attend Ejike's wedding looking like a cow. He chuckles to himself. He would have felt better about rubbing his victory in Ejike's face if she looked anything near presentable. Anyway, he loves a good wedding. Lots of beautiful women to feast his eyes on.

"How do I look?" Rachel asks nervously. She has decided on another outfit that is less fitting but unflattering. At least, she is comfortable. Doug's wearing an old white native outfit he has worn several times before, but he still looks good in it. She swallows as she awaits his feedback.

He barely looks at her. "You look fine, dear. Let's go."

Rachel breathes out and makes her way downstairs, where the nanny is feeding Ezekiel. Gloria had agreed to come in exchange for taking next Wednesday off. Rachel gives her some instructions before joining Doug outside. He has chosen to take her Mazda, which he still loves to drive every now and then. She slides into the passenger seat, and they are on their way to the wedding.

***

Ejike looks around at the guests seated in the reception hall. He's all alone in his loveseat since his wife left to change into her second attire. The MC has been talking up a storm, producing waves of belly-aching laughter from the wedding party. Ejike brings his glass of champagne to his lips as he giggles to the latest knee-slapper.

His attention returns to a certain table. His friend is not looking like herself today. There has been this air of depression around her lately, but Rachel actually looks like she's in hell right now. He's sad to see her this way, but his attention is soon turned to the centre stage, where a beautiful woman in red has begun to sing.

Ejike gulps when he realises who the woman is – his bride. He hadn't expected this performance from her. He always knew she could sing, but her voice is powerful and angelic as she belts out "I Turn to You" in the style of Christina Aguilera. He listens to the lyrics as she serenades him, their eyes connecting, and their hearts binding with each word. *God, she is amazing!*

Impulsively, he rises to meet her on the stage and draws her in for a passionate kiss when she has sounded the last chord. The applause from their well-wishers is deafening, but in spite of it, all he can hear is the loud beating of his heart. He loves this woman, and he made the right choice.

***

Oh, wow! And she sings, Doug marvels, as he watches Ifeoma in awe. She is incredibly beautiful, and he has to admit, if anyone won between him and Ejike, it was Ejike. *This babe is the full package!* He rises up to give her a standing

110

ovation, while loudly cheering and joining the whistlers as the newlywed couple kiss.

Rachel stays seated, her gaze fixated on the television screen close to their table, which captures the whole scene in true colour. Closing her eyes, she takes a deep breath. At least he is happy. And honestly, she is happy for him. She wants him to be happy. He deserves it. And she says a silent prayer for his marriage and hers too.

A new song comes on, and the friends of the bride and groom hasten to join them on the dance floor. Rachel opens her eyes to see that Doug has gone too. She sees him congratulating the happy couple before going off to dance with his friends.

There's nothing left for her to see and do at this wedding. She would rather go home and be with her baby. She will just go and greet Ejike and Ifeoma, and let Doug know she's leaving. He can take an Uber back if he wants to stay.

***

Ejike spots Rachel as she approaches him on the dance floor. His hold on to his bride's waist as she dances, grinding her behind seductively against him, remains intact, even as Rachel draws nearer. She suddenly stops and waves at him as though afraid to come closer.

So, she's leaving. Well, he isn't surprised. Not only does she look out of place, she looks absent. He nods in acknowledgement, giving her a slight smile.

Ifeoma turns around in his arms and goes down low, twerking her butt and causing a small commotion from their audience. *Oh, she is naughty…and it's on tonight!* He draws her closer when she has risen, and they grind their hips to the music. They enjoy being the centre of attention until they notice that someone else has broken into their circle, drawing attention to himself.

Ejike watches as Doug leads a line-dance routine. Ifeoma, who doesn't know him, but sees her friends following his routine, decides to join the train, laughing aloud happily when she misses steps. Ejike decides to sit out the routine and returns to his loveseat. How typical of Doug to steal the limelight, he thinks, a little irritated.

***

Doug feels a tap on his shoulder and turns to see his wife. He continues dancing, looking at her expectantly to say what she wants to.

"I'm going... I'm tired."

He nods. "Okay. See you later," he replies and turns his back to her. He's having a great time and has no patience for a party-pooper.

One of his favourite party jams comes on, and instinctively, he begins a dance routine, inviting a couple of people to join in. Soon, the whole dance floor is following suit, and he can't but feel pride at being the inspiration for the performance. When the song is over, he notices the bride was among his followers, and she's looking at him as he continues dancing.

"You're a really good dancer!" she shouts through the music.

"And you have the most amazing voice!" he replies. She beams. He extends a hand. "I'm Doug. Ejike's friend."

"Oh..." she mutters. *The Doug.* "Nice to meet you, Doug. Where's your wife?"

"She's gone home... Baby's calling!"

"Oh, right. Take care," Ifeoma says, before looking about for her husband. She spots him on their loveseat and eagerly makes her way to him.

Doug continues dancing until the floor clears, and he heads back to his table to observe the final part of the festivities.

***

"First of all, I give God the glory for making this day possible. If He had not done a work in me, I might have missed out on this beautiful woman you see right here," Ejike says to his guests, raising his glass to his beloved. "I also want to thank my parents, my greatest mentors; in life, in business, and in love. I wish my marriage will be as strong and enduring as yours! To my brother, Ekene... You've been my best friend from time, and it's ride or die with you, man! And to my beautiful queen, here's to forever; happily ever after!"

"To happily ever after," the congregation responds as they clink their glasses in a toast.

Ejike winds his hand with his wife's, both of them beaming at the success of their day. When they have drunk, they bring their lips together for another kiss, and Ejike whispers in Ifeoma's ear, "My woman, my everything..."

Ifeoma beams, and her smile bursts into full on laughter when the song begins to play. It takes her a moment longer to realise that the artiste is actually in the building. The commotion begins from the right entrance until Patoranking gets to the dance floor and begins his rap. Ifeoma can't help the scream that escapes her lips!

She throws her arms around Ejike, and they begin to dance. "I love you," she cries into his ear.

"I love you too, Babe!"

***

Doug is slightly awestruck to see Patoranking performing live until he realises the opportunity it presents for his music business. He needs to locate his manager so they can talk about a collabo. He looks about earnestly to see who he might be able to get information from. His eyes spot a familiar face and recognition comes with the awe of her new look. Damn, is that Bose?!

"Hey, Doug! How are you?" she drawls.

"I'm fine, Bose. Damn, you look good! Nice haircut," he says, his eyes trailing down south. She's definitely eager to get off the dating bench, he thinks.

Bose beams, pleased that her new look could command such a reaction from Doug. "Where's Rache?"

"She left early. And you're late…"

"I came for the after-party," she replies flirtatiously. "Weddings are depressing when you're single."

"Hmmm… I see. Then you came at the right time. Let me get you a drink."

"Thanks," Bose beams and then looks about the hall. There are certainly a lot of beautiful women about, but Doug has just given her the confidence boost needed to hold her own. She takes a seat and waits for him.

When Doug comes back, Patoranking starts singing "Happy Day." The pair turn to the stage and watch as the happy couple dance. Doug and Ejike lock eyes for a few seconds, enough for Doug to read concern on Ejike's face. Doug smiles, thinking Ejike must be wondering why he is still at the wedding, talking to single women, instead of at home with his wife. *Na him sabi*, he snickers to himself before returning his full attention to Bose.

Her short dress has risen up to reveal full, fair, smooth thighs. He looks up to see her watching him scope her and smiles sheepishly. "So, how is it you're still single?"

CHAPTER FIFTEEN

It's the subject we can't avoid. SEX!

It's the most talked about subject, yet, it is the most embarrassing and most misunderstood. A lot of the embarrassment and misunderstanding is to do with those who feel they are in power or control, communicating false messages to those who feel, or are made to feel, powerless about this thing called sex. And for a lack of knowledge and understanding, the people perish indeed...

Rachel pauses in her writing. She's preparing for the next show of her radio series, The Marriage ABCs. This week's theme is "Sex and Sexuality", and it's one that has given her much trepidation, as she feels little qualified to talk about it. Rachel has invited a sex therapist to weigh in too, which makes her feel better as the session won't be built on her thoughts alone.

Sex serves the biological purpose of procreation and sustenance of the human race. It is primarily biological. But it is also a social, emotional, and physically enjoyable activity between two people of the opposite sex. However, there is another law that guides us in how sex should be practiced, and who should engage in it. It is a spiritual law of love and wisdom.

Rachel smiles. *Not bad*, she thinks. *Trust God to assist with some inspiration.* She's aware that a lot of people may disagree with her Christian perspective on the issues, but she strongly holds them and is encouraged that her station also promotes

Christian values. However, she's well aware of the challenge that bodes Believers who obey the teaching to abstain from sex before marriage. It seems like it will be an issue to prepare for too, knowing her listeners.

Sexual compatibility is not an exact science, unfortunately. You can't know who you will be sexually compatible with, especially if you have been chaste (not kissed) in courtship. It can be disheartening having to work on your sex life when you've just begun a marriage, and you expected that you would be delirious with happiness. It can also hurt your pride or self-esteem to know, or think, that you are unable to satisfy your mate in bed.

If you are single, you might be wondering how you can prevent yourself from experiencing such disappointment without disobeying God and 'sampling' sexually, as your mates may do and encourage you to do. It is good for you to remain faithful to God and keep yourself for your spouse. There are other and more important factors in play for you to enjoy a happy marriage. If you are following God, He will lead you to the right person, with whom you should share not only spiritual and emotional compatibility but also sexual compatibility.

Hmmm... She really wants to believe that, but she's struggling to with her own experience. Rachel puts down her pen and decides to take a break from further writing.

The truth is, Doug hasn't had sex with her since the night of the games' night at their house, over a month ago. In fact, he has barely touched her and has even stopped saying "I love you" altogether. It feels as though her confrontation about his feelings, or lack of, caused him to drop his pretence and freed him to be as cold as he wanted to be. She still can't believe all he said in response to her cry for a real connection was "okay". Rachel swallows.

How is she supposed to talk about love and marriage publicly when she's going through such a loveless one? She feels like such a phoney. But she's committed to see the series to completion. Rachel wipes away tears from her cheeks. Maybe more inspiration and guidance will come from above. She has to believe that there's hope, even for her situation.

***

It's another Saturday, and Rachel's home alone with her baby. She hasn't seen her husband since Friday morning when he left for work. He'd sent a message in the evening about working late but made no mention about staying out all night. Rachel reached out to him this morning, but he is yet to return her call and message.

Her shoulders heave with a sigh. This behaviour is becoming too typical. She's beginning to feel like a single mother. This is definitely not what she signed up for, loneliness in marriage. The way things are going, she fears that Doug is carrying on an affair as he seems to be so contented and happy to be disconnected from her.

The other day, she caught him in a lie, but he stood by it so strongly that she began to doubt herself. But she had known, when they married, that he had a distant relationship with the truth. She keeps looking back at the night he proposed, thinking about what he said about wanting to make her happy. She knows now that even that was a lie. How had she been so deceived?

Rachel picks up her phone to call a friend. But who can she confide in? Unfortunately, she has lost touch with most, and she doesn't feel like she can talk about her feelings with Rochelle or her step-mother, as they've never been close. She decides to call Bose.

"Hey, Rache! It's been a minute, how *nau*?" Bose answers the phone jovially.

"Hi Bose… I'm good, how are you?"

"I'm fine, hon. What's up?"

"Nothing much… Just at home with Ezekiel. How about you?"

"I'm going for my cousin's wedding today. I'm at the salon, getting made."

"Oh, cool… That's nice."

"You don't sound too happy. Everything okay?"

Rachel hesitates. Now doesn't seem like the right time to have such an intimate discussion. "Yeah, I'm fine. Missing my friend is all. Maybe we can meet for ice-cream or something tomorrow if you're free."

"Sounds cool. I'll let you know if I can get away. Or, maybe we can do next weekend."

"Yeah, sure. Just let me know. Have fun today!"

"I will! Kisses to Ezi!"

Rachel sighs as she ends the call. Yeah, it would be better for them to speak in person. She does feel a little better after the call, though. She returns her attention to her seven-month-old, who has begun crawling. They grow so fast, she smiles.

***

Rachel doesn't hear from her friend that weekend, and Bose seems too busy whenever she tries to reach out during the week. With no confirmed date nor time for their meet-up, Rachel feels more desperate about talking to someone about her feelings and challenges in marriage.

She'd considered reaching out to Ejike but, aside from not wanting his pity, she doesn't think he would be the appropriate shoulder to lean on. Since his wedding day, they haven't exchanged words, by phone or text. It's better that way… To be faced with his new love would be terribly devastating, considering her emotional state. Also, she'd addressed temptation on her marriage series last week, and she was reminded that she mustn't be foolish enough to fall into it.

Unity is the theme for this week, another thing dearly lacking in her marriage. Rachel realises that their problems will not go away with their current approach of disregarding and ignoring them. She longs for an occasion to speak with Doug about their marriage; their intimacy and relationship.

Maybe they can finally be united about seeing a marriage counsellor, even if they can't see eye to eye on other things.

He's home tonight. As usual, he's transfixed on the television, with his laptop nearby as an alternative, acceptable distraction. They have just had dinner, and now is as good a time as any.

Knowing him, though, there will never be a good time to want to talk. It's either he's too tired, or in a hurry, or busy. He always seems to have a reason why *now* is not a good time for her to require his attention.

"Can we talk?" she finally manages to say.

Doug turns to look at her. He's distracted by the television and quickly returns his gaze to it, while asking, "What?"

"Can you mute the television or pause it, please? I need to talk to you."

He sighs deeply, rolls his eyes, and reduces the volume slightly. "I'm listening. What is it?"

She swallows, unsure how to begin. "I...I think we need to see a marriage counsellor..." He sighs. She continues, "I don't feel close to you, and you don't even touch me anymore."

"Are you not a marriage counsellor? We don't need a marriage counsellor. You just need to understand what I need, and do it..."

Rachel is dumbfounded. *What does that even mean?* "Even marriage counsellors need therapists. A mediator that they can trust. I can't counsel you." *I can hardly get you to listen to me!*

"Look, it's simple. I'm just trying to work to provide for us. The studio is very demanding, and it needs a lot of money to run. I have to do other things for money because your dad didn't give me enough to start. I need like 10 million to get off the ground. Maybe you can talk to him about that or something..."

"This is not about money… Why are you making it about money?"

"Don't be so naive… What are you bringing to the table? It's all on me to provide. Maybe if you had a better-paying job, things might be more relaxed around here."

"Doug, even poor people have romance. They communicate and get along. They plan together and enjoy each other's company. We have so much, we don't even have to pay rent! But we can't even talk for five minutes without arguing."

"Maybe you should try that submission thing you preach about then," he retorts, before returning his attention to the television.

***

Rachel's shaken by her talk with Doug. What he said about submission is making her question herself and whether or not that's the real problem in their marriage. Maybe she isn't submissive enough.

She thought that by avoiding arguments and confrontation, and by being a dutiful wife, she was submissive to her husband. Obviously, she has her own mind and opinions, but she usually lets things go and does things his way. Now he says he wants her to talk to her father about giving him more financial assistance. It seems like something she can do, but it doesn't feel right. In her opinion, her father already does too much for them.

Doug has gone to bed, and she's alone in the living room re-watching one of her favourite series, Girlfriends. The sitcom always puts her in a good mood or takes her mind away from her cares. However, as she watches today's episode, she sees some similarities with her own life.

It's the scene where Monica returns to William, after breaking up with him for quitting his job. Monica begins to plan his next business move, and William is surprised that she doesn't want to do something more romantic to celebrate their reconciliation. But she replies, "This is us!"

The words resonate with Rachel. *Is this what Doug wants from me? Is this how he sees us?*

She heads to their bedroom and finds him lying on the bed. After telling him about the scene, she asks if that is what would make him happy.

"Yes. That's what I want from you," Doug replies grimly.

Rachel swallows. She nods and then sighs. Now she knows. Maybe they can be happy this way.

But deep down, she knows it will never be enough, and she will never be happy being a glorified business manager instead of his beloved wife. She returns to the living room to be alone and think more on what Doug has just revealed.

I can't do it, she thinks. Even if she could ask her father for more support, she can't keep up the job of campaigning for her husband. It's just not her nature and definitely not what she signed up for. And there is no assurance of the love and care he promised when he married her, even if this condition he has set is met. He has shown that he is not trustworthy nor in this for love. But what can she do now he has made it plain to her what he wants from their marriage?

Rachel gets down on her knees, moved with anguish to cry out to her Father.

CHAPTER SIXTEEN

"Lord, I don't know what to do. My marriage is in trouble, and I don't know how to fight for it, how to save it. I feel like it was wrong from the start, but I also know that there's nothing impossible for You to do. Please, God, help us to overcome our problems and love each other the way we should.

"Please help me to get past the hurt I feel, the disappointment, and the pain. Help me to see things Your way, and give me the strength to love Doug unconditionally. It feels so hard because I too am human. I need love too. But I pray that You will be enough for me, and I can be Your minister in this marriage. Lord, please help me!" Rachel pleads.

She pauses to listen for a word from Him. A scripture comes to mind; *"Be on guard. Stand firm in the faith. Be courageous. Be strong. And do everything with love."* She looks it up on her phone and learns that it's from 1 Corinthians 16:13-14 of the New Living Translation. Rachel meditates on it, especially verse 14. The New King James Version says *"Let all that you do be done with love."*

From her meditation, Rachel realises that she has been driven by fear, distrust, and anger towards her husband, and not by love. She turns to the chapter on love, 1 Corinthians 13, and studies it again, verses 4 to 8 being focal. She prefers the wording of the New International Version, which reads:

"Love is patient, love is kind. It does not envy, it does not boast, it is not proud. It does not dishonor others, it is not self-seeking, it is not easily angered, it keeps no record of wrongs. Love does not delight in evil but rejoices with the truth. It always protects, always trusts, always hopes, always perseveres. Love never fails."

After meditating on it awhile, Rachel returns to meditate on 1 Corinthians 16:13. She knows her faith is being tested by this trial. The temptations to blame God, to doubt Him, or to disobey, and look out for number one are strong. But she is reminded of the cross Jesus bore and calls her to bear also.

God, please, I need more faith to honour You in my marriage…and I need Your grace to stand. Please help me!

Abide in Me, for without Me, you can do nothing… Rachel perceives the Holy Spirit, as a gentle whisper filters through her thoughts. Encouraged, she remains on her knees, meditating on those words, and crying intermittently for strength to endure.

***

"That was "Hello" by Adele, requested by Dami from Ikoyi. I really love that song. It's one I think everyone can relate to," Rachel speaks into her microphone at the studio. "So, this is the week of love, with Valentine's Day coming up on Sunday. It's also the V week on The Marriage ABCs series. Tomorrow, I'll be on with Pastor (Mrs) Idowu, who is also a marriage counsellor with a lot to contribute to our theme, "Victory in the Vine." You don't want to miss it! Next up is a new hit by Justin Bieber, "Love Yourself," requested by Obi from Maryland…"

She takes off her headphones as the song plays on the air. *The week of love indeed.* It's her second Valentine's Day as a married woman, but she doubts that there will be any celebration of it in her house. She's been praying and fasting intermittently, as she's still breastfeeding, but her marriage feels as cold as ever.

Rachel has had to admit the truth to herself that she was not in love with her husband when she agreed to marry him. She had accepted the teaching that the emotional element of love was not so essential and thought her feelings would deepen with time. She now realises, however, that those emotions would have been great stimulants in her fight for her marriage. Right now, her only motivation appears to be religious duty. Her will to fight does not originate from her heart…

"A penny for your thoughts…" Dongjap says.

Rachel looks up at him and gives a small smile. She doesn't want to delve into her issues with her producer, but he looks genuinely concerned. A sigh escapes her lips. "Do you believe the emotional, romantic element of love is an essential part of real love?"

"Hmmm…" Dongjap mutters, pursing his lips. "Why you asking? I thought you covered this on The Marriage ABCs already?"

"Yes, but everyone has their opinion. I want to know yours…"

"I actually agreed with your perspective and thought more on it. I think the emotional aspect is like the engine oil of love, which makes everything work more smoothly… Without it, there's just a lot friction."

"Yeah… Friction…" Rachel mutters.

"Everything okay with you and Doug?"

Rachel puts on a brave face and nods. "Yeah, we're good." *It's nothing God can't fix…*

The light on line two is flashing, and Rachel seizes the opportunity to disengage from Dj and her thoughts.

"Hi Caller, what's your name, and where are you calling from?"

"Hi Rachel. I'm Steve. I live in Oshodi."

"Nice to meet you, Steve. Are you ready for Valentine's

Day?"

"Not quite. I'm nervous. I'm in love with my best friend, but she doesn't know how I feel. I mean, I've never told her..."

"Oh, really? Well, you can't let the opportunity pass you by. You have to tell her. What's her name?"

"Yewande. We've been friends since high school, but things just kept getting in the way..."

"Is she listening?"

"I've sent her a message to tune in... She just did! Can you play "Thinking Out Loud" by Ed Sheeran? I think of her every time I listen to the song."

"Awww, that so sweet! You got it! Happy Valentine's to you both! Yewande, this is for you, from Steve..."

Rachel smiles and sits back as the song plays, happy for Steve and Yewande. Closing her eyes, she prays that such pure love that Ed sings about is still possible for her. She can only hope.

***

"Victory in marriage is guaranteed when we are connected to the Vine as branches, and we abide in Christ, who enables us to do all things," Pastor Idowu says with a smile. "Problems arise in marriage when we try to do it in our own strength, with our own wisdom, depending on our limited and fickle love. Marriage, though of the world, requires divine empowerment to succeed. If you want to succeed, you have to submit to the divine!"

"Hmmm," Rachel mutters. "What if one person is trying, but the other isn't committed?"

"The marriage can still be saved," Pastor Idowu replies. "Though it is hard to do so alone, two people giving up and being selfish and unchristian in a marriage is a definite failure without revival! But if at least one abides in Christ, and is dependent on Him, we can call upon Him to arise on our behalf and fight with us for our marriage. And such faith always moves God to act on our behalf."

"Wow! That's a really tough call…"

"Yes, but this is what is required of each one of us in marriage; to be Christ to our spouse and to love them as Christ loved and loves us. And even the worst sort of marriage can be turned around!"

"I can imagine that a lot of wives and husbands will find this hard to accept. I mean, some people are in very abusive marriages. What would you say to them?"

"I'd say look at me. I did it. I abided with my husband though he was a philanderer from day one! In fact, the first month of our marriage, I wanted to throw in the towel! I actually caught him in bed with our house-help!"

"Oh my God!"

"Yes, oh my God! My heart broke to a million pieces, and I packed my things to leave that very night. And guess what…" Rachel looks on at the pastor. "He didn't try to stop me or beg me or anything. He didn't even come after me. I went back on my own about a couple of weeks later when my mother told me that it was God who would fight for me and deliver me if I would just honour His word and my vows."

"Hmmm… That must have been excruciating! I mean, it sounds like he didn't even care for you at all."

"It *was* excruciating. And you know, things didn't change right away. But I made up my mind that his actions were not going to affect my faith in God. I abided and had three children for him. It was not in my time nor power, but God eventually took hold of his heart…and what do you know, we pastor a church today, and counsel many married couples."

"Amazing! I mean, it's awful what you went through, but it's great to see how God came through for you. It's a bit like how Daniel was in the lions' den. His faith was greater than his circumstance, and God honoured his obedience."

"Exactly!" Pastor Idowu beams. "So, if you are going

through a challenge in your marriage, and you fear that you cannot survive it, take courage! Trust in God. Victory is guaranteed in the Vine. Abide in Jesus, learn from Him, follow Him to that cross where He died, and die too…to self, and rise up and live for Christ in your marriage."

"On that note, we'll take a break. When we come back, Pastor Idowu will answer your questions. Don't touch that dial!"

***

Rachel's thoughts are on yesterday's show with Pastor Idowu. She hasn't been able to stop thinking about it in relation to her marriage. It felt like God was confirming the word He gave her last week; *Abide in Me, for without Me, you can do nothing.*

Rachel prays for more leading and direction, surrendering her will to Him. *Not my will but Yours be done, Lord.* After some more time in prayer, meditation, and worship, she finally feels ready to face the day.

Rachel exhales, feeling relief from the burden she has been carrying. She smiles, thinking it's going to be a good day. She can do what it takes to save her marriage because God is with her, and He alone can make a way where there seems to be none. The joy abides with her as she sings worship songs while attending to her daily chores.

Rachel breathes in the sweet aroma of the prawn fried rice she has just prepared. Tasting it, she confirms that it's her best yet.

She picks up her phone to send Doug a message, inviting him to join her at home for lunch. He does so on occasion, usually dropping by unannounced to get some food. Sometimes, he calls ahead to enquire and asks her to pack lunch for him to take away.

However, she feels that she should make more effort today. It is Valentine's week, and rather than wait for Doug to show his affection for her, there's nothing wrong with her making the first move. Since it's her day off, she has the afternoon free. She packs up a small picnic basket and gets herself ready to visit her husband at his studio.

In the seven months that she's been back, she's ashamed to realise that she's only visited Doug at his studio on three occasions prior. She had just returned with Ezekiel then, and Doug was still kitting out the studio with furniture and sound equipment. Rachel is pleased to see that it is looking rather professional and well-equipped now. She admires the wall painting behind the receptionist's desk, as she announces her presence.

"He's in a meeting, Mrs Olumide. Why don't you take a seat, and I'll let him know you're here," the young lady says.

But just as she's completing her sentence, Doug opens the door to his office and looks somewhat surprised to see Rachel. The woman holding hands with him as they exit the room appears more shocked to see Rachel standing in the hallway, holding her basket. Rachel feels her heart drop to the pit of her stomach at the sight before her.

What is Bose doing here? And why is she holding hands with Doug?!

To her astonishment, they do not separate their hands but walk towards her, as though it is a very normal thing for them to be together this way. Rachel makes a point of fixing her gaze on their clasped hands, before returning to look at her husband's face.

"Hi, Rachel," Bose says awkwardly. *What is that smile on her face?!*

"You should have told me you were coming…" he says. Doug turns to Bose, gives her a hug and a kiss on the cheek, before saying, "I'll catch up with you later."

Rachel can't bring herself to look at Bose, as she walks past as if she had never seen nor heard of Rachel in her life. Rachel's fuming as she looks at Doug, waiting for an explanation. It doesn't come.

He takes the basket from her. "Thanks, dear. You saved me a trip. Next time, call first. I'm very busy today," he says as he returns to his office, leaving her standing there frozen, as though she had been slapped in the face.

CHAPTER SEVENTEEN

By the time Rachel gets home, she has convinced herself that it couldn't possibly be what it looked like. Things have been off between her and Doug for months, so his disregard for her today isn't totally unusual. But it still doesn't explain what Bose was doing there, why they were holding hands, and why Bose behaved so aloof. Had she offended Bose or something?

Rachel dials her friend's number. After a few network connection issues, the phone finally rings, but no one picks up. She tries again and gets a busy signal. Rachel decides to reach her via WhatsApp instead.

"Hi Bose. Can we talk? I've been trying to reach you."

The message delivers, but the blue ticks don't appear. Rachel decides to exercise more patience and get her chores done. However, she struggles to concentrate and returns repeatedly to see if she has gotten a response. It doesn't occur to her to send Doug a similar message. When he comes home, she'll broach the subject. She just wants to hear from her friend first.

When, by evening, she hasn't gotten a response from Bose, though the two blue ticks indicate that her message has been read, and Doug hasn't returned home nor been in touch, Rachel doubts herself again. What if it *is* what it looks like? What if there is something going on between Doug and

Bose? How long has it been going on? Is this why Bose has been distant since she returned from the US? How could the two people who are supposed to love and care for her do this to her?

It's late when she finally decides to send Doug a message. *"Hi, dear. Are you coming home tonight?"*

"Still busy here. Don't keep dinner," is his response.

Moments later, she gets another notification. It's Bose.

"Hi, Rachel. How are you?"

"I'm fine. And you?"

"I'm great. What's up?"

"I was surprised to see you at Doug's studio today. What were you doing there?"

"We're working on a production. I thought he told you."

"He didn't. You should have told me too."

"Why? Am I your husband? I don't answer to you."

Rachel pauses at the change in Bose's tone. *"You're my friend, Bose. If you're working closely on a project with MY husband, I should know about it!"*

"Exactly, you should know about it. Your marital problems don't concern me. Just don't try to act like we're best friends. It's funny that you even want to claim we're friends."

"What? Why are you talking like this?"

"Don't worry about it, Rachel. I'm busy now. Later."

Rachel can't believe that's the end of her conversation with her friend. What does Bose have to be mad about? But the thing that bugs her the most is Bose's reference to her marital problems, especially as she'd actually sought her out to talk about it. Now she knows that would have been a big mistake.

***

Rachel hears the front door open, shut, and lock. She checks her phone for the time. 2:20am. Sadly a typical time for Doug to return home.

She hasn't been able to sleep thinking about what

happened today and her subsequent conversation with Bose. She lies in bed waiting for the bedroom door to open, but the next sound she hears is from the television downstairs. Doug has apparently chosen to spend his night in front of the TV again, instead of in their bed.

Rachel mulls over going to meet him downstairs, but she knows now isn't really the ideal time, and they'll likely end up arguing. She'll have to find time in the morning, or sometime tomorrow, to talk to her husband. Closing her eyes, she settles into sleep.

Doug is asleep on the sofa when she goes down to open the door for the cleaner in the morning. Rachel wakes him up and waits for him to climb the stairs to their bedroom before letting Rose in. Afterwards, she goes to the nursery to breastfeed Ezekiel before getting herself ready for work.

Gloria arrives by 9am in time to relieve Rachel and look after Ezekiel. At this time, Doug is just stirring from sleep. Rachel lingers in the hope of talking to him about Bose. Her body shakes in anticipation of the confrontation.

She sits on her side of the bed waiting as he rounds off his morning prayer. When he's done and sits up in bed, she opens with, "Good morning."

"Good morning, dear," he replies.

"I made toasties. They're in the microwave."

"Okay, thanks."

"I want to talk about what happened yesterday…"

"What happened?" he asks without a trace of guile.

"When I brought you lunch, and you were heading out of your office with Bose…"

"Okay…"

"You were holding hands…"

"And…?"

"I don't like it…" Doug rolls his eyes. "And I was surprised to see her there. Why didn't you tell me you were working together?"

Doug sighs, stands up, and heads to the bathroom. "I didn't think I had to. She's your friend, don't you guys talk? Besides, what's not to like?"

Rachel rises to follow him. "It's not right, Doug. How would you like it if I was walking about holding hands with another man?"

Doug huffs. "It's really not a big deal, Rache. I don't have a problem with it…"

Rachel frowns. "Well, I do. Please stop it, because you will send off the wrong message. You're supposed to protect our marriage."

"Don't tell me what I'm supposed to do, Rachel. If you want to read meaning into it, that's on you," he replies conclusively, shutting the bathroom door to end the argument.

***

It has been a month since that exchange with Doug, and Rachel has tried not to let her imagination run wild thinking about what her husband could be doing with her friend, who has refused to communicate since. He said there was nothing going on, and she really doesn't have much of a case. Plus, she's too busy looking after her child and trying to be a good wife to be an effective detective.

But it's been hard.

"One thing I need you to take away from this series is, however wonderful marriage is, however ordained and holy your union is, marriage itself is not your purpose for living and should never become your centre," Rachel speaks into her microphone emphatically. "Your spouse cannot and should never become your everything – God forbid! Marriage is and should be one of the things in this life that add meaning, beauty, and joy to our lives, but without it, we can still live full, beautiful, and impactful lives."

Rachel is airing her last show in The Marriage ABCs series, themed "Zealous for Life." Today's episode is short and sweet, and she doesn't have a guest speaker. While preparing for it, she made a decision about her radio career. It had been fulfilling and an opportunity to minister, but she no longer felt right about teaching or counselling others about marriage, knowing hers was in such a mess. She needs to get out of the limelight and take care of herself and her family.

"Life itself is the most precious gift God has given us on this side of eternity. To be alive, be able to think and reason, feel, enjoy, laugh, breathe, smile, sing, dance, and talk… These are all pleasures we take for granted. We were supposed to enjoy living, be fruitful, have goals and strive to achieve them, have family and friends, and discover our world, appreciating all of God's creation and creatures…"

Twisting her wedding band on her left hand, fourth finger, Rachel pushes through her show, engaging her listeners and taking regular sponsored breaks. It's the shortest show in the series, but it feels like the longest. Rachel's relieved when she gets to the last few minutes and wraps up the show with some parting advice.

"Remember, God is enough. Your spouse is extra. They are meant to help. But God has got you, and if they will not do what they were called to do, what they promised to do, God will make other help available to you. His arm is not too short. His resources are not too limited. And His grace is more than sufficient."

Rachel sighs as she hangs her headphones, while a jingle plays on the radio. She'd submitted her notice to leave instead of renewing her contract earlier that morning. After today's show, she wishes that she'd thought to do so earlier, so that today would have been her last. She's eager to move on to the next chapter of her life.

"You alright?" Dongjap asks, concern etched on his face.

Rachel nods, but the feelings she's been fighting to hide bubble up and spill out, causing her to sob, her shoulders heaving even as she tries to fight the cry. Dongjap goes to her and gathers her in his arms. He says nothing at all as he strokes her back. He has seen enough to know there's trouble in paradise. Maybe, one day, Rachel will let him in and talk about it. But for now, his shoulder is available.

***

"Hey, Rachel. How are you?"

Rachel looks at the message from Dongjap and pauses. Since the day she broke down in tears at the studio, about two weeks ago, he has been reaching out almost daily. She knows he's only worried about her, but she doesn't want to encourage his behaviour. She doesn't need a man-friend who pays her more attention than her husband.

"Hi, Dongjap. I'm fine. How are you?"

"I'm good. How's Ezi?"

"He's good too. Thanks."

"Sure. You're welcome."

Rachel sighs and closes their chat. She takes note of his new display image. It's a scriptural passage, one of the verses she had shared on her last episode of The Marriage ABCs. Was it a coincidence, or had Dongjap finally found Jesus?

"That he would grant you, according to the riches of his glory, to be strengthened with might by his Spirit in the inner man; That Christ may dwell in your hearts by faith; that ye, being rooted and grounded in love, May be able to comprehend with all saints what is the breadth, and length, and depth, and height; And to know the love of Christ, which passeth knowledge, that ye might be filled with all the fulness of God," (Ephesians 3:16-19 KJV).

Rachel smiles as she reads the encouragement and prayer by the apostle renamed Paul. It is just what she needs, and she suspects that others would find the scripture timely too, so she copies the image to share as her display picture also. Moments later, she gets another message from Dongjap.

"Nice DP! ☺*"*

Rachel responds with a smiley face.

Scrolling through her WhatsApp chats, she notices some

new display images from her friends. Ekene's picture catches her eye, and she selects it to get a closer view. It's one of him and Ejike, which would have been taken on Ejike's wedding day. It's a beautiful shot, and the groom looks ecstatic, as though he was captured mid-laughter. Rachel smiles and opens her chat with Ekene. He's online.

"*Lovely DP,*" she writes. "*How are you?*"

"*Hey, Rachel*" Ekene responds cheerfully. "*It's been a while. I'm good. And you?*"

"*I'm fine, thanks.*"

"*Yeah, thanks!*" he replies to her compliment of his display picture. "*You're joining us tonight?*"

"*For what?*"

"*Ejike's birthday. It's today. I thought you guys talk...*"

"*Oh, really? I didn't know. Well, it's been long we talked.*"

"*Oh, okay. Well, I'll forward the details. If you are free, you should come.*"

"*Thanks, Ekene.*"

"*No problem. Later.*"

Rachel sighs as she reads through the exchange. She's sad that she and Ejike have drifted apart and no longer talk. After his wedding, she'd chosen to give him space, with the belief that he would contact her after his honeymoon if he wanted to. But he never did, and she didn't think it right to reach out to him, especially being as unhappy as she has been.

But if there was ever a time to reach out, it would be now.

"*Happy Birthday, Ejike! I hope it's your best year yet* 😊"

Coincidentally, he's online. His response comes soon after.

"*Hi, sis! Long time* 😊 *Thanks!*"

Sis? Ejike never calls her 'sis'! It doesn't feel nice nor close. It feels distant. Perhaps, that's how he hoped for them to be.

Rachel's desire for further communication dies with his reply. She rather closes their chat and puts her phone aside.

It beeps moments later, and she goes to check it, half-hoping it's a "How are you?" from Ejike. But it's just Ekene sending the invite to Ejike's party.

Rachel puts her phone on silent and closes her eyes, hoping to escape the agony she feels at the realisation that Ejike is well and truly over her.

CHAPTER EIGHTEEN

The view from the 15th floor of Eden Enterprises' 16-story building in Ikoyi is breath-taking. Being the tallest building for miles, the whole floor is surrounded by floor to ceiling windows, making the fluorescent spotlighting in every room redundant during daylight. Rachel watches as cars speed along the Third Mainland Bridge, which connects Ikoyi with Ikeja. It's her second favourite view from the high-rise building.

Her first is the amazing landscape of the Atlantic Ocean, seen from her father's office. She's in his waiting room, while he's engaged in a meeting. His assistant informed him of her presence about 20 minutes ago, so she's hopeful that he will soon be available.

The sounds of chatter and laughter cause Rachel to turn towards the direction of Chief Eden's office doorway. Two executives have exited the room, and they both acknowledge her presence with a nod and a smile as they pass by. She curtsies slightly in greeting, before entering her father's office.

"Rachel, how *nau?*" he says jovially, a pleasant smile on his face as he beholds his first daughter.

Rachel beams from ear to ear and goes to give Chief Eden kisses on his cheeks. After a brief hug, she leaves to take her seat in front of his expansive desk. A widescreen television hums quietly as a reporter shares the news at 1pm. Rachel turns to it briefly before returning her attention to her father.

At almost 70 years of age, Chief Eden is the most energetic and the happiest man Rachel has ever known. If not for the full head of grey hair on his head, it would have been easy to confuse him for a 50-year-old man. He still stands tall at 5'8 and sports a slim, athletic build, owing to his dedication to healthy eating and regular exercise. An impressive man, even before you open his resume. Rachel exhales.

"Everything okay?" Chief Eden asks his daughter. She looks like she's carrying the weight of the world on her shoulders.

"Yes, Daddy," Rachel says with a small smile. "How are you?"

Chief nods. "Fine, thanks." He keeps a steady gaze on Rachel as she fidgets across the desk.

"Good," she mutters and then swallows. "Dad, I want to discuss a business idea with you…"

"Sure. What is it?"

"I want to open a spa and resort, catering especially to mothers…"

"Hmmm, okay. Have you prepared a proposal or a budget?"

"Yes, Dad. It needs a bit more work, but I want to run by some of my ideas with you first."

"There's no rush, Rachel. Develop your proposal, and let's talk when you have it. How's Doug?"

"He's fine. Thanks again for your support with his studio."

Chief shakes his head and smiles. "No problem, dear. All for my baby!"

Rachel beams. She remembers Doug's appeal for additional funding, but she knows her dad too well. He will require a well-thought-out proposal before upping his investment, and she doesn't have that to present to him. Still, she broaches the topic.

"Doug is working on some new collaborations, and…and…" Rachel stutters, not knowing how to ask for more money from a man who has given so much already.

"Let him come and see me if he needs my help with anything," Chief Eden interrupts, sparing Rachel the trauma.

Rachel nods, getting the message. Chief doesn't like unnecessary middle men. She smiles shyly, rising to take her leave.

"I'll work on my proposal and send to you next week."

"No problem, dear."

With a kiss on his cheek, she exits his office.

***

The noise of the television competes with the pitter patter of rain drops outside, and the occasional thunder. It's a very rainy Saturday in April, which has stranded Doug in his house since morning. He has used the opportunity to catch up on all his television programmes, though his body yearns for sleep.

On the two occasions Rachel has sought to switch off the television, after observing that Doug had fallen asleep, he'd stirred and stopped her. So, now he lays, snoring on the sofa, with the TV blaring, as Rachel changes Ezekiel's diaper on his playmat.

At eleven months, with increased mobility, Ezekiel demands much more attention than before. The small playpen she'd bought to restrict his movement failed to sufficiently engage him, so Rachel opted for a larger playmat, which he adores, for him to crawl around on, with supervision. When he's a little older, she's looking to get the gated play-yard fence.

Rachel muses as she observes her son playing. She'd completed and emailed her proposal to her dad on Thursday, but she's yet to hear from him. She's still got another two months at the radio station, and she's eager to get started on her new business if she gets her father's backing.

Doug stirs awake again as the credits roll on another show. He looks out through the window, as though with longing. The clouds are fading, and the heavy rain has turned to sunny showers. After an hour, the flooded streets will become passable again. He'll go to the bathroom now and get himself ready to go out.

Rachel watches as Doug rises up and climbs the stairs to their living quarters. She'd been enthused when it started raining early in the morning, thinking they would be able to spend time together as a family and talk. But she should have known it'd make no difference. Rising up, she puts Ezi in his walker and goes to the kitchen to boil rice for lunch.

Doug is back down, just as Rachel finishes setting up the table. "I'll take mine with me," he says.

Rachel carries his plate back to the kitchen and serves his food in a takeaway pack. He's already outside when she returns to the living room. She goes out to meet him, his food in a nylon bag.

She has questions about where he's going, why, and when he'll be back, but he's obviously in too much of a hurry for that to be well received. Maybe when he gets back, they can talk.

"Thanks," he mutters as he collects the bag from her, puts it in the back seat, and settles behind the wheel.

The next sound is the horn for the security guard to open the gate.

✳✳✳

"So, you're quitting the radio? Why *nau*?"

Rachel's distracted by her niece's chatter, as Jen shows off the number of words she knows, as well as the number of toys she owns, to a fascinated Ezi. Occasionally, Ezi sobs in frustration, usually when his cousin grabs one of her favourite toys from his reach. Jennifer's nanny is supervising the pair as they play in Jen's playroom, across the hall. Even as big as Rochelle's house is, the noise carries into the living area, where Rachel's visiting with Rochelle and Ekene.

Rachel turns to Ekene, who's waiting for her to answer his question. She finds it hard talking about her decision to leave the studio. How can she tell people that being out there emotionally for others, and talking as though she has it all together, makes her feel like she's standing naked and covered with bruises? Or that she feels like people must know the thoughts and feelings she's battling to stay hidden, and when she can no longer keep it together, she'll be a laughing stock?

"I just feel it's time for a change..." she says at last.

Ekene nods as if he understands. "Do you know what you want to do instead?"

"Yeah... I'm opening a spa for mothers," Rachel beams. Her father loved her proposal, and they have already begun to draw up the legal papers for her company's registration.

"Oh, cool!" Ekene replies. "Why just mothers?"

"Well, I am one, and I think we are an under-served clientele..."

"How do you mean?" Rochelle interjects.

"I think it would be nice to have a place that helps expectant mothers prepare for motherhood, supports first-time moms with resources to cope, and provides affordable day care for working moms. All the services will be geared to making motherhood easier and more enjoyable for women. It will be like a place away from home where moms can hang out with other moms and get pampered, while their children are well looked after by trained nannies. I don't know anyone else doing that."

"Wow! I want to go there," Rochelle cries.

Rachel laughs. "I got the idea after I had Ezekiel. It's been so hard to organise play dates for him, and I never seem to be able to do anything for me anymore."

"Will there be a gym too?" Rochelle asks, excitedly.

"Yes, of course. It's like a woman's paradise, but with

motherhood in mind. I'm calling it Haven for Moms."

"That sounds great, Rachel! How does Doug feel about it?" Ekene asks.

"He thinks it's a good idea." She swallows. Truthfully, they haven't spoken much about it, though Doug's aware that she's setting up a spa with her father. If anything, he seems envious of the investment Chief is making to help Rachel set up the spa as opposed to funding his studio.

"Well, I hope you'll be open before the new year," Rochelle says, a glint in her eye. "We're expecting number two!"

"Oh, wow!" Rachel beams and studies her sister closer. If she hadn't said anything, Rachel would never have thought to ask, as Rochelle's chubby frame makes it hard to know if she's carrying extra weight or baby weight. "How many weeks are you?"

"Six weeks, so it's still early," Rochelle replies.

Rachel watches as Ekene kisses the top of his wife's head fondly. Somehow, she knows that it wasn't just for her benefit, but is a reflection of his deep affection for her. And Rochelle is positively glowing, like every beloved wife ought to.

"Congratulations!" Despite the pang of jealousy at their seemingly happy home, Rachel is truly pleased about their news.

***

Rachel can hardly believe that almost a year has passed since she delivered her son. With just two weeks to his birthday, she has started on plans for his big celebration. She'd initially wanted a small event at home with just a few friends and family. But after stumbling on some one-year-party themes on Pinterest, she's excited about throwing a themed party now.

"It doesn't have to cost more. It's really about creativity, imagination, and resourcefulness," Folusho, an old friend from NYSC camp, says.

"That's true, actually. I once went to a party where the children made the decorations as part of their party fun," Ihotu, a new friend from Church, chimes in.

"Nice... I'm not sure I'll do that, though," Rachel says candidly. "I was thinking something more classical, like a Disney-themed party."

"Hmmm... But have you noticed that most Disney films are geared towards girls?" Rochelle asks. "I can only think of Peter Pan for a boy's party..."

"You know, I never realised that. Most Disney movies are centred around princesses," Rachel marvels. "Hmmm... But a Peter Pan themed party would be very creative, I guess."

"Actually, there are quite a few. What about The Lion King? Aladdin? Pinocchio?" Seun, Rachel's friend from work, suggests.

"There's also The Jungle Book..." Ihotu adds.

Rachel beams. "Yes, I love The Jungle Book. It will be a great theme. Let's do that!"

Rochelle, Folusho, Seun, and Ihotu nod in agreement. "In that case, can I suggest an outdoor party?" Ihotu says.

The ladies agree, and they settle on the compound of the Eden mansion to hold the birthday bash. Rachel puts Ihotu in charge of the decor. Folusho takes on the responsibility of catering for the event, and Rochelle, who has a few friends with infants and toddlers, takes charge of the guest list. Rachel and Seun are left to plan the games and activities.

Rachel smiles happily as she imagines how the day will be. She's elated that Seun, Folusho, and Ihotu honoured her invitation to help plan for Ezekiel's first birthday. Folusho was one of her bridesmaids, but they've hardly kept in touch. Rachel is a little disappointed that Bose ignored her invitation. Even though she'd only arranged the meeting a couple of days ago, she'd been hopeful that it would be an opportunity for them to resolve their issues.

"Have you got a photographer, Rache?" Folusho asks. "Because I know a guy..."

"Oh, please, send his contact!" Rachel replies. "I want to do a pre-birthday shoot at home too," she adds, turning to look at the celebrant.

"Oh, look at him go," Ihotu exclaims as she observes Ezekiel successfully take a few steps towards his nanny. "Is that his first time?"

Rachel's breath catches at the sight. She nods. "Yes... And I almost missed it..."

"He's really the cutest," Seun says. "You and Doug are so lucky! I can't wait to get married!"

Rachel turns to her friend, her expression serious. "Actually, you can. You must wait for the right person because there's absolutely no rush."

She returns her attention to her son and ignores the puzzled look on her friend's face.

CHAPTER NINETEEN

Ihotu really outdid herself with the decorations. With a very small budget, she managed to achieve a forest-feel outdoor party design with different shades of green and brown balloons, red and orange ribbons hanging from the trees, and The Jungle Book poster backdrops between the palm trees that line the Eden's garden. Thankfully, the sun has been cooperative and stands shining brightly, high in the sky.

The food vendors Folusho recruited have all arrived and are setting up their stands. Fake bananas and monkeys hang around the fruit stand, where the children can get various fresh fruits, fruit drinks, popsicles, and other fruity treats. In contrast, a burger joint, offering hot dogs, burgers, and fries, is set-up across from the fruit stand. A little further to the right, the two-layer, nutty, birthday cake sits on a confectionery stand, surrounded by cupcakes, brownies and other sweet treats.

"Wow! This is great! Well done, Babe."

Rachel's thrown aback by the sudden arm around her shoulder. She hadn't seen him coming. She turns to look at her husband, and he gives her a kiss on her lips, followed by a grin. He's holding a plate of jollof rice and chicken and munching happily away. She lets out a big sigh as she looks around the garden again. Few guests have arrived, and the party is yet to start.

"Thanks. I had a lot of help," she says.

"Hey, Rache!" Rachel turns to see Seun. "Hi, Doug."

"Hi, Seun. How are you?" Doug asks.

"I'm fine, thanks. Congratulations!"

"Thanks," he replies. Giving Rachel's shoulder a squeeze, he makes his exit. "I'll see you later."

Rachel nods and smiles, before turning to Seun again. "Thanks, dear. Did you get the craft games?"

"Yes. Where do you want them?"

***

It's hard to tell who's having more fun, the grownups or the children, as they play "Who's That Baby?", a party game where people share their old baby photos, and others have to guess who is who. While the adults find it amusing and are taken down memory lane, the kids are driven to hysterics by their parents' childhood pictures and the stories they regale them with.

Actually, it looks like Doug is having the most fun. Rachel hasn't seen him laugh so hard since…well, their wedding. He seems to have something funny to say about every single photograph, as he exercises his role as the compere for the event.

Rachel looks up at the banner displaying all the digitally enlarged baby photos submitted. As she was the one who collated the pictures and designed the banner, she's not allowed to partake in the game. They are now on the last photograph. Rachel's gaze is drawn to the owner of the photo.

"*Na girl be dis?*" Doug chuckles. "This baby fine, *oh…*"

Rachel turns her gaze back to the picture. She can see why someone would be in doubt about the baby's sex. The child in the picture has big curly black hair and large bright eyes, framed with long lashes. There was no doubt that it would grow into a stunner. She looks back at the mature version.

Rachel's shocked to find Ejike staring back at her. She quickly looks away and tries to keep her gaze from returning in his direction. His beautiful wife is by his side, her long, jewelled fingers on his right thigh. Rachel wonders why they bothered to come. It's not like they have kids... But then again, she'd left Rochelle in charge of the invites.

Rachel feels a tap on her shoulder and turns to see Folusho. "Hey, What's up?"

"Can we start distributing the food packs now? Some parents have been asking?" Folusho asks.

"Oh, not yet. We need to cut the cake first. We'll be doing that next. Thanks!"

Rising up, Rachel makes her way to the cake stand to make preparations for the next item of the ceremony.

***

"Congratulations on Ezekiel's first birthday, Rache!"

Rachel looks up to see Ifeoma, Ejike's wife, smiling down at her. The lady is tall and graceful, definitely a match for her husband. Rachel plants a smile on her face and makes to embrace Ifeoma. "Thanks for coming."

Ifeoma hugs Rachel back. "No problem at all. How can I help?"

Rachel looks about and then back at Ifeoma. "I think everything's taken care of..."

"Oh, please. I wanna be useful. What are you about to do?" Rachel thinks Ifeoma's laying on her American accent thick. She'd never noticed that before, and she wonders why Ifeoma feels the need to impress.

"I'm just preparing for the cake cutting..."

"So, you need to gather the kids together, right? I can do that," Ifeoma says before rushing off to talk to some children nearby.

Rachel sighs, surprised but also anxious about Ifeoma's behaviour. She looks about for Ejike and finds him sitting in the same spot, engaged in a conversation with Ekene and

Rochelle. Rachel signals to the photographer and indicates for Doug to announce that the children should gather for the cake cutting.

As the children position themselves behind the cake, Rachel carries the celebrant from his nanny. Ifeoma arrives with more children and helps with their arrangement, so that the taller kids stand at the back. Rochelle strolls into the shot with Jen just in time.

After the birthday song and the cake is cut, the photographer takes the group photo of the moms and their children, followed by the celebrant and his extended family, then his immediate family. Doug takes Ezi from Rachel and wraps his arm around her for the last family shot. And it's a beautiful one.

***

The last two days, the rain has been pouring as though it is making up for staying away all weekend. Rachel lies in bed as the wind sends rain drops smashing against the window by the side of her bed, causing lines of rain to descend down the glass. She should get up and start getting ready for work, but she's also contemplating calling in sick. The way it's been raining, the gutters would have overflowed, and the traffic won't let up for another three hours.

She turns on her pillow and sighs. Doug must be thinking the same thing because he's still in bed. She watches as he takes in a deep breath and lets out a snore. She should at least get up and make him a nice breakfast, seeing as it's their wedding anniversary today. They haven't spoken about any plans, though.

Rachel sits up and swings her legs off the bed. Nature's calling, and now, she's wide awake. Doug stirs in bed with a snort and rolls on his side, facing her. She turns to look at him. His eyes are open, and they meet.

"Happy Anniversary," she greets.

He smiles and mumbles, "Happy Anniversary," before

shutting his eyes again.

Rachel rises up, slips her feet into her slippers, and heads for the bathroom. Perhaps today will be a good day after all.

Doug is kneeling on his side of the bed, praying, when she returns from the bathroom. Rachel's a little disappointed. She was hoping they would have prayed together today. Deciding to take the initiative, she kneels beside him.

Sensing her presence, Doug prays louder. "Thank You for another year of marriage, Father. This year will be better than the last. Help us to submit and love each other, and bless our home with more children."

"Amen," Rachel mutters.

"No weapon formed against us shall prosper... We shall be the head and not the tail! I decree and declare that we shall be strong and do exploits..."

"Amen."

As Doug reverts to speaking in tongues, Rachel continues to utter quiet prayers for herself and their home. Finally, Doug says, "In Jesus mighty name we have prayed, amen!"

He turns to Rachel, gives her a brief kiss before going to the bathroom. Rachel remains kneeling as she waits to hear from God, searching her spirit for His peace.

***

To celebrate their anniversary, Rachel makes a big English-style breakfast for them to share. They exchange cards as they eat. Doug also bought her a small box of Ferrero Rocher, her favourite chocolates. Rachel smiles and thanks him as she receives his gift.

After wolfing down his breakfast, Doug settles in front of the television to let it digest. The heavy rains have now subsided, leaving drizzles as the clouds give way for the morning sun. Rachel decides to get herself ready for work. She can still make it on time, and besides, this is her last full week until her notice is served, and she becomes self-employed.

Doug's on the phone when she comes back downstairs. Ezi's standing in his playpen, his hands outstretched to be carried. Rachel carries him briefly before putting him down again. He cries at their separation, but she soothes him.

"Mommy will be home before you know it," she says with a kiss. She still hates to leave him each day.

Rachel walks over to Doug and kisses his cheek, before heading out to her car. She's feeling good about their time together today. It's the first time in a long while since she has felt optimistic about their marriage. Maybe because they prayed together and enjoyed a meal without arguing, she muses.

Upon arriving at the studio, Rachel takes a moment to share a message on social media about her anniversary. She uses one of the pictures from Ezekiel's birthday party with a short caption.

"To God be the glory, today we celebrate another year of marriage and friendship. I thank God for His faithfulness and blessings. Happy Anniversary, darling xoxo!"

Throughout the day, the likes pour in, and Rachel responds to all her well-wishers. But though Doug 'liked' her post, he doesn't comment nor post on his page about their marriage. And like every other day, he doesn't call or text. When he eventually does, in the evening, it is to tell her that he will be working late at the studio.

The sadness, which is her usual companion, returns.

***

Rachel has just climbed into bed when her phone vibrates with a call. She reaches for it and is surprised to see who's calling. Gladly, she slides her finger across the screen to take the call.

"Hey, girl," Rachel says.

"Hi, Rachel," Ihotu replies. "I hope this isn't a bad time."

"No, it isn't. What's up?"

"Oh, nothing really. I just saw your post on Instagram.

Congrats on your anniversary!"

"Oh, right. Thank you."

"You've actually been on my heart all day, and I was thinking I'd send a message. I decided to call when I saw your post."

"Oh, yeah…?" Rachel mutters, feeling anxiety arise in her belly.

"Yeah…" Ihotu pauses. "I think the Lord wants me to encourage you today. I don't know what's happening in your life, I know we haven't been all that close, but if you need someone to talk to or pray with you, I'm your girl. I hope you know that."

A lump forms in Rachel's throat, as she resists the urge to pour out her emotions on her friend. Though they haven't known each other long, Ihotu has always been a genuine person, whose passion for the Lord is obvious. A tear escapes her watery eye, and she wipes it away. Rachel longs to believe that the call is inspired by God, but what if it's not?

"Are you there?" Ihotu asks. "Are you okay, Rachel?"

Rachel nods and speaks at last, "I'm fine. Thanks for reaching out, Ihotu. I appreciate it."

"Are you sure you don't want to talk?" Ihotu presses on. "I mean, if you don't feel comfortable enough to talk to me about it, I'll understand. But I think maybe you need to talk to someone… Maybe a pastor or a counsellor?"

"I'm fine. Thank you," Rachel says with finality. "I'm talking to God."

"Okay, then. Have a good night, dear."

"Good night," Rachel says and cuts the call. Giving in to her emotions, she sobs into her pillow.

CHAPTER TWENTY

"You're so naughty!" Rachel hears Doug chuckle into his phone. Her eyes fling open, while she remains still on the bed, intent on hearing more. "Thanks, dear. You bet! Alright, see you later."

She can just imagine the grin on his face. It seems obvious to her that he was just talking to a lady, but what's the crime in that? It's not like he isn't allowed to talk to women. By now, Rachel's aware of his frequent interactions with different women for his work. The challenge remains proving that the relationships are neither professional nor platonic.

But today, the calls have been coming in since dawn, prompting Doug to rise early to prepare for work. When his phone goes off again, Rachel gives up on sleep and sits up in bed. She can tell from his tone that it's his mother on the line. Even when she has nice things to say, he's too busy for her too.

"Thanks, mom. Yes... I will. She's fine. He's fine too. I have to go. Yes, I'll call. Not now, mom! OK. Bye!" He hangs up and continues combing his hair in front of the mirror.

"Happy Birthday, Doug!" Rachel says. She pulls open a drawer and brings out the gift she'd bought and wrapped for him. Going to him, she gives him a hug and then his birthday present.

"Thank you, babe," he says with a smile. He opens it, and seeing a black, leather-strap, Braun Classic watch, beams. He gives her a kiss on her lips and puts on his new wristwatch.

Rachel beams, happy that he likes his gift. "I was thinking it would be nice for us to meet for lunch today. Can you make time?"

"I'm sorry, dear, it's going to be a busy day. If anything changes, I'll let you know."

"Okay..." Rachel mutters, concealing her disappointment. "Have a great day."

***

Rachel is startled from sleep by the ringing of her phone. She hastens to pick up before it cuts. "Hello?"

"Delivery from Cakes and Creams. Please, I need directions!"

Oh no! She'd forgotten about the cake she'd ordered. Rachel directs the dispatch rider to her gate and collects the 12-inch birthday cake. She should take it to Doug. Today *is* his birthday.

She checks the time. It is just past one thirty. If she hurries up, she can make it to his office by 2:30pm. Maybe he will be able to make time for lunch after all. She packs some of the food she'd prepared in case he decided to come home for lunch and heads off to Obalende.

Due to some traffic along her chosen route, Rachel makes it to Doug's studio a few minutes later than anticipated. She gets help from the security guard to take the cake inside, while she carries the food behind him. Rachel's surprised to see so many people hanging around in the small reception. Some are eating slices of cake and others, small chops.

She comes to a complete stop as she realises what is happening. The security guard has dropped Doug's cake on top of the receptionist's desk and is on his way out. The party guests have become aware of her presence in their midst, but all she wants is for the ground to open up and swallow her whole.

As Doug is nowhere in sight, Rachel walks to his office and opens the door. This time, she's not overly shocked to find Bose there. She takes in the scene.

The other woman rises from the desk, where she'd been sitting, a chicken drumstick in her hand. Doug, who's standing beside her, is caught in mid-laughter as he turns towards the door. A smirk creeps on his face.

"Hi, Rachel… Everything okay?" he asks.

Rachel keeps her hand on the door handle to steady it against the trembles threatening to overtake her body, as she's filled with rage. "What's going on here?" she manages to ask with a steady voice.

Doug raises an eyebrow, as if it's an odd question. "It's my birthday! Some friends decided to surprise me. What does it look like?"

Rachel is breathing hard, fighting to stay calm with each breath. *How dare he try to make me look stupid?!* "I mean, what's happening *in* here?!"

"*What?* Can't you see I'm talking to my friend? What's your problem?"

Rachel swallows. So, he wants to keep pretending that he and Bose are just friends, while this is the second time she's caught them in a compromising situation?

"Bose, what are you doing?" Rachel glares at her frenemy. All she wants is for someone to tell her the truth.

Bose looks at Doug and then at Rachel. "I think he just told you. *Jeez!*" she laughs. "By the way, I brought chicken. You want some?"

Doug giggles as they both watch Rachel, who looks like she's about to blow a fuse.

Realising that they both intend to taunt her with their relationship and embarrass her among his friends, clients, and staff present, Rachel backs away from the door. Turning around, she hurries to her car and drives away.

***

Rachel can hardly believe what happened today at Doug's studio. How could he do that to her? What had she ever done to deserve such cruel treatment? And what had come over Bose?! *Why are they doing this???*

She feels so embarrassed as she remembers how Doug's friends had looked at her when she arrived. She could have sworn that a couple of them snickered as she ran out. What must they think of her? Surely, they are all aware of Doug's indiscretions, since he doesn't seem to want to keep his affairs hidden from them. How will she ever face them again?

Rachel's curled in a ball on her sofa as she cries. She really is the biggest fool. She'd entered her marriage with doubts… But she thought she'd been acting in faith. However, she can see so much clearer now that it had been fear… The fear of being alone, of missing the right one…and the fear of being hurt by someone she deeply loved.

The last one surprised her to admit. She'd believed Doug was a safe choice because her heart was not that invested. She thought she was being wise and using her head to make the right decision, instead of following her heart and potentially having it broken by Ejike…but look at her now. Doug never cared for her. She, too, had been his safe bet!

There's a knock on her bedroom door. Rachel doesn't want to answer, but she knows she has to snap out of it and face her life. Wiping her face with the sleeve of her blouse, she opens the door.

"I'm ready to go, ma," Gloria says. "Ezekiel is sleeping."

Rachel nods and thanks the nanny. She follows Gloria downstairs to lock up after her and then goes to Ezekiel's room. She curls up on the armchair, the tears at bay, but her mind in turmoil.

She can't live like this… She can't keep lying to herself

that what she has with Doug is a marriage. *I can't do it.*

***

July 9th, 2016

Dear Diary,

I think my husband is having an affair with my friend, Bose. I've suspected them for months, and yesterday, when I found them together in his office, they just mocked me! I can't believe this is happening, and I don't know what to do.

Last night, Doug didn't come home, and he didn't call or text to say he'll be working late or anything, like he usually does. I slept in my son's room all night. I can barely stand to be in our room now. I just feel so angry!

***

Rachel drops her pen, tears running down her cheeks, unto her diary. She shuts the book and gives in to her anger.

She can't keep up with the pretence any longer. This charade of a marriage! She doesn't have to put up with this shit! If anyone has anything to lose, it's Doug. She needs to quit with this loyalty crap and call out the wolf for who he is!

Before she's too far gone, the counsellor in her kicks in, reminding her of all she knows and has been taught about marriage. The sacrifice it is, the relationship it signifies, the message it brings to a world lacking love, and the responsibility it holds, not just to her child but to society in general. Marriage was never supposed to be easy, and even if she believes there was no love in hers from the onset, she must have been prepared to face this outcome and weather the storms, with God's grace holding her up. She just has to tap into that grace and refuse to give up…

Rachel falls on her knees and cries out to God.

"Jesus, I'm Your child! I only ever wanted to be in Your will. I kept myself, and I trusted in You. How did I end up in this sort of marriage?!

"Do you have a plan in this? Was this part of Your will for me, like how You let Joseph be sold into slavery that he

157

may bring about a greater deliverance of his people and the world? Lord, I don't feel strong enough to endure the trials he did. I don't think I have enough love or faith. Please, Lord, increase my faith and give me greater grace to go through this trial and accomplish Your will through it.

"Father, I am in so much pain. Please help me to fix my gaze on You as Christ did on the cross. Please have mercy on me and fight for me. Lord, I want to feel Your presence and Your loving arms around me. Please, Lord, I need You!

"Jesus, please teach me to love like You do. Please help me to forgive them… Please remove every trace of bitterness and anger from me, so that I am not moved by vengeance, but trust in You to make all things good. Lord, in this trial, be my joy! Amen."

The tears subside, and Rachel grows still. She feels strength return to her; body, mind, and spirit. She abides and listens, and the Lord ministers to her, reminding her that she doesn't have to go through this life alone and afraid. She has power and great resources in Him.

In her mind, she sees Ihotu, her Christian friend who reached out to her on her anniversary. She knows she should reconnect. God has sent her help and fellowship in her time of need.

***

Ihotu picks up on the second ring. "Hi, Rachel! How are you?"

Rachel feels immediate relief to hear a friendly voice. She lets out a deep sigh. "I'm fine… Well, actually, I'm not. That's why I'm calling…"

"Okay. I'm here for you, girl. What's going on?"

Rachel tells Ihotu about the latest development in her marriage, and as they discuss, she recounts the back story to her relationship with Doug. Ihotu is a listening ear, a sounding board, and a friend. She doesn't pass judgement, and she has little advice to give.

"There are many perspectives here, but the only right one is God's. He is the only one who knows all and sees all, even searches the hearts of men. Every day, we need to remember this and lean into Him so that we don't make unrighteous judgments," Ihotu says eventually. "I'm currently reading this devotional that's helping me to take every thought captive for Christ and learn to see things from His perspective. Would you like to join me?"

Rachel nods. "Yes, I would."

"Great! Let's start with prayer," Ihotu says. "Father, thank You for bringing us together to learn from You and grow into Your image. As we study Your word, please grant us wisdom, knowledge, and understanding. In our dark moments, we ask and trust You to enlighten our paths according to Your great mercy, amen."

"Amen."

***

September 19th, 2016.

Dear Diary,

Tomorrow's my 35th birthday. I can't believe I'm already in my mid-thirties. Despite what's happening in my life now, I know I have so much to be thankful for. I have been so blessed. I am healthy and strong, and I have friends and family who care about me.

Most especially, I'm grateful for my son and my dad. When I look at my son, I see my gift and a reason to keep fighting and smiling each day. And my dad has been such a blessing to me. He's constantly pushing me to reach for the stars and supports me to achieve my dreams.

I'm also thankful for my friend, Ihotu. Over the last couple of months, we've grown quite close. She's been a Godsend, someone I can talk to, confide in, and pray with as I'm unable to do with my husband. She reminds me to keep making effort every day, to give him daily grace as I receive from God. I just hope I can be a strength to her as she's been to me.

I don't have any plans for tomorrow. It's a weekday, so I'll be working. We're leasing to buy a three-story building in Lekki, which we are currently renovating for the spa. It's perfect! It has so many rooms, and I know just what to do with each. We're hoping to complete the renovation, design, and furnishing by December, so we can launch in time for Christmas.

My new business has been a welcome distraction. It's certainly helped to keep my mind off whatever Doug is doing. Things have gotten to the point that we don't even talk anymore. We're basically housemates because he hardly sleeps in our room, let alone our bed. I try to talk to him, but it's real hard to be shut down all the time.

I'm just hanging in there because I have to believe God can turn it all around. Ihotu said I should just focus on doing my part, being available, humble, and loving, and leave the rest to God. I'm really trying. If I can get through the day without letting his actions dictate how I behave, then it's a good day. I hope tomorrow will be another good day.

CHAPTER TWENTY-ONE

Ejike looks at the notification on his phone and pauses. He hadn't forgotten. He'd saved the date three years ago and had been thinking of it for the last week. He has really missed her friendship, and today presents an opportunity for them to reconnect. But what scares him is how much he longs to hear her voice.

Before he can change his mind, he dials her number. Rachel picks up on the third ring.

"Happy Birthday, Rachel!" Ejike greets cheerfully.

"Thanks, Ejike," she replies. "How are you?"

"I'm great, dear. How are you? How's your day going?"

"It's okay. I'm fine."

Though she sounds friendly enough, he can tell there's something wrong. It's her birthday, she's supposed to be way happier.

"Are you alright, Rache?" he prods. Maybe she's upset with him or something.

"Yes, I'm fine," she says. "Thanks for calling. I appreciate it."

Not wanting to hang up nor give up on finding out if everything is cool between them, Ejike persists, "So, any plans for today?"

Rachel sighs, but he can tell she's not smiling. "Not really."

He expected that she'd say more. It sounds like she wants to, but she's holding back. "Are we cool?" he hears himself ask.

Why he can't let it go is beyond him. He just knows that he's not happy – *content* – with their exchange today. Like, it's been so long, they should be catching up.

He can hear her hesitating. At last, she speaks, "Yes, we're cool. Why shouldn't we be?"

"I know it's been a while since we spoke. I thought I'd see you at my birthday party, but you didn't come. I guess I should have reached out sooner."

More hesitation. "It's okay. I'm just going through some things at the moment. It's not about you…"

"Hey, you can talk to me… What's going on?" Ejike asks, his tone coming off more intimate than he'd wanted.

"It's just life, y'know. Marriage, motherhood, work… It's not as easy as you'd think. But I'm pulling through, by the grace of God."

Her effort to sound cheerful fails woefully, the edge in her voice, distinct and obvious. Something's definitely wrong, could it be what he's thinking? Ejike has been worried about Rachel since he saw Doug and Bose talking at his wedding reception. Actually, he'd been worried even before. In the US, she'd given off some vibes, and he'd suspected then that all was not well in her marriage, but he'd chosen not to interfere. But now, he's not sure that's the way to go.

"Is everything okay with you and Doug?" Ejike finally asks, waiting with bated breath. A part of him wishes she would say there's no problem so that he can continue to hope for the best. Still, he longs for her to confide in him, though he doesn't know what he'll do if he discovers that his suspicions are right.

Rachel's effort to laugh it off comes across as a muffled cry, as she huffs. And she huffs again. It sounds like she's on the verge of tears. "I don't know…" she finally confesses.

"I don't know what's going on with him."

Ejike feels something twisting his heart. He's pained that she sounds so hurt. *That bastard! What has he done now?!* Thankfully, with a little more prodding from him, Ejike gets Rachel's perspective on her marriage. And when he finally ends the call, he's filled with a blinding rage.

***

The door to his recording studio swings open suddenly, disrupting his current production. Doug scowls as he turns to confront the intruder, but is surprised to see Ejike fuming at the doorway. *WTF?!*

"Excuse you!" Doug yells at him.

Ejike heaves each word out, "Did you or did you not say you were never going to hurt her?"

Doug looks at Ejike perplexed for a few seconds then bursts out in laughter. "You're kidding me! You're fucking kidding me, right?!"

Ejike steps closer. "Don't make me ask you again, Doug! Did you not make that promise to me?"

"Who the fuck are you?!" Doug turns on him, matching his rage. "Seriously, who the hell do you think you are, barging into my office and asking me that fucking question? Have you lost your mind?!"

"Out now!" Ejike shouts.

"Or what?!" Doug stands his ground. With a shake of his head, he adds, "You're married for God's sake. Have some fucking self-respect!"

"Let's settle this outside, unless you want me to redecorate this studio with your face!"

Not finding it at all funny anymore, Doug throws the first punch. Ejike dodges it and lands his own, right in Doug's gut. Doug pushes him, and Ejike pushes him back against his studio equipment and goes after Doug's face as threatened. Doug evades the punches and kicks Ejike. A few more blows are thrown, with some choice words flying in the air.

Eventually, there's relief from the kicks and punches as the men are separated by the other two people in the studio, the sound engineer and the recording artist. Doug wipes his nose and scowls when he sees blood. His shirt is ripped, and his body hurts. But at least his opponent did not leave without a scratch.

"Get out of my studio!" Doug shouts, shaking himself free of his employee. "Don't ever show your ugly face around here again! And you better stay the hell away from my wife!"

Ejike also shakes himself free and points a threatening finger at Doug. "Don't for a minute think this is over!"

"She's my wife! I'll do whatever the fuck I want…and there's nothing you can do about it!" Doug says with a smirk. Ejike huffs, but the security guard enters the room at this point. "Now, get the fuck out!"

***

Getting out into the sun, Ejike looks down at himself. He looks a mess. What had possessed him to fight Doug like that? How was it to make things better for Rachel?

Ejike swallows. He just couldn't stop thinking about the day he let Doug go after Rachel, knowing he wanted her too. He should have fought for her. She should have been his wife, and she would have been cherished and adored. She deserved that. And now, he feels responsible for her pain…

But Doug was right. There's nothing he can do for her anymore. She's not his wife, and he has his own woman to protect and love. Yet, his fury at Doug's behaviour refuses to subside.

Ejike gets into his car, lays his head on the headrest, and takes a deep breath. What does this mean? Does he still love her? Will he always love her? What about his wife?

Yes, he would have fought to defend her honour too. What happened today was not about Ifeoma. He just can't stand to see someone he loves – *cares about* – be so badly treated. It doesn't mean that he's still in love with Rachel.

But Ejike knows deep down that he's lying to himself. And there's nothing he can do about that either. This is his life now... She did this to him.

Starting his car, Ejike pulls away from his parking spot.

***

Apart from her emotional conversation with Ejike this morning, it's been a pretty easy, uneventful day for Rachel. She's been receiving calls, texts, social media mentions, and gifts all day. She also posted on her timeline about her birthday and lots of people have been dropping comments on it.

Rachel's excited about tonight. She has plans to meet up with Ihotu, Folusho, and Seun after work, at Ice Cream Factory. Ihotu organised the hangout after confirming Rachel had no plans with Doug or her family today. Rachel hopes it will stop her from continually rehashing the conversation she had with Ejike this morning.

She really didn't want to go into the details with him, but it was as if Ejike could see right through her. Even over the phone. It took her back to their time together in the US, when they'd been so free with each other. Speaking with him today made her feel like she was truly special to someone, to him. But she'll have to be careful to guard her feelings, now that he is married. Even if her marriage is falling apart, she mustn't endanger his.

Rachel looks at the curtain fabric samples before her and makes a choice. She's been at the spa since morning, supervising the contractor in charge of the renovations. She's hungry now, as she skipped lunch, so she's calling it a day and heading back to her car.

Her phone rings just as she starts the engine. Rachel answers the call on the hands-free connection.

"Hi, Dj!" she answers cheerfully.

Rachel's surprised when her former producer begins to sing, "Happy birthday to you, happy birthday to you, happy birthday, dear Rachel, happy birthday to you!"

She laughs with a joyful heart. "Thanks, Dj! How are you?"

"I'm fine, dear. How are you? I hope your day has been awesome."

"Yes, it's been good, thank you," Rachel replies. "How are things at the station?"

"It's dry without you," Dongjap says. "Seriously, though, I've missed you."

Rachel feels warm in her chest at his words. "I've missed you too." And it's the truth.

"I hope we'll stay in touch, not just on our birthdays, sha…"

"Sure. Why not?" Rachel laughs. "Thanks for calling."

"No worries, dear. I'll holla at you later."

Rachel's feeling so much better than she was this morning. All the love she has received from her friends almost make up for that lacking in her home. For her birthday, Doug gave her five thousand naira, enclosed in a birthday card. It seems he couldn't decide on a gift, or maybe he hadn't found the time to buy something himself. Rachel's not sure what it means, but she's determined to be happy today. It's her day!

***

Rachel's surprised to hear Doug's horn at the gate just moments after she gets into the house. She'd branched and used the N5,000 he'd given her to get herself a nice meal out, as she wasn't expecting company with lunch. She smiles, thinking maybe Doug has had a change of heart.

However, she is startled to hear the door slam with his entry. Rachel practically jumps from her position on the sofa and turns to look at the door, trying to figure out quickly what might have happened. The fury on Doug's face is unmistakable. She stands frozen, waiting for him to express his grievance.

Doug rather huffs and paces around the room. He doesn't

seem to know what to say or do, making Rachel even more afraid of how this confrontation will turn out. She decides to speak up.

"What's the matter, Doug?"

He manages to smirk. "Like you don't know!" he retorts.

Rachel's now thinking of her conversation with Ejike. Surely, he wouldn't have said anything to Doug? That would be very stupid of him! "I don't know what's going on..."

Doug shakes his head and sneers, "You are just a pretender, aren't you?! You act like you're this holy princess when you're nothing but a slut!"

Rachel gasps. "How dare you?!"

"Shut your filthy mouth!" he barks at her. "If you're not opening your legs for him, what will give him the audacity to come to my office and fight me, as if you're not my wife?!"

Rachel's hand swings to her mouth in shock. Is she hearing right? Did Ejike really go and fight Doug? For *her*?

Though it warms her heart to think that he cares so much, she now has the problem of dealing with the aftermath of his momentary madness. "There's nothing going on with me and Ejike! I've told you like a thousand times!"

Doug smirks, "I didn't say his name, but you knew it was him, didn't you? Perhaps you know why he would be so stupid to do a thing like that...?"

Rachel backs away as Doug inches closer. "I don't know why he did what he did..."

"You didn't go crying to *lover boy*?" Doug taunts.

Rachel stops when she hits a wall. She looks about for an escape, or maybe something she can use to protect herself. Doug has never raised his hands to her before, but she fears now that it's about to change.

"I didn't," she replies with boldness she didn't know she had. She straightens herself, determined not to cower. If he lays a hand on her, she doesn't care what anyone says, she's not going to stick around to be his punching bag, on top of all the crap she's been dealing with.

Doug grabs her by her upper arms and glares down at her as he presses her against the wall, the threat imminent. "Liar!" he hisses and shakes her when she still doesn't cower.

Do it! Rachel feels emboldened. It's the exit she's been waiting for. "Do it!" she taunts, glaring back at him.

Doug drops his hands from her arms and steps back. He has too much control for this shit! "Be careful, Rachel. Be fucking careful!"

Rachel watches as he turns around, walks to the door, and slams it, just like when he came in. She finally gives in to the shakes and crouches on the floor. Something tells her that things are about to get a lot worse in her marriage.

CHAPTER TWENTY-TWO

Rachel's of two minds about going to meet her friends tonight. On the one hand, she could really do with the company, the treat, and getting out of her house. But on the other, she really just wants to be alone, curl up in her bed, and watch television. However, knowing the only reason Gloria agreed to stay later is because of her birthday outing with her friends, Rachel decides on the former.

Ice Cream Factory enjoys a coastal breeze, being by the edge of the Lekki Peninsula. Rachel takes it in as she sits under a canopy outside, waiting for her friends to show up. *Lovely*… It's really one of her favourite things. She's already glad that she came out despite how badly she'd been feeling.

Her phone vibrates, and she brings it out of her purse to check the message.

"How's your day going?" Ejike had sent.

Rachel wants to ignore him. After what he did today, she's not at all happy with him. She decides rather to confront him. *"Why did you go to Doug's studio to fight him? Why would you do that?!"*

"I'm sorry. I don't know what came over me. I was just so angry. I hope he didn't do anything to you…"

"What are you going to do about it?!"

Moments later, her phone rings. He's the one calling. She sighs and picks it up.

"Did he hurt you?" Ejike asks, his voice filled with both concern and threat.

Rachel shakes her head and answers, "No."

"I don't want to know what I would do, Rachel. I just know I can't let him treat you that way," Ejike lets out a sigh. "But if he had done anything to you tonight, it would have been my fault, and I don't know how I'd live with myself. I'm really sorry... Forgive me?"

Rachel exhales, feeling appeased but also emotionally touched. She swallows. "I do... And I'm sorry I got you involved."

"You didn't do anything wrong... Okay? I'll just have to think of a better way to get through to Doug..."

"No, please. I don't want you to do anything. I'm fine, okay? I can take care of myself..."

"Yes, I'm sure you can. But everyone needs someone to care enough to fight for them. You can't stop me from being that friend..."

Hmmm... Rachel chuckles, thinking about how insistent he'd been in Chicago too. "Yeah, you're really quite stubborn!"

Ejike laughs. "I'm glad you know that. And that we have an understanding..."

Rachel giggles. She can see Folusho has arrived and is parking. She should end this call.

"So, how can I make it up to you?" Ejike asks.

"You already have. Thanks for calling."

"You've got somewhere to go?" Ejike objects.

"Let's just say you're not the only friend I have in the world," Rachel giggles. "It's still my birthday, you know?"

"Touché!" Ejike giggles. "No worries. I'll holla at you later. Have a good night, Rache."

"Thanks..." Folusho is standing by the canopy, and so Rachel refrains from mentioning Ejike's name. "Good night."

Cutting the call, she stands up and hugs her friend. "Hey, darling!"

***

The tide has shifted, and Rachel feels joyous surrounded by her friends on her birthday. Tonight's chat with Ejike has done wonders for her mood, and she almost forgets about the miserable life she's been living with Doug. Folusho and Seun chalk up Rachel's boisterous mood to being the celebrant, but Ihotu senses that something has shifted in Rachel's world. She observes her friend keenly as they chat.

When the others say their goodbyes, Ihotu is the last to call it a night. She observes Rachel as she scoops the last of her ice-cream into her mouth. "I'm happy to see you in such a good mood, Rache," she says at last.

Rachel smiles as though she's been caught stealing candy. "Yeah, I'm feeling good."

"That's great! How are things with Doug?"

Rachel's lips twist into a frown, as she raises her brows. "Nothing's changed over there…"

"Oh… But something about you is different…" Ihotu gives a knowing smile.

Rachel grins again. Why can't she keep this one to herself? But she knows if she wants to stay out of trouble, she'll have to be accountable to someone. With a sigh, she confesses, "It's Ejike…"

"Hmmm… Your brother-in-law?"

"Well, my *half-sister's* brother-in-law…" Rachel giggles.

"What a way to get technical," Ihotu laughs. "So, what about him?"

Rachel leans her head back as the feelings she's been trying to keep at bay all night rise up in her. *Wow! Such strong feelings.* She breathes out a sigh. "He got in touch with me today… And we got to talking."

"Oh… About Doug?"

Rachel nods. "I told him. I didn't plan to, but he seemed

to know something was up, and I kinda wanted to talk about it, so..." She swallows.

"Okay... So, did that make you feel better? Talking to him?"

Rachel nods again. "But he confronted Doug, today. He actually went to his studio, and they had a fight." Ihotu listens patiently. "Then Doug came home and was mad at me. Anyway... That's what happened."

"Hmmm... It seems Ejike has strong feelings for you. Isn't he married?"

Rachel nods, her expression glum. She feels an old pain in her heart.

"But you have feelings for him too... Wow..."

Rachel rests her face on her hand and takes some deep breaths. "I don't want to, but he's so wonderful," she cries at last. "I love him so much!"

"Hmmm..." Ihotu ponders. *This is bad.* "That must be really hard for Doug..."

Rachel looks up at Ihotu, perplexed. *What does she mean that it's hard for Doug? What does he care about it? It's hard for me!*

"Obviously, he knows about your feelings for each other," Ihotu says, as if to explain. "It must be painful for him knowing you don't love him, and that you'd rather be with someone else."

Rachel ponders with bated breath. Why has she never thought about it like that before? As hurt as she feels that Doug doesn't love her, it never occurred to her that he could be acting out because *she* doesn't love *him*. All she wanted was to feel his love. She was sure she'd return it if he gave it... But now, she doesn't want to think about how he feels, only how she feels.

"I don't know how to get rid of these feelings for Ejike. I've tried, but it's like, they just hide, and the moment I see him or hear from him again, I'm drowning in it. Maybe I can never get over it..."

"If that's the case, then you'll probably be in misery forever. You're both married. I don't see your happily ever after with Ejike. Just pain, betrayal, and heartbreak if you continue in your feelings."

Rachel looks at Ihotu, haunted, her eyes wide with trepidation. The pain hits her like a tsunami, and Rachel bursts into tears. She wants someone else's husband; she knows it as clearly as she knows she doesn't want her own. And the thought that she'll be captive to these feelings for a lifetime makes her want to… She can't think it.

"No temptation has overtaken you except what is common to mankind. And God is faithful; He will not let you be tempted beyond what you can bear. But when you are tempted, He will also provide a way out so that you can endure it," Ihotu recites the NIV version of 1 Corinthians 10:13 by heart. She looks at Rachel, who looks overwhelmed with pain and guilt, and reaches out her hand to her friend. "God knows the way out of this, Rachel. You just have to let Him show you, and give Him your whole heart."

Rachel sobs as her friend holds her. She knows what she needs to do. No one needs to tell her. She has to cut Ejike off, just as Jesus said. *If your right hand offends you, cut it off…*

***

The days that follow are agonisingly painful for Rachel. She ignores calls and messages from Ejike in her effort to cut him out of her life. But he becomes even more frantic, probably anxious that something unfortunate has happened to her.

"Rachel, why aren't you picking my calls?"

"Is everything okay? Did Doug hurt you?"

"Is it something I said or did?"

"I'm really worried now. What's going on?"

"Please, just talk to me so that I know you're okay, and I won't bother you anymore…"

Rachel's picks up her phone, feeling a need to put him out

of his misery. *"I'm fine, Ejike. There's no need for you to be worried."*

Immediately, her phone rings, but she ignores it. Why is he not getting the message? It rings again, but she doesn't answer.

"I think we already established that I'm more stubborn than you... Lol!"

"Come on, Rachel. Pick up, let's talk."

"No problem, Rache. If that's the way you want it, I'll leave you alone. I'm sorry for bothering you."

Rachel exhales after receiving that last message. *Wow, can he not see how he's coming across?* She shouldn't have to point that out to him. She's sure he's a praying Christian... He's probably just acting out of concern for her. At least he has finally gotten the message.

Rachel shuts her eyes from both relief and pain. Now, she has to stop wanting him to want her...

***

A couple of weeks later, Rachel's at the spa. Her office was among the first rooms to be completed and furnished. The small ensuite room, overlooking the Lekki-Ikoyi toll bridge, holds a standard executive desk and swivel chair, two visitor chairs, a two-seater sofa, a filing cabinet, and some shelving space. Rachel's thinking of getting a small television as well.

Sitting behind her desk, she's happy to realise how serene the neighbourhood is. Apart from some clanking sounds in her building, caused by the ongoing renovations, there's not a petrol generator to be heard for miles. And since they are not on a main street, there's little traffic noise too.

Rachel smiles to herself as she wipes her hand across her desk. It's a bit dusty. She might need to hire a cleaner now. She was hoping to put it off longer. Currently, she only employs a security guard to man the gate, day and night, and clean the compound. She's already started interviewing for an admin position, as the work of preparing for their opening is piling up.

Today, she has just a couple of meetings; one with a tech company she's working with to design their website and app, and the other is with a woman's network, which she hopes will partner with them to help get their first clients when they are ready for the trial opening in about two months. Rachel decided to come in early to check on the contractor and prepare for her meetings. As she's all set for her first meeting, Rachel relaxes by browsing her social media applications.

There's a knock on her door. Rachel looks up to see the security guard. She raises a questioning brow.

"There's someone here to see you, ma."

Thinking it's the representative from the tech company, she says, "Let him in, thanks."

"Hi, Rachel…"

Goosebumps arise on the back of her neck upon hearing his voice. The last time she saw him would have been at Ezi's birthday party, and even then, they hadn't spoken. Looking at him now, it feels like a lifetime ago. But what is he doing here?

As if in response to her thoughts, he says, "I was driving by your street when I saw your car parked outside, and I figured this must be your new office."

"Oh, okay…" Rachel stays seated.

He moves away from the doorway and into the room. "You okay, Rachel?"

She swallows. "Yes, I'm fine, Ejike. Are you okay?"

He nods. "I am. So, aren't you going to show me around?"

Rachel looks into his face. It's plain to see that marriage has had an effect on him. His full cheeks are telling of his improved nutrition.

Rachel's feeling chuffed that she's finally been able to

shake off some of her pregnancy weight. She'd struggled to at first, but after deciding to take a break from her contraceptives, seeing as she wasn't getting much action down there, and in order to stop the side effects of bloating and weight gain, the weight began to fall off noticeably. With consistent exercise and attention to her diet, she'd been able tone her body and keep the weight off too.

She stands up, as if to show off her regained figure, and leans against her desk. "I'm kind of busy at the moment. Maybe we can arrange something," Rachel says but wishes she hadn't.

"You mean, you'll take my call now?"

Rachel lets out a deep breath. "What do you want from me, Ejike? What's this?" She gesticulates between them.

He shrugs. "I thought we were friends... You just...cut me off. Why?"

Shaking her head, she replies, "I don't want to be 'friends' anymore. I don't think it's healthy for either of us."

Ejike nods slowly and strokes a finger along one of the visitor chairs closer to him. With his other hand, he massages his forehead before he turns to her, his eyes holding hers. "Why do you feel that way? Why now?"

Rachel looks down and fidgets with a pen on her desk. "I think the real question is why you can't let this go..." she manages to say, and then looks back up at him.

Two long, thick fingers touch her chin and lift her head towards his, where his soft, full lips take possession of hers, in one swift manoeuvre. Rachel is knocked breathless and immediately feels her body respond to his touch, even as his other hand grasps her hair, pulling her closer for a deeper kiss. Her weak arms fumble, as she tries to find some balance.

She should stop this. Pull away. Fight him off. But she gives in to it, resting her hands on her desk, until he releases her. And she's just hanging there, her lips supple and bruised, waiting to be taken again. Rachel exhales and opens her eyes to look at the man who has just rekindled her flame. She swallows and pulls back at last.

She wants to scream at him, but all that comes out is, "Wh…why did you do that?"

Ejike puts his hands safely back in his trouser pockets as he beholds her with dark eyes. "I've just always wanted to know what that would feel like." *And oh my God! I'm in trouble.* He licks his lips.

"Oh," Rachel mutters, feeling slightly dizzy as she sits back down. She's still trying to think of what to say in response when there's another knock on the door.

They both turn to look at the visitor.

"So, Rachel, I'll take you up on that tour, okay? Let me leave you to it," Ejike says before making his exit.

CHAPTER TWENTY-THREE

Rachel can't stop reliving Ejike's kiss. Every time she closes her eyes, it's like she's taken back to that moment in time. But the wicked man hasn't called her since! *What an ass!*

How can you kiss a woman like that and not call her for two days?!

She doesn't want to call him. She shouldn't. If anything, she should stick to her plan to cut him off, and even block him. Though she never planned to, after the tomfoolery he pulled, he deserves to be blocked completely!

Rachel jerks her head, as if to shake the thought of Ejike from her mind. She has to focus on her work. She needs to finish at the office and head over to her father's for a business meeting. He'd sent her a message to meet him by 4pm.

She lets out a sigh as she clicks on a link the website designer sent her. The website looks good, but she's thinking pastel colours would look better. She'd told him she wants a touch of pink for the theme design, but the site colours he'd chosen look fit for a little girl's birthday party. Rachel quickly shoots off an email with her feedback and then shuts down her computer.

Being so close to the toll bridge, she's in Ikoyi within 15 minutes, owing to some traffic. Rachel parks her car, walks into Eden Enterprises, and takes the special elevator that only stops at the penthouse. As the elevator rides up, she checks her reflection in the mirror. She loves the way her new blouse hugs her frame and even makes her look slimmer.

Smiling to herself, Rachel steps off the elevation into the executive waiting area. She greets the security men and the receptionist standing by, before turning to the other visitor waiting to see Chief Eden. Rachel freezes when she sees who's seated on the armchair looking up at her, an amused expression on his face.

"What are you doing here?!" she hisses, before looking about to make sure she hadn't raised any brows.

"It's lovely to see you too," Ejike replies, not bothering to change his expression nor position. His eyes follow her as she takes a seat, darkening as he admires her figure in a black, high-waisted skirt and fuchsia-pink, narrow-sleeve, satin blouse.

Rachel sits down on the two-seater sofa, which is farthest from Ejike, and checks her phone for the time. She still has five minutes until her meeting time. She takes a deep breath.

She will not let Ejike's presence get to her. She's a grown woman, who's here for business, and she'll definitely comport herself professionally. However, she can't help throwing a glance in his direction once more. The fingers that he'd rubbed on her scalp, while *assaulting* her with his lips, now lay on his thighs. And surely, there's an expensive wedding band on the fourth one. *How dare he?!*

"You can go in now," Lanre, the receptionist, says.

Rachel's surprised when Ejike also rises up to enter the MD's office. She's tempted to ask him '*what for*', but wisdom prevails, and she decides to wait and observe what's happening. She follows behind him to enter her dad's office.

Chief Eden looks up at his visitors and smiles. "Oh, so you're both here! Good."

"Good evening, sir," Ejike greets with a slight bow. Chief

Eden stands up, stretches out a hand to Ejike, and slaps him on the back. Rachel swallows, as she watches their warm exchange.

"How's the family?" Chief asks.

Ejike nods and smiles. "They're fine, sir."

"That's good."

Ejike takes his seat and watches as Rachel greets her father.

"Hi, dad," she says. She goes over to him and hugs him, planting kisses on each cheek.

"How are you doing, Rachel?"

"I'm fine, dad. How are you?"

"I'm good. So, let's start," Chief says, going straight to business. "Ejike contacted me with a great idea, and I thought, since it's your business, it's best you're looped in straight away. Ejike, why don't you tell Rachel what you told me?"

"Thank you, Chief. Well, it's not such a big deal... I've been looking for something to invest in, mostly real estate, but also business ideas that I believe will yield profit with the right investment. When I visited your office earlier in the week, I saw an opportunity. A place like that will require a substantial investment, and since we're family and all, I thought it would be perfect. I mean, if that's okay with you...?"

Rachel can hardly believe her ears. She swallows, not knowing what to say. Ejike's looking at her waiting for a response, and she realises that her father's eyes are on her too. "Ummm... *Hmmm*... Well, I want to see if I understand... You want to come as a *partner*?" Rachel passes a quick glance at her father.

"Well, yes. Just as an investor, until you turn your profit and buy me out. I'm thinking after five years should be sufficient. But I'm easy," Ejike says, and then looks at Chief Eden for backing.

"I think it's a great idea. More capital in the beginning is always good. It will save us borrowing from the bank too," Chief adds. "Do you have a problem with Ejike coming on board, Rachel?"

Rachel quickly shakes her head. "No, I don't. Thanks, Ejike."

He turns to her and beams, "You're welcome."

"Great, that's settled. Then we can go over the financial documents and get the ball rolling. You two should get better acquainted," Chief says, smiling at the two youngsters before him.

***

Rachel walks briskly to the elevator, eager to get away from Ejike. But just as she enters it, she hears him tell the security guard to hold the elevator. He does, and Ejike thanks him as he enters and stands beside Rachel. They both stand apart as the doors close.

The second they do, Rachel turns to Ejike. "What sort of game are you playing?!"

Ejike sighs. "I wish I knew. All I know is I don't want to lose you," he says sincerely.

Rachel swallows. "What are you doing? We're married to other people!"

"And whose fault is that?!" Ejike replies sternly. Rachel is stunned to silence. "Do you think it has been easy for me, Rachel? I've tried to deny it, and I've tried to hide it, but there's no getting over you! So, even if I can't have you as my wife...damn it, I'm still going to have you in my life!"

He's looking at her with those mesmerizing eyes again, and she's melting, aching for him to lay claim to her lips once more. But the elevator dings, and the doors open. With their eyes locked, they both step off the elevator.

Rachel's the first to look away. She walks with her hands in front of her, as if she's afraid that he'll try to hold her. Getting to her car, she unlocks and opens the door. Ejike comes up beside her.

"Look, don't think too much about it. I'll try to control myself when next I'm around you. I know this is difficult, but we have to figure out a way to be in each other's lives... Okay?"

Rachel nods, and without giving him a glance, enters her car. He's still standing by her car and is indicating for her to wind down. Heaving a sigh, she does.

"You don't look like you should be driving right now. You want me to give you a lift?"

"I'm fine!"

Ejike huffs, a smile curving his lips. "You are one stubborn lady... But I think I love that the most about you." He sighs. "Okay... Please just wait for like five minutes before you start driving. I'd hate for anything to happen to you. I'll call you later."

Rachel swallows and ignores him. She watches him through her driver side mirror, as he walks away. How's she supposed to explain this new development to Doug?

***

"He did *what?!*"

It's unusual to hear Ihotu exclaim. Rachel's been dreading the moment she would confide in her friend about the happenings of this week. She still can't believe all that's happening herself.

"Wait... Back up. You said he came to your office and *kissed* you?"

Rachel nods.

"And then he spoke to your dad about joining your business as an investor?"

"Yeah..."

"Okay... Now, I'm a bit confused about the last bit..."

"He said he is going to try to control himself around me, and that he just wants to stay in my life..."

"Wow... Wow... Do you know what this reminds me of?"

"What?"

"The time Jesus' disciples couldn't cast out an evil spirit, and Jesus said it would leave only with prayer and fasting. Do you know that scripture? I think it's in Mark 9."

"Yes, I'm familiar with it. But, are you saying Ejike is evil? Or that he has an evil spirit?"

"Well, I'm not saying that... But he is basically standing opposed to you obeying God... It doesn't look good."

"But he's a believer. He loves God..."

"And apparently, he loves you more... And worse, he wants you to love him more too. This will be a hard bond to break, so I think we'll need to do some fasting too."

Rachel gawks at her friend, incredulous. She hasn't fasted in a long time, and she doesn't really want to. Also, wouldn't getting rid of Ejike adversely affect her business now? Her father would never understand why she'd jeopardize her dream spa by burning bridges with Ejike, who he sees as family.

There has to be another way. Rachel nibbles her lip and looks away.

***

It's Sunday evening when Ejike finally calls. Rachel's been anticipating his call since Friday night, after he left her in the parking lot of her dad's office. She's not sure what she'll say or how she'll behave. All that she knows is, despite her better judgement, she really wants them to be friends too.

"Hi, Rachel," Ejike greets gently.

She swallows. "Hi, Ejike."

He laughs aloud. "Wow, you sound so mousy. Are you scared of me now?"

Rachel giggles. "What can I say? You're my boss."

"Please, don't be like that. This isn't a professional relationship. We're friends."

"Don't you mean *family*?" she corrects.

Ejike chuckles. "Yes, that too." He sighs deeply. "Isn't

this better?"

"What? What's better?"

"That it's all out in the open now... No more pretending. No more lying to ourselves about how we feel. We can just be cool."

"Well...except we are lying to our spouses."

"Are we really? Ifeoma knows that you're a special friend to me, it's not a big deal. And Doug... Well, he's certainly not clueless."

"Hmmm... I think if they really knew how cool we're being, they won't be too cool about it themselves."

"Yeah, well. As long as we're not acting on it, there's no harm, right? At least we've got a good release now. We're no longer trying to hide from each other. It's a compromise I can live with."

"Hmmm... Okay," Rachel mutters. *I guess so.*

"So, how was your day, dear?"

"It was okay."

"Did you go to Church?"

"Yup. You?"

"Yeah..." Ejike replies. "And how are things with Doug?"

"It's the same."

"Hmmm... Did you tell him about our partnership?"

"I honestly don't know how..."

"Why don't you leave that to me? I'll tell him."

"Really? I'm not sure..."

"All he needs to know is that the investment is from my family. He doesn't need to know it's personal."

Rachel breathes out. *That seems easier.* "Okay, thanks."

"You're welcome."

"And thanks. For the investment."

"You're very welcome. I'm always happy to help you." *My love...*

"I have to go now..."

"No problem. I'll call you later. Have a good night,

Rache."

"G'night."

Rachel hangs up the phone. She's having conflicting feelings, but the greatest is a feeling of happiness that she gets to have Ejike in her life after all. She knows it will be hard. There will be temptations ahead, but isn't that a given with life? All they need is discipline not to give in to their romantic feelings for each other.

It's certainly better than trying to live without him.

CHAPTER TWENTY-FOUR

December 10th, 2016.

Dear Diary,

It's nearly three months since I wrote last. So much has happened since. My birthday was…special. I honestly can't think of a better word for it.

The truth came out about me and Ejike. We were finally able to admit our feelings to each other, after I opened up to him about what's been going on, and he decided to go and fight Doug at his office. Needless to say, things have gotten worse between me and Doug.

After he came home and accused me of being a slut, he left and didn't come back home until that Friday. Even then, we didn't talk. He basically does whatever he likes now and no longer bothers to send me a text to let me know if he'll be coming home or not. I've also had a couple of people tell me about seeing him with a girl or a woman at some club, restaurant, or whatever. I've been too busy trying to set up my new spa to be bothered, honestly.

In fact, I love it when he's not around. I don't have to cook, and I don't feel like I have to go and say anything to him. I never miss him. All we talk about are the bills, repairs, and the shopping I do for the house. Oh yeah, Ezi too. He actually shows very little interest there. Thankfully, Ezi hasn't ever been sick. He only gets a slight fever after his immunisations.

Anyway... Despite this, I'm happy. Haven for Moms is coming along so well. I just love being my own boss! And Ejike has been a great help to me too.

Actually, he's an investor, so he comes around often to check on his investment, lol! We talk about work, life, everything... And he has linked me with so many of his contacts, that I wonder how I would have done it without him.

Yes, Ihotu thinks I'm making a big mistake by not cutting Ejike off from my life. But the truth is, she's not in my shoes. She doesn't know how it feels to love someone so much that it feels like you will die if you never see them again. And it's not like I haven't tried. Ejike and I have both tried to stay out of each other's lives, but we've decided that, as long as we're not doing sinful stuff, there's absolutely nothing wrong with us enjoying each other's company.

Well, apart from that kiss he gave me in my office – our very first kiss – nothing else has happened. He's kept his promise to behave, and we don't even hold hands or anything. Sometimes, when I want to, it really hurts that I can't. But I just think that if we start fooling around, then what we have will end, and then I won't get to have him at all. It's been a good enough motivator to keep things platonic.

I'm still praying through it, though. Some days I feel like I can't pray because of how bad things are with Doug. Some days, I just want to run to Ejike and ask him to run away with me. Some days, I feel like the worst person in the world, especially when I wake up after having hot dreams about us making love. And some days, I don't even want to live...

But it's knowing that he loves me, that God loves me, and that I have Ezi that I am able to push through and live for the happy moments. I just pray it gets easier.

Next Saturday, we're launching Haven for Moms. We did

a soft launch on the 1st, and the spa is currently open for a few special patrons, but we won't be open to the public until after the official launching. As you can imagine, I'm super excited! I really hope it will be the beginning of better things for me.

***

Now that Ezekiel is walking, and even talking, Rachel doesn't feel so alone when it's just them at home anymore. She often engages him in chatter, enjoying their banter. Rachel watches Ezi playing with his alphabet mat in his yard, and smiles at his new childish fascination with building words.

She rises up to prepare his lunch. While setting up the table, her phone begins to ring. It's most likely Ihotu or Ejike. They are the two people who call her the most these days.

"Hi, Rache." Rachel's elated that it's Ejike and smiles from ear to ear.

"Hey, what's up?" she replies.

"Nothing much... How are you and Ezi?"

"We're good... We're just about to have lunch."

"That's cool."

"Have you had lunch?"

"Not yet... So, any plans after?"

Rachel laughs. "You know me, *nau*... I'm a homebody. I do have a few things to do ahead of the launch, *sha*. Why? What's up?"

"Nothing... Just wondering if you'd like to meet... I missed you this week."

"Yeah... It's been very busy with the soft opening. I've hardly had a moment to myself, so I'm going to veg out real good tonight. That's if Ezi will let me," Rachel laughs.

"Okay. So, I can stop by with some suya?"

"Are you looking for someone's trouble, *Oga*?! *Biko*, stay in your house and send the suya by Uber!"

"*Na wa oh*! So, you'll eat my suya, but you won't see me… This life is not fair, *oh…*" They both laugh. "It's okay, dear. I can take a hint."

Rachel cracks up. "*You*, take a hint? You're very funny, Ejike! How's work, *sha*?"

Rachel beams as Ejike catches her up with the latest from his office. He offhandedly mentions that his wedding anniversary is next week too.

"Oh, okay," Rachel replies, the enthusiasm gone from her voice. "Congratulations to you guys."

"Ifeoma wants us to get away for the weekend, but I don't want to miss your launch. I mean, *our* launch!"

"Well, you gotta do what you gotta do…"

"We can do dinner, though… Maybe just do a night at a hotel…"

"Too much info, Ejike!" Rachel interrupts. Why does he act like it's not a big deal to her that he has a wife he loves and pampers?

"Sorry… I just… Sorry. I wanted you to know."

"It's okay. I have to go now."

"Sure. I'll send the Uber! It will contain my apology…"

"Yeah, whatever! Later…"

"Bye, dear…"

***

"*Hi, Doug. I thought I should remind you that tomorrow's the launch of my spa. I hope you'll be able to come.*"

"*Okay.*"

Rachel sighs with relief when she receives the response from Doug some minutes after sending her reminder. She'd told him about it when they'd settled on the date a month ago. She'd also reminded him on Sunday. He'd come home after Church and spent the whole afternoon sleeping on the sofa.

Whether or not he comes, the launch is going to be lit. She just doesn't want his absence to raise needless questions.

But his response is encouraging.

"Thanks."

***

"Congratulations on your launching today, Rachel!"

Rachel beams upon seeing the message from Rochelle. Her half-sister's back in Chicago waiting to deliver her second child. Rochelle travelled with her mom in October, and they're expected back in early February with a bouncy baby boy.

"Thanks, dear! I wish you could be here 🙁*"*

"Don't worry, I'll be there soon to patronise you! Lol!"

"Yes, oh… I can't wait 😊*"*

Rachel sighs and puts away her phone. Today's the day! She gets down on her knees and commits it to God.

***

"Welcome, Mrs Rachel Eden-Olumide, to Haven for Moms, *a nurturing place for nurturing mothers…*"

Rachel smiles at the compere she'd hired for her launch, who has just announced her entrance into the building. The formal ceremony is yet to start, but the invited guests are all receiving special mentions as they arrive and are taken on a tour of the grounds by dedicated ushers. Ejike's idea. Rachel beams upon sighting him, but it dims when she notices his wife by his side. She looks on at the other seated guests and goes to greet them all.

"Rachel is the visionary of Haven for Moms, an idea that came to her when she returned from having her first baby in America. In her own words, *"The compound effects of pregnancy, delivery, and parenting on mothers is so enormous compared to the services available to meet their physical, emotional, psychological, and financial needs. It seems cruel that a place such as this isn't readily or freely available to women everywhere. So, I see this as a social impact initiative as much as it's a profitable enterprise…""* the compere continues his introduction of the CEO.

"Rachel is a graduate of Stanford University, in California, where she studied Communication. She is also an MBA holder, and until recently, a beloved radio host on 94.2 Urban FM. She's an amazing woman with a big heart, and a lot to offer the citizens of this great nation. Rachel is married to Douglas Olumide, an up and coming music producer."

"Wow, Rachel! This is a great accomplishment, congratulations!" Ryan says as he gives his sister a hug.

"Thanks, Ryan! Have they shown you around?"

"Yes, it's beautiful. I'm so proud of you!" Ryan replies.

"It's a really good one, Rachel. I can't wait till I get pregnant so I can make this my second home," Cassie says.

Rachel reaches out to hug her. "Me neither, dear…"

"Hey, little sis." Richard stands up for his hug. "This is wonderful! I'm so bummed it's only for women…"

"Only for *mothers*," Cassie says with a sulk.

Rachel giggles. "They need it! Thanks for showing up, guys. I hope you'll stay for the formal ceremony. It shouldn't take more than an hour."

"We're here, dear," Ryan says. "Where's your bobo?"

"He's coming," Rachel says, her smile unwavering.

***

Rachel spots Doug entering just as the ceremony is about to start. By then, the special guests, being the Governor's wife and the Permanent Secretary for the Ministry of Women's Affairs, had arrived and had been shown around the entire complex, with Rachel as their guide. Several members of the press, and Rachel's dedicated photographer and videographer, had accompanied them to take shots and clips for their press releases and social media promotions.

Chief Eden had arrived in time to welcome the special guests too. He is now seated with them on the high table, where two other board members are sitting, waiting for the ceremony to start. Ejike opted to sit among the guests, leaving the seat beside Rachel vacant. Rachel watches as

Doug approaches the high table and greets everyone, one by one. When he gets to Rachel, he kisses her cheek before settling down beside her.

"Welcome, Mr Douglas Olumide, to Haven for Moms, *a nurturing place for nurturing mothers…*" the compere says.

Thankfully, he doesn't say more by way of introduction. The compere starts the ceremony by inviting one of the board members to say the opening prayer. The prayer is short, and Rachel is invited to talk about her vision for the place.

"People have asked me, why not just open a spa for anyone who wants it? Why only mothers? Won't that limit your profit? Yes, another spa may not have been a bad idea. There are not that many in Nigeria, but we don't need another spa as much as we need a place that focuses on and caters to the needs of mothers.

"As one, myself, I can still remember how it feels to be pregnant. It wasn't simply a physical change in my body, but a psychological shift in my mind. I suddenly had new anxieties, so many questions, and my body no longer felt like it was mine. And that's before the baby comes, and so many other things change, physically, emotionally, and financially for the mother.

"Yes, in our culture, many women have their own mothers or mothers-in-law available to assist with the demands of a new baby. But who's there to help with the self-image crisis when your body hasn't bounced back months later? Some women go through post-partum depression, and for many, the anxiety of being replaced at work by a skinny, single woman or even a man, is very real!"

Rachel looks at her captive audience, some of which are nodding along. "So, for me, it isn't a question of why only mothers, but why are the needs of mothers being overlooked in society?" After saying more about her vision and the services Haven for Mom offers mothers, Rachel ends her talk with, "Mothers are known for their selflessness and sacrificial love, and with many words, they are often praised. But more than words, they need support, understanding, and a *break!* At Haven for Moms, we make sure every nurturing mom has a nurturing place too. Thank you."

A round of applause follows as Rachel steps off the podium and returns to her seat. Rachel's eyes meet Ejike's in the audience briefly, but it's long enough for him to communicate his adoration, as his dark, brooding eyes light up with a curve of his lips. She sighs as she settles in her seat.

Doug reaches for her hand, squeezes it, and whispers, "Well done, dear." Rachel smiles at him before looking back at the compere, who is now introducing the next speaker.

CHAPTER TWENTY-FIVE

Rachel has been putting in late hours at the spa all week, since their opening on Saturday. They are booked solid with different events until the New Year. Today, Event Room A is the venue for a baby shower, the first they are hosting at Haven for Moms. The party of thirteen women is scheduled to start at 5pm, and they've booked three spa treatments for the entire group.

Event Room B is vacant tonight. Rachel plan to turn it into a training room during the weekdays, when demand for events is lower. The two rooms are separated by a room divider such that, when opened, they become one big event hall, big enough for ten round tables, seating ten persons each. Rachel smiles, thinking of how the large hall came in handy during the launch.

With a fully stocked crèche, a mommy and baby's room ideal for breastfeeding, and nannies on ground until they close at 9pm on weekdays, Rachel has practically moved into the spa. An added benefit is that Ezekiel now has friends to play with, as some working mothers are already taking advantage of their day care services. And with an in-house cafe and restaurant, she doesn't even need to go out for meals anymore.

Switching off her laptop, Rachel puts her head down. The problem with this setup is that she never ever wants to stop working, until she's run to the ground. Even at this early stage, she's finding that there's always something to do. She could really do with something to take her mind off work for a while.

Rachel sighs and looks up at the bare wall in front of her. She still hasn't gotten the television for her office. The only place they hooked up televisions is at the gym on the top floor. For the sake of a peaceful, relaxing ambiance, she'd decided against having a television at the cafe. And instead of televisions, Haven for Moms provides tablets for the children to use for entertainment and self-learning.

Rising up, she decides to go to the cafe. She passes some women on her way there. They look like they belong to the baby shower group. Rachel watches as they follow the signs to Event Hall A and smiles. The administrator she hired is standing by to assist the party goers, so she can take a mental break. She continues to the cafe.

At the cafe, she orders a cup of tea and settles down at her favourite spot, the one with a view of the Lekki-Ikoyi toll bridge, which also gets a good breeze. *Hmmm...* Yes, this is relaxing. Along with the calming instrumental music on low through the ceiling speakers, it's easy to forget one's worries here. Rachel shuts her eyes as she lets the music do its work.

"Wow, I almost don't want to disturb you..." Rachel hears a familiar voice say. She opens her eyes and takes in the sight of him, as a smile blooms on her lips.

"And yet you do..." she teases.

Ejike sits down across from Rachel and smiles. "How are you?"

"Something wrong with your phone?" she replies, tongue in cheek.

"I prefer to see you when I ask... So, how are you?"

"I'm fine... Been very busy, though."

"I can imagine. That's why I thought I should give you some space."

Rachel shrugs.

"You're mad?"

"Why should I be?"

"I thought we've stopped lying to each other…"

Rachel sips her tea. "Have we?"

Ejike leans in, his eyes penetrating hers. "You know *I* have… I missed you. And I got you something."

Rachel raises an eyebrow, but it seems he wants her to ask. "What?"

He slides over a small jewellery box. Rachel sits upright. The box is too small to contain a necklace…well, a good one that is. She looks up at Ejike. "What is this?"

"Open it…"

Sucking in her breath, Rachel opens the box and releases it when she sees the ruby, diamond-studded, white gold earrings. "They're beautiful. They look expensive."

"Well, of course!" Ejike beams.

"Why?"

Ejike sighs. "Consider it an early Christmas gift or belated congratulations on your launch."

Rachel closes the box and pushes it back across to Ejike. "They're nice, but I don't need expensive ear-rings. Thanks, though."

Ejike looks at her, a frown on his face. "So, if they were cheap, you'd take them?"

Rachel shakes her head. "I don't need any gifts from you, Ejike. Thanks, but I'm good."

"It's not 'cause you need them, Rachel. I'm giving them to you, because I want you to have them," Ejike says, pushing the box back across the table.

"I don't want them!" Rachel slides them back.

"Enough with the stubbornness, already!"

"I thought that's what you *love most about me*…" Rachel says in a mocking voice.

Laughter bubbles up in Ejike's throat, causing his

shoulders to heave. "God, I love you! You're going to kill me, Rachel."

Rachel fights a smile and shrugs.

"What do you want from me? I'm sorry I didn't call or come by sooner... We just got back from Dubai yesterday. I swear, I haven't been able to stop thinking about you. And when I saw these earrings, I could just imagine them adorning your beautiful face. That's why I want you to have them."

Rachel fights the tears threatening to fall from her eyes. To stop him from further talking, she reaches out to collect the box of earrings. "Thank you."

"You're welcome," he says, reaching across to stroke her chin. He giggles when she slaps his hand away.

***

"There's nothing at home to eat!"

Rachel's surprised to get this message from Doug in early January. They'd been living separate lives for so long that she forgot that she's still supposed to be playing 'wife'... She'd figured that with her new job, he'd be understanding, at least at this early stage. Seriously, she can't even remember the last time he came home to eat.

"Sorry, I've been busy. What do you want me to make you?"

"Anything, I'm starving!"

"Okay. I'll be there soon."

Hmmm... Has he run out of money that he can't get food outside like he usually does? Or has he run out of women's houses to go and have dinner? Or are they all broke too? Rachel wonders in amusement.

She decides to go to a fast-food joint and order some cultural dishes. As they do not cater to a lot of customers, food takes a while to prepare at the cafe. It's late afternoon, and she plans to return to her office, so she leaves Ezekiel there with the nannies.

Doug's on the sofa watching television when she gets home. Rachel greets him as she walks to the kitchen to warm and serve the food.

"I thought you were going to cook…" Doug says from behind her. He frowns at the packs of food she has opened to warm.

Rachel huffs. "Really? I thought you said you were starving?"

"If I wanted to eat this junk, I'd have bought it myself."

Rachel lets out a frustrated sigh. She turns to him. "So, what do you want me to do?"

"Go and buy some foodstuffs and cook! Be a wife for God's sake!"

Since when did you want a wife?! "Doug, I left work to bring food for you. And if there's no food in the house, it's because you stopped showing an interest months ago. Am I just supposed to cook food that will waste?"

"I've told you already…"

Rachel stands with folded arms, seething. She wonders what could have come over him to make him start demanding that she "be a wife"? She was quite sure he wanted nothing from her.

Opening the cupboards, she finds a packet of spaghetti. There are canned vegetables to make a nice sauce. She'll chop up the roasted chicken she bought and do a stir fry.

Twenty minutes later, the meal is ready.

Rachel sets up the table and serves the food. Doug gets up and goes to sit down. He wolfs it down without a thank you, as Rachel tidies up the kitchen. She'll have to do some shopping and stock up this afternoon. Thank goodness, she isn't that busy today. She sighs.

When he's done, he drops his plate on the kitchen counter, mutters "thanks," and slaps her bum. Rachel jumps with a start. *How weird! He better not think he's going to get any!*

Rachel collects her handbag from the dining table, ready to go back out, but finds Doug sitting up on the sofa. "I want to talk to you," he says.

She pauses and looks at him. He indicates for her to sit, and she does. "I need to borrow some money…" *Hmmm, so there's the why…*

Rachel swallows. "How much?"

"N500k."

"I don't understand. Why?"

"I owe somebody. I'll pay you back, I promise."

As if! Rachel knows the money is as good as gone if she 'lends' it to her husband. Even his contributions to their upkeep at home have discontinued, which was another reason she stopped stocking up the fridge. And now he's asking to borrow money…?

"What makes you think I have that much?"

Doug eyes her. "*Per-lease!* You can't tell me you're not making money at the spa."

"Doug, we're barely making a profit. We're putting more in than we're getting out right now."

"But you have to put in, don't you? You can lend me from there."

Rachel huffs. He hasn't given her any justifiable reason to part with that much money… But he's her husband, and ideally, they should have one purse, except their disunity hasn't allowed room for such a trusting partnership.

She does have some money in the business, but she really doesn't want to start spending from it, especially when it won't be coming back to the company. Personally, she doesn't have anything near that amount, unless she sells her new earrings… *Nah…*

"I'm sorry, I don't have that kind of money to lend. I can send you N100k, if you can manage that, though."

"Okay. Thanks."

***

Time really does fly when you're having fun! Rachel smiles and sniffs the new flowers she'd ordered for the spa, as part of getting the place ready for Valentine's week. They have so many bookings by expectant fathers for their pregnant wives. However, there are only a few spa treatments booked for wives not currently pregnant, but with children. All but one of those appointments were booked by grown children for their moms.

Rachel peeps through the glass viewer on the door of Event Hall B, where an antenatal class is ongoing. Haven for Moms has got quite a few regular members now, so they are able to pay trainers to run classes on different things all week. Rachel likes the yoga class and occasionally joins in. Oh, how she loves her job!

Leaving the event hall, she decides to check on Ezekiel before returning to her office. On her way to the crèche, she spots a familiar face in the hallway. The woman is standing by the reception/admin desk, looking a little lost.

"Hi, Ifeoma... What brings you here?"

"I wanna see you," is all she says. Rachel thinks she looks a little jittery.

Rachel nods. "Let's talk in my office."

Rachel goes to settle behind her desk, while indicating for Ifeoma to take a seat on one of the visitor chairs. "Or maybe you'd prefer the sofa..."

Ifeoma stands still, her hands clutching her expensive handbag as though she's afraid it would be stolen. "I'd prefer if you'd leave my husband alone!"

Silence. Rachel and Ifeoma lock eyes. Rachel swallows, then lets out a breath. "*Sorry?*"

"Don't try to lie to me! I know what's going on between you and Ejike! You're even wearing the earrings he bought in Dubai on our anniversary getaway! Please, just leave my husband alone."

Rachel instinctively touches the jewel on her right ear. Her heart is racing within its cage. "I'm sorry you felt you had to come here, but I'm not doing anything with Ejike. We're just friends..."

"I thought you were a Christian woman?! I used to listen to your programme…that Marriage ABCs… I know you know better! Please, stop trying to break up my marriage, and focus on your own!"

And with that, Ifeoma turns around and walks briskly away from Rachel's office. Rachel's stunned, so much that she doesn't hear her phone ringing. Suddenly, she has a blinding headache and a pain in her chest that feels like someone broke a knife in it.

She puts her head down on her desk, feeling dizzy, until the vibration from the phone alerts her of the caller. She reaches for it and cuts the call, without knowing who's calling. Why does she feel like she's about to faint?

Rachel stumbles to her sofa and lies on it, closing her eyes against the spinning. On her desk, her phone continues to ring, but she doesn't hear it. All she wants is for the spinning to stop and for sleep to take over.

CHAPTER TWENTY-SIX

Sleep doesn't come. Rachel stays lying on the sofa, feeling like she's free falling. She's felt this way before, she realises.

This feels like when she was hanging on to Onyeka, her Catholic boyfriend, even though she knew their relationship was doomed. She'd vowed that she would never put herself through such torment again. But now, here she is, desperately in love with a married man!

Oh, God! Why does this keep happening to me? What am I doing wrong?

She can't stay like this. She needs to go home, where she can have some privacy. Where Ejike will not come looking for her. She needs to leave this office now…

Rachel manages to get on her feet, grab her phone and her bag, and walk out of the spa, occasionally leaning on the walls for balance. Can she drive? No. She walks back to the cafe and orders an Uber.

Though she's struggling to keep her eyes open, she manages to complete the order and respond to the driver when he says he's outside. She'll have to come back for Ezekiel. She needs to sleep this off and is in no condition to take care of a baby.

Rachel gets into her Uber and fights the urge to lie down in the back seat, as he drives away.

***

Ejike parks outside Haven for Moms. For some reason, Rachel hasn't been taking his calls. He hopes she'll be free for lunch today.

As he walks in, he sees that her car is still parked outside, so she must be in the building, if not in her office. On getting to her office, he finds it empty. He decides to check the cafe, while calling her phone. Now, it's just saying it's switched off.

When he doesn't find her in the cafe, he checks the crèche before finally asking Lolu, Rachel's admin, where her boss is.

"She should be around here somewhere. She didn't tell me she was leaving, sir. I can go up to the spa rooms to see if she's there."

"Yes, please do that," Ejike says, puzzled about the whole thing. He sits on the waiting stools and looks up expectantly when Lolu returns a few minutes later.

"She's not upstairs, sir. I checked the gym too. She probably went out."

"Does she have an appointment now?"

"None, sir. Mrs Ifeoma was here earlier, but she didn't stay long. Maybe Madam went home to pick up something."

"Ifeoma was here?"

"Yes, sir."

"Oh, okay. Thanks!" Ejike says, bolting from the building. What was Ifeoma doing at the spa?

***

Upon getting to her home, Rachel stumbles into the living room and falls unto her sofa. She's able to stretch out on the three-seater, and her body feels ready to sleep now. The spinning has reduced, leaving behind a thumping headache and hunger pangs. But she just wants to sleep now.

Her sleep is interrupted by a horn at the gate. It's probably Doug, she thinks. She can't deal with him now, but she doesn't have the strength to climb the stairs. She rather stands up to look for some paracetamol and maybe something to quieten her angry stomach in the kitchen.

There's a knock at the door. Very unlike Doug. "Who is it?" she shouts.

"Madam, Mr Ejike Okafor is here to see you…"

"I'm not feeling fine. Tell him I'll call him later."

"Rachel, are you okay? Please, let me in," she hears Ejike shout.

"Please, I'm not feeling fine. I'll talk to you later…"

"I know Ifeoma was at the spa today. Let's talk about it."

"Please, Ejike! There's nothing to talk about. Just leave me alone."

There's sudden silence, and Rachel hopes it's over. She finds the paracetamol and swallows two tablets with some water. There's some bread and egg in the fridge. She'll make do.

Rachel hears the gate closing, a sign that her unwanted visitor has gone. She breathes out a sigh, feeling better already.

***

It's 5pm when Rachel stirs from her nap. Her headache is gone, leaving behind heartache. *It's over!* Rachel's shoulders heave as she weeps.

She'll never look in his face and feel joy in her heart again. She'll never see the twinkle of desire for her in those dark, beautiful eyes. She'll never feel the sweet bliss just to have him near nor hear his hearty laughter again. She has to let him go, whether she wants to or not, because he belongs to someone else…

Reaching for her phone, she puts it back on. Thankfully, it stays silent for a while. When she finally feels ready to return to her office, it rings.

"Hello," she says, as lively as she can manage.

"Hi, ma. When are you coming back to the office?"

"I'm on my way. Is everything okay?"

"Yes, ma."

"How's Ezekiel?"

"He's fine, ma. He has been napping."

"Okay. Thanks, Lolu."

With a sigh, she cuts the call, puts her phone in her handbag, and heads out the door.

***

After a cup of coffee and a slice of cake from the cafe, Rachel feels more like herself again. She'll put in two more hours at the office, then go home. Lolu has sent her a maintenance report, indicating areas and equipment in need of repair at the spa. Rachel takes a moment to look through it before approving the budget.

The next thing on her agenda is their planned promotions for March to celebrate women, particularly mothers. A non-profit organisation for vulnerable women sent her a proposal about an event they want to hold on the International Day for Women. They'd like to use the grand hall, but Event Hall B is supposed to be running regular training that day. Rachel's still musing on a compromise when there's a knock on the door. She looks up just as the person opens it.

Rachel had thought to lock it, but she reasoned that she'd rather he come in than cause a scene at her doorway. She sighs on seeing Ejike. Rachel thinks he looks despondent, but that's not really her problem now, is it?

"Ejike, please, I'm busy. Let's talk another time," she says, returning her attention to the schedule for March in front of her.

"Why are you trying to shut me out again, Rache? I thought we'd gone past this…"

She shakes her head, still refusing to look at him. "Ejike, I can't do this…"

"Do what?"

"Be in your life…"

The words cut to his heart. *This can't be happening!* "We're not doing anything wrong!" he says, taking a couple of steps closer.

Rachel finally looks up from her work. "Stop deceiving yourself, Ejike. This isn't right. I can't lie to myself about it anymore..."

"Look, I know it's complicated, but..." he says, walking over to her side of the desk.

She puts out a hand to prevent him from coming closer. "Complicated for me, *convenient* for you! You get to have your cake and eat it too, while I have to watch you having a marriage..."

Ejike huffs. Taking her hand captive, he draws her to himself. Rachel is astonished by the motion, and the strength he shows extracting her from her seat in a single move. "You think I'm having my cake and eating it too? If that was the case, then you and I would be making love..."

Rachel gawks at him and swallows. They are so close that she can feel his heart thumping. *"Every damn day!* You feel me?" he asks, drawing her even closer to feel him, his eyes revealing his intentions. Rachel sucks in a breath, her body trembling with passion. *"Yeah, that's right.* But we're not, because I'm trying to do the right thing."

Finally gathering the strength, she pulls her hand from his grip and pushes her way out of her enclosed position, edging closer to the sofa. "Then do it! Be single-minded! Ifeoma needs you, so be there for her..."

Ejike turns around to face her again. Narrowing his eyes, he asks, "What did she say to you?"

Rachel shakes her head, still trembling from being so close to him. "That doesn't matter. I'm a woman, and I know how it feels when your man loves someone else. I can't do that to her, not anymore."

Ejike takes a hold of her hands again. "Rachel, please, don't do this! I don't want to live without you... I can't do it."

Rachel struggles to be free of him, but his grip is fastened. "I can't live with you like this! I'm not happy..." she cries.

"Oh..." Ejike loosens his hold, while still holding her hands. He thought they were both happy...

"Ejike, if you love me, and if you love Ifeoma, then you owe it to us to make at least one of us blissfully happy. I know it can't happen with you and me, but you can still live happily with Ifeoma. Please, go home and take care of your wife, the way you'd want Doug to take care of me..."

"Is that what would make you happy...?" he asks, searching her eyes.

Though blurred with unshed tears, she holds his gaze and nods. "Yes, it would."

"Okay..." Ejike lets go. He steps back and paces, then takes a seat on the sofa, his head in his hands as he continues to deliberate his next move. He shakes his head at his dilemma. *This is not fair!*

Maybe he should just walk away. *No, I can't. Why can't you let her go*, he asks himself? Then he thinks about her smile, her laughter, her wit, the way she makes him feel whenever they're together, their kiss... *Oh, God, the kiss!* Many nights have passed since with him dreaming of taking possession of those soft lips again and not letting go until they are both sweating and writhing with ecstasy.

He'd doubted before because they hadn't spent any real time together before she got married. He'd thought it might have just been infatuation. But after their time together in Chicago and these few months of getting to know her well, even with kissing off the table, he'd realised that he didn't marry his best friend. He didn't marry "the one". And now, the woman he loves wants to leave him for good?

"What if I choose you?" The words come out so quietly that both of them wonder if he really just said them. Ejike stands up and looks down at Rachel, speaking softly, "If I can't have you both, then I choose you."

Rachel can't believe what she's hearing. She gapes at him, stunned for a moment. "You can't. I'm married," she finally manages to say with quivering lips.

Oh, God, why?! "You might be married to him, but you're mine," Ejike says, seizing her passionately and silencing any objection with his lips pressed against hers.

Rachel leans into him, matching his passion. She wraps her arms around his neck, and Ejike lifts her into his arms. He places her gently on the sofa, as they continue to snog. He breaks away briefly to mutter, "I choose you," sending Rachel into emotional ecstasy. Desperately, she clings to him, as they make out on her sofa.

***

Doug has been home for thirty minutes with no sign of Rachel. He sends her a WhatsApp message asking when she'll be home. However, though delivered, the message appears not to have been read. Annoyed, and finding nothing in the fridge to eat, he gets ready to go out again.

At the gate, he inquires, "Madam no come home today?"

"Yes, sir. She come for afternoon. Brother Ejike also come, but he no stay, *sha.*"

"*Ejike?*"

"Yes, sir. Mr Okafor, Madam's in-law."

"Okay, thank you," Doug says as he drives out of the compound.

Doug decides to take a detour and pass by Haven for Moms. Upon spotting Ejike's car outside, he parks his own and enters the building. He heads straight for Rachel's office.

Not bothering to knock, he tries the door. It's unlocked and opens. But Rachel's not at her desk. She's lying on her sofa, half-dressed with a man between her legs.

Saying nothing, Doug shuts the door and walks back to his car. He pulls out of his parking spot sufficiently to drive forward and ram Ejike's BMW 5 series, causing the bumper to fall off. Satisfied with that vandalism, he drives away spitting obscenities into the air.

***

Ejike and Rachel turn to look at the door at the sound of someone opening it. Rachel never wanted the door locked so that she and Ejike would never use the privacy to fool around. She had also hoped it would prevent such an event as this. But it seems they got carried away today.

There's not enough time for them to separate, but time enough to see that they've been caught in their affair. Rachel wants to rise up, but she's pinned under Ejike, whose reaction time is way too slow. Finally, Doug shuts the door, and Ejike rises from his position. Rachel sits up and buttons her blouse. Standing, she pulls her skirt down and sits again, heaving a sigh.

Is she supposed to chase after Doug? It doesn't look like Ejike wants to. If she did, what would she say? That she's sorry? She loves him? She never meant to hurt him?

No, she's afraid that she doesn't even care that he knows. She's only worried about what he'll do with the knowledge. But seriously, how much worse could her marriage get?

Ejike sits on the sofa next to Rachel. "So, that's that…"

"What do you mean by that?" *And why is he being so calm? Did he want this to happen?*

Ejike sighs. "Now everybody knows."

Rachel gets his meaning and sighs too. "But we didn't do anything… We just kissed!"

"They'll never believe us. And for that, I'm sorry."

Rachel swallows and rests her head on his shoulder, his arm around her. "Me too."

CHAPTER TWENTY-SEVEN

Ejike gets out of the Uber and walks towards his gate. He is let in by the puzzled security guard, who carries his briefcase and follows him to the door. Using his keys, Ejike lets himself into the house.

A surprised Ifeoma rises up to greet her husband. "Hi, darling. Welcome home," she says with a hug and a kiss. "What happened to your car?"

"I had an accident. It's at the mechanic."

"Oh, are you okay? Poor baby," she coos sweetly. Ifeoma collects his case from the security and puts it by the stairs, before returning to the living room, where Ejike is now sitting and pulling off his shoes. "Here, let me help you with that."

He sits back and relaxes. "Thank you."

She smiles up at him. Pulling off his socks, she tucks them into his shoes, and then takes them to the bottom of the stairs, next to the briefcase. When she returns, he has put on the television and is relaxing on the sofa.

"I made you seafood coconut macaroni with grilled chicken salad. Do you want to eat at the table or should I bring it in a tray?" Ifeoma asks, though she has already laid the table.

Ejike looks up at her. She's wearing one of her pretty dresses and looks very beautiful. "I'll eat at the table, thanks."

"Great!" she beams. She checks the food is still warm and goes to get the jug of water from the fridge. Sighing, she sits and waits for her husband to come to the dining table.

The clock in the kitchen says it's 9pm, quite late to be having dinner, but she promised herself that she'd always wait for her husband to come home before eating. He usually returns between 7 and 8pm, except during the weekends, when he occasionally stays out later. She figures he's late today because of his car accident. However, she'd smelt a woman's fragrance on him when she'd hugged him at the door. It is the same fragrance she perceived from Rachel when she visited her office.

Ifeoma swallows. So, he was with Rachel tonight. Her friends had told her never to confront the mistress, but she had been sure that Rachel would be different. What if all she had done was give them a reason to laugh tonight? Ifeoma shuts her eyes against the taunting image.

She opens them when she hears Ejike walking towards the table. Throwing on a smile, she watches as he pulls out his seat and settles at the table. His wedding band catches her eye. *Does he take it off when he's with her? Does he even love me at all?*

"This looks nice," Ejike says.

Ifeoma beams. "I used the recipe book I bought in Dubai. I hope you like it."

Ejike nods and tucks into his meal. He observes Ifeoma from the side of his eye. She seems nervous, like she wants to ask him something. He tries to keep his cool and continues eating quietly.

"So, how was work today?" she asks.

Ejike nods and mumbles, "Fine."

Ifeoma notices that he doesn't ask about her day. She decides to volunteer information. "Cool. Mine was good too. I got some orders for Tok's wedding, next month."

"That's good," Ejike says without looking at her.

"I also stopped by at Haven for Moms…"

That gets his attention. He turns to her. "Hmmm… I was informed…"

"Oh. Okay. So, you saw her today?"

"If by her, you mean Rachel… Yeah," he says, returning Ifeoma's gaze. "She seemed upset. What did you say to her?"

Ifeoma is taken aback. "N…n…nothing, really. I guess I was just concerned because you've been spending so much time there lately."

"If you are concerned about anything, you ask me… I thought you knew from Chicago that we're close…"

Ifeoma swallows. "How close?"

Ejike smiles and shakes his head. Is there really any point in lying now? Then again, what's the point in divulging all? "We're just close, okay?"

Ifeoma's eyes are clouding with tears. "Do you love her?"

Ejike doesn't look at his wife when he says, "Yes."

The tears break free, and Ifeoma pushes back her chair to leave the dining table.

***

Rachel drives into her compound expecting to see Doug's car under the canopy, but he's not home. She parks and carries Ezekiel from his car seat before entering the house. She wonders if Doug will come home tonight.

She still hasn't called nor sent him a message since he caught her with Ejike. Honestly, she doesn't know what she'd say. What would she want him to say if the roles were reversed?

Well, the last time, he and his companion had mocked her, but then again, they weren't exactly in a lovers' embrace as she'd been found in. Actually, Rachel still couldn't prove that Doug has been involved with Bose or any of the women he's been seen hanging around with. All she has are her suspicions, some hearsay, and the fact that he hasn't touched her for over a year!

Anyway, back to her current situation. She knows that even if she wouldn't pick his calls nor respond to his messages, she'd feel so much worse if she thought he didn't care enough to try to appease her. With a deep breath, she brings out her phone.

His phone just rings out with each dial. After three attempts, she settles for reaching him via WhatsApp.

"Hi, Doug. Are you coming home?"

"I'm sorry about what happened today. Please come home, let's talk about it."

"We didn't do anything, I swear. I know how it looked, but nothing happened."

"I'm at home, now. Please, we really need to talk."

All messages are received, with no indication that they've been read. Rachel puts her phone away and goes to attend to her child. Ezekiel needs a bath before she tucks him into bed.

***

Ejike carries his briefcase and shoes up the stairs. It seems, in her upset, Ifeoma left them. He finds her in their bedroom, blowing her nose into a hanky. He feels really awful to have hurt her like this. She has been a really good wife, so he can't fault her on anything.

Quietly, he takes off his clothes and puts them in the wash basket. Grabbing a towel, he enters the bathroom. Why does life have to be so complicated? Why is it that his romantic feelings for Ifeoma evaporated like menthol months after their wedding, but his feelings for Rachel are like stinky cheese that have only gotten stronger with time? He smiles at the analogy.

Ejike closes his eyes as the water washes over him. What is he going to do now? He'd told Rachel that he would choose her, and he meant it. So, does that mean he's getting a divorce? Or will they just allow themselves to be together, even though they're married to other people? It would be easy for Rachel seeing as she married an ass, but Ifeoma's quite a catch. Would he later regret his decision?

Towelling dry, he walks back to his bedroom. Ifeoma's still nursing a handkerchief on the bed. She'll want to talk to him. He doesn't even know what he'll say to her.

"Why?" she finally asks, when he's slipping on his boxes. He turns to look at her and sighs. What can he say? "Is she better in bed than me?"

He should have known that's what she'll be thinking about. At least he can honestly say he doesn't know. He tries to control the smile on his face, especially at seeing Ifeoma's horrified expression. Swallowing, he says, "Actually, we've never done that..." *Yet.* He bites his bottom lip.

Ifeoma's mouth is agape. Clearly, she doesn't believe him. "You expect me to believe that...?"

"I think you know me better than that, Ifeoma," Ejike says, settling in the bed beside her. "Remember, I didn't touch you before we married..."

Actually, I don't think I know you at all... Ifeoma swallows. "So, why are you doing this? Is it me? Do you not love me?"

Ejike looks at her and feels sad. He can't tell her he doesn't love her... It's just not the same. "Of course I do."

"Then, what is it? Whatever it is, I'll change," she says desperately, reaching for his hands.

Ejike closes his eyes against the guilt, clasping his hands together. "I'm sorry, Ifeoma. If I knew how to switch off my feelings for Rachel, I would have. I just don't want to lie to you about it anymore."

Ifeoma nods her head, lies down, and turns her back to him. How is she supposed to fight for her marriage when she's just not good enough? The tears continue to stream down as she lies in bed, heartbroken.

Ejike checks his phone, intending to send Rachel a

message. However, he sees a message from Chief Eden.

"I'd like to see you tomorrow. Please let me know what time will be best for you."

***

Rachel's in bed sipping a cup of tea. She's not quite ready to sleep and is still processing all that happened today. She'd never have imagined that this is the way things would go with her and Ejike. She'd been ready to give him up, but there he was *choosing* her, fighting for them again.

She'd thought she had all the knowledge and wisdom about marriage, but look where she's ended. Like Ejike said, they were in this situation because of her. Maybe it not too late for them... Maybe it's time she started listening to her heart instead of running from it...

Her phone sounds with a notification, and she looks at it on the bedside table. Speaking of her heart...

"Hey, babe," he'd written.

"Hey, babe," she types back.

"How are you?"

"I'm fine. Home alone. Well, with Ezi."

"Hmmm... No word from Doug?"

"None. What about Ifeoma? Did you guys talk?"

"Yeah... I told her about us."

"Wow. How's she taking it?"

"Better than I imagined, actually."

"I feel so bad..."

"I know. Me too. But if we keep denying what we feel, it's not going to be good for anybody."

"Yeah, I was just thinking the same thing. Like how I didn't follow my heart in the beginning, and we ended up in this mess."

"Exactly. So, please, don't try and shut me out again. We're going to figure this out."

"I love you so much, Ejike. I never thought I could love anyone like this!"

Ejike sends a link to a video he'd been listening to. It's

Mario's video to his hit song, "I Choose You". *"I love you too, Rachel. I choose you!"*

Rachel's heart leaps when she sees it and reads his caption. *"OMG! You're going to kill me saying that 😊"*

"I mean it."

"I choose you too, Ejis 😊"

"You better! I'll see you tomorrow."

"Can't wait! Good night, babe 😊"

"Good night, Rache 😊"

Rachel smiles to herself as she gets under the covers. Mario's song is on repeat, as she listens to it, musing on the lyrics. *Is it possible to be happier than this?* She wants to say her night-time prayers, but she's anxious that she might hear something contrary. Instead, she closes her eyes and mutters, "Lord, I just want to be happy. Please, watch over us tonight, I pray, amen."

As she relaxes to sleep, her phone sounds again. She quickly checks it. It's from her dad.

"Rachel, meet me at the house tomorrow by 12 noon."

***

Ifeoma's not in bed when Ejike wakes up the following morning. He's relieved about that and gets himself ready for the day. He goes downstairs to find her sitting at the dining table, all dressed for work, the table set for breakfast.

"Good morning," she greets. No 'darling' today, he observes.

"Good morning," he replies. He drops his briefcase by the sofa and goes over to check out the spread. Tempting, but he can only have a quick breakfast today. "Thanks," he says as he puts half a pastry into his mouth. Yummy!

"I want a baby."

Ejike almost chokes on the food in his mouth. He gawks at Ifeoma. Coughing, and drinking some water, he regains his composure. "I'm sorry?"

"You said after our first year, we can start trying… But since our anniversary, you've been putting me off. I don't want to wait any longer."

"And you think *now* is the time to start trying for a baby…?" Ejike asks incredulously.

"Yes. I'm not getting any younger, and if you decide to leave me…" she trails off.

Ejike can hear the pain in her voice. He looks at her. She's skilfully applied her make-up today that if he didn't know better, he'd never suspect that she'd been crying. Oh, he's a real bastard to do this to her!

Ifeoma swallows. "I just want a baby."

"Can we talk about this later, please?"

"When?"

"Tonight. When I get back from work. I promise." That should give him some time to think about it.

"Okay, thanks," she says, standing up to leave, her head held high.

CHAPTER TWENTY EIGHT

"Good afternoon, Dad and Mom. Thank you for this occasion to express my grievance. I really didn't want it to come to this, but Rachel has given me no choice, and I don't know what to do anymore," Doug says.

Ejike looks over at Rachel, who's seated on the opposite side of the Eden's grand dining table, next to her husband, her head bowed. He hadn't expected such a meeting when Chief had invited him over to the house last night. He swallows as he looks at Doug. *What is he trying to pull?*

"I don't even know how to begin, so I'll just start with why I called this meeting. Last night, I walked in on my wife having sex with Ejike in her office."

Rachel gasps and gets a stern look from Chief Eden. She takes the cue to keep her mouth shut. Mrs Eden is shaking her head disapprovingly, while Ejike is resting his head on his hands. She turns away, unable to look at Doug as he continues his tale.

"I have suspected them since she travelled to Chicago to have Ezekiel. She kept telling me nothing was going on, that he was just helping her, and they are family, so nothing can ever happen. But my gut was telling me otherwise...

"When she got back, she was distant and withdrawn. She stopped showing me any affection, she always used Ezekiel as an excuse not to be intimate or even to do anything around

218

the house. I put up with it because she had just given birth, and I wanted to be supportive. But it just kept getting worse. She doesn't even cook or stock up the house anymore.

"I remember she was really miserable around the time Ejike got married. It brought back my suspicions about them. But he was married, and I hoped that would be the end of it. I mean, they are both Christian, and she's even a marriage counsellor. So, I put it out of my mind.

"And then, on her birthday, Ejike barges into my office to fight me over something she must have told him. I think we'd had a small disagreement or something, but she'd obviously been talking to him about our problems. It was then I knew something was really going on between them, even though she denied it when I confronted her.

"But yesterday, I finally saw for myself, and…" Doug stops to cry and wipe his tears. "God, I…love her so much!"

Rachel finally turns to Doug, mouth agape. *You've got to be kidding me!* How the hell is she going to defend herself against such a bullshit performance? She decides to hold her tongue until spoken to.

Chief Eden clears his throat and speaks up. "Rachel, what do you have to say to what Doug has reported about you and Ejike?"

Rachel swallows. "I just want to say that we were not having sex when Doug came to my office…"

"I saw him on top of her, and they were practically naked!"

"Actually, I was fully clothed!" Ejike corrects.

"We'll get to you, Ejike," Chief chastises.

"We were kissing, but nothing more," Rachel says.

"And was that the first time?" Chief asks.

Rachel hesitates, and Mrs Eden huffs, shaking her head accusingly. "It was our second kiss."

"Please, I don't know why we are counting how many times, or whether they had sex or just kissed. Obviously, there's something that's been going on with them for a long time, and it has been affecting her marriage," Mrs Eden says.

"I agree," Chief says. "I don't think the details are what's important here. What's more important is why this is going on and how we can put an end to it."

"Can I speak, Chief?" Ejike asks.

"Go on."

"Yes, this has been going on for a long time. Even before Rachel got married. I was in love with her, but I didn't make my feelings known in time. However, Doug knew from the beginning, and since I was in Port Harcourt, he moved in fast, and before I knew it, they were getting married.

"I went to the States to get away from it all. But then Rachel came to have her baby, and I wanted to help her like I'd helped Rochelle the previous year. Nothing happened between us in Chicago, it was purely platonic. I was also seeing Ifeoma then." Ejike takes a deep breath. "I feel like part of the reason I got married was because I was trying to escape my feelings for Rachel. After I got married, I didn't speak with her for months, until I called her on her birthday. It was then that I found out that Doug was messing around with Rachel's friend, Bose. That was what caused me to do what I did and go to his office that day."

Ejike swallows. He's happy to have both Mrs Eden's and Chief's attention. "After that, I realised that my feelings for Rachel hadn't died like I'd wanted. In fact, they are stronger now. I love Rachel. So much... She's not at all like Doug describes. She's a good and faithful woman. Yes, Doug caught us kissing. But that only happened because I wouldn't let her go. Rachel keeps trying to push me away, but I thought we could just be friends. But now I realise that can't happen, because I want more..."

Hmmm... Chief muses. "Who's Bose?" he asks Doug.

"She's a mutual friend. She's been doing back-up vocals for me at the studio."

"And you're having an affair?"

"No, we're not," Doug denies.

"Were you ever?" Rachel asks, thinking he might be hiding behind the use of the present tense.

"No, we were not," he replies and swallows.

"What made you think there was something between them?" Chief asks Rachel.

"Well, on a couple of occasions, when I visited his office, I found them looking quite intimate. They were holding hands and stuff..." By the look on Chief's face, it's clear he isn't convinced. "Plus, Bose has refused to talk to me since the first time I saw them and confronted her about it... And Doug hasn't touched me in over a year...so..."

Hmmm... Chief and Mrs Eden exchange looks. "Okay, so let me get this straight... Ejike, you're in love with my daughter?"

"Yes, sir."

"And your wife?"

"She knows. I told her last night."

Mrs Eden chuckles. "You people are unbelievable!"

"And Rachel, are you also in love with Ejike?" Chief Eden asks.

Rachel nods. "Yes, I am."

Chief sighs. He looks sympathetically at Doug.

"So, Doug was right," Mrs Eden says. "I can imagine how your relationship with Ejike must have put a strain on your marriage. And I suspected something when I was with you in the US." She turns to her husband. "They used to carry on like lovers, but you will never hear her on the phone with her husband for more than two minutes! Am I lying, Rachel?"

Rachel swallows and says nothing. She looks across at Ejike. He, too, is looking a little defeated.

"So, I guess it's left to Doug. What do you want to do? Do you want a divorce?" Chief asks.

"No, sir. I don't believe in divorce. I just want my wife back. I can forgive her if she will stop what she's doing and let us work on our marriage."

Mrs Eden's frown is converted. "It's that simple. Forgiveness. There's no marriage that can break where there is forgiveness."

"So, Rachel... What do you have to say to your husband?" Chief asks.

Rachel looks at each of them, from her dad, to her step-mother, to Ejike, then to Doug. "I don't know if it's that simple..." she finally says.

"He's offering you forgiveness on a platter. What is the problem again?" Mrs Eden chastises. "Is it Ejike you are looking for? Does he not have his own wife?!"

"I don't think Doug loves me. I don't think he's being sincere..."

"You don't think he loves you, but have you shown that you love him? Look, forget about Ejike, and face your marriage! Whatever you think you have there, that one is a lie, *oh*! When you said your marriage vows, for better or worse, it means, even if you don't feel loved, you must still love your husband!" Chief nods his head in agreement. "And when they say "forsaking all others", it means you cannot carry Ejike enter your marriage. It's just you and Doug until death do you part..."

Rachel swallows. She looks across at Ejike, tears gathering in her eyes. Mrs Eden huffs.

"Ejike, I'm quite disappointed in you," Chief says. "When you said you wanted to join Haven for Moms as a partner, it never occurred to me that you had such interest in my daughter. I would never have allowed it."

"*Partner?*" Doug asks, obviously hearing it for the first time.

"She didn't tell him, *nau*," Mrs Eden speculates.

"Yes, Ejike has a substantial stock in Haven for Moms, obviously his means to keep ties with Rachel. I think we will need to rectify it immediately... They cannot continue to have such a partnership, in light of everything," Chief says.

Rachel can't believe how her world is crumbling. She wipes tears from her eyes as she sits listening. And the worst part is the way Doug has managed to come off, not only as the injured party, but as the gracious one too. Or has she really been deluded this whole time because of her feelings for Ejike?

"Please, can I speak?" Ejike asks. All eyes are on him as he takes the floor. "First of all, I'm sorry for how this came to light. But Rachel and I are both grownups. If we want to be together, we will be together."

"Grownups, indeed! Wait until I tell your father about this nonsense you're trying to pull, throwing your money around and breaking up my daughter's marriage. *Na only you get money?!*" Chief rebukes.

"*No be* trust fund?" Mrs Eden adds mockingly. "If your father cuts you off for disgracing him, will you be able to talk…? *We are grownups… Mtcheeew!*"

"Actually, ma, I make my own money…"

"*Abeg*, it's enough!" Chief hisses. "Stop embarrassing yourself."

In the silence that follows, Ejike can swear he sees Doug snicker. This is exactly what he wanted. *Poor Rachel!* He looks at her and all he wants to do is wrap her in his arms and carry her away from all this. But now, he's facing a much bigger obstacle than Doug – her family.

"Look, I think we've spent enough time on this. Rachel, what you've done to your husband is unforgivable betrayal, yet he is ready to forgive you. I'd implore you to repent and work on your marriage. I think you also need to re-examine your relationship with God," Chief says. "Doug, on behalf of my daughter, I apologise. Thank you for your forgiving heart. Please be patient with her and help her win this battle with the devil. We know that he is the one that wants to break up your marriage."

"Thank you, Daddy!" Doug says, bowing the knee. "Thank you, Mommy. I will love her through this. I appreciate all your help."

"It is well with you, my son," Mrs Eden says, nodding to show her support.

"We will still talk about this later. I have a meeting to go to," Chief says, standing up.

Mrs Eden rises up and follows her husband. Ejike is the next to rise up. He doesn't have anything else to say. Without looking at Rachel or Doug, he walks away.

Rachel wants to follow after him and cry, "I choose you!" Why does she not have a choice in this matter? How can she stay in her marriage feeling like this? Is this a death sentence?

"Rachel…"

Rachel turns to see Doug looking at her. He is really looking at her. He looks genuine and broken. She swallows.

"I forgive you. And I'm sorry."

Rachel blinks. What is he apologizing for?

"I'm sorry I made you feel like I didn't love you. I guess I've always suspected that you'd rather be with Ejike and felt like I wasn't good enough for you. It made me insecure. Can we start again? Please?"

Rachel swallows. Was she wrong about him? Has she been the one sabotaging her marriage from the get go by comparing them? All she knows now is that Doug seems really genuine, and she really has no choice but to honour her vows, for better or for worse. There's no harm in giving it one more go.

She nods. "Okay. And I'm sorry too. I'm sorry I let Ejike come between us."

Doug hugs Rachel, and she hugs him back. Chief and Mrs Eden pass by on their way out and smile when they see the reconciled couple.

"Love covers a multitude of sins!" Mrs Eden says.

Rachel stands up and goes to hug her. "Thank you, Mom.

Thank you, Dad." She hugs him too.

"That's what we're here for, baby!" Chief says fondly, kissing his daughter on her head.

And Rachel sighs. She can't believe it was that easy.

CHAPTER TWENTY-NINE

Ejike's mind is consumed with the events of the last 24 hours, and he's unable to focus on work. Feeling a desperate need to be alone with his thoughts, he decides to leave early. How could he let things get so out of hand? How could he not have exercised more self-control? He hadn't even sought God's help but dove into his feelings like a kid, oblivious to the consequences, especially to the woman he sought to love.

Reflecting, Ejike is quite embarrassed at all that he's done in the last six months since his reconnection with Rachel on her birthday. Though he felt in control of himself, he now sees that he was only able to pursue after her by silencing his conscience. The more time they spent together, the harder it got to stay away from her or control his growing feelings. Naturally, his prayer life took a dive because he couldn't deal with his guilt over his infidelity.

He'd promised himself and God that he would never be that man again. He wanted to be the kind of man who cherished his wife. But he has failed woefully.

As wonderful as Ifeoma is, Ejike knows now that he never loved her enough. His confession at Chief's mansion today about his reason for getting married had been eye-opening for him too. He knows God hates divorce, but He hates lies too. What kind of man would he be if he strung Ifeoma along, only to hurt her later, if and when he does fall in love again?

And will he ever love again? Will he ever get over Rachel? *God, I just want to do the right thing!*

Upon getting home, Ejike heads straight to his bedroom and climbs into bed, fully clothed. He can't remember the last time he napped during the day, but he's not feeling well. His emotional sickness is having a toll on his body. As he lies in bed, the tears he won't let anyone see fall freely. What a trip that he would be crying over a woman…

***

Ifeoma's heart races with excitement upon finding her husband's Lexus, which he had driven today, in the driveway. It can only be a good thing that he is home at this time. Perhaps, he has had a change of heart.

Eagerly, she lets herself into the house and makes her way upstairs, after confirming that he isn't in the living area. When she finds him asleep on their bed, his shoes still on, she goes to his side. She assists him to remove them and his socks and puts them away. Sitting beside him, she watches him sleep.

Curiously, she touches his forehead, but it's not warm. Ifeoma exhales. He must be tired. He stirs and turns to her in a jerky movement, as though he doesn't know where he is. She swallows.

"Hi, dear," she says. "Are you okay?"

Ejike rises and sits up in bed. Conscious of how he might look, he heads straight for the bathroom to freshen up his face. Walking back into his bedroom, he finally replies, "I'm fine. How are you?"

Devastated. Heartbroken. What do you think? She shrugs.

When he says nothing more, she asks, "What do you want for dinner?"

"Don't worry, I'll help myself when I'm ready. Thanks."

Ejike walks across to the L-shaped sofa in their bedroom and sits down, cradling his head in his hands. He should take

Panadol for this headache.

Ifeoma doesn't understand his action. Why not sit on the bed next to her? She slowly makes her way over to him and sits down with some distance between them. "Can we talk now?"

He shrugs. She sighs. She looks at him. "So, can we start trying...?"

He shakes his head slowly, and she's shocked. She never expected he'd say no. "Why?"

He looks at her, and their eyes meet. "I'm sorry. I don't want to have a baby with you. I want a divorce."

Ifeoma jerks back as though she's been stabbed in the heart. She stays frozen, unable to speak, while Ejike resumes his position of cradling his head. *This has to be a cruel joke.*

✳✳✳

Rachel's feeling a little weary about her reconciliation with Doug this afternoon. After her parents left, he escorted her to her car and hugged her again before pecking her on the lips.

"I'll come home early tonight so we can talk some more..." he'd said before getting in his car and driving out of the compound.

Rachel knows that she needs to put Ejike out of her mind, but it's been hard. Whenever she starts thinking things might work out with her and Doug, she feels like she's betraying Ejike. And she feels like she's losing him a second time. She's so confused, she doesn't know what to do.

At the office, Rachel keeps looking at the sofa where she held Ejike in her arms, as he uttered sweet words in her ear, kissing her, and making promises to satisfy her forever. She closes her eyes against the memories. Will she have to get a new sofa? In all her life, that was the happiest moment, she thinks as she begins to cry.

Rachel dabs her face with tissues. She owes it to herself, she owes it to Doug, and she owes it to Ezekiel to give her marriage a second chance. God hates divorce, and she knows that the only way she, or anyone for that matter, can stay in a marriage is by crucifying her flesh. It's time she carries her cross with joy and stops complaining about it.

As she works, she half-expects Ejike to call, to text, to walk through the door and tell her he cannot live without her. But the hours go by, and she doesn't hear from him. It's getting dark out... She should go home.

Oh, mehn, she forgot that Doug said he'll be coming back early... Was she supposed to cook? She's really not in the mood. She'll send a message and find out where he is.

"Hi, Doug? What time will you be home?" She words it that way, hoping he'll assume she's there already.

"I'm almost there... Did you cook?"

"I haven't had the time."

"Okay, let me branch and get some dinner for us. See you soon x"

"Okay, dear. Thanks."

With a sigh, she packs up for the day.

***

Rachel gives Doug a weak smile as he walks through the door. She rises up, knowing she has to make more of an effort. He's trying too.

"Welcome home," she greets, smiling brighter.

Doug smiles and hands her the bag of packed food he'd purchased from a fast-food joint nearby. He tells her all the things he bought for her and himself. As she goes to serve the food into plates, he puts on the television and settles down on the sofa.

When she returns with his tray, he indicates for her to place it on the stool near him. She does and pulls up another for her meal. They eat as they watch the television. Rachel suppresses a sigh.

When they're done eating, and she has packed the trays away, he invites her to sit closer to him on the sofa by tapping on the space next to him. Rachel draws closer, and

Doug makes to kiss her, but she recoils.

"I thought we were going to talk," she says.

"About what?"

Rachel blinks. "About the problems in our marriage…"

Doug shrugs. "Everything is fine now. Like your parents said, it was just Ejike that was coming between us, and we've resolved that."

Schwoooh, Rachel can hardly believe it. She massages away a headache. "I think we have more issues than Ejike, Doug. I really think we need to see a counsellor."

Doug frowns. "There's nothing a counsellor will tell us that we don't already know. It's just money down the drain." He sighs. "We just have to make more effort to listen to each other and to be sensitive to each other too. I'll do my part if you will…"

Rachel's still struggling to let the issue go. "Okay… But what about Bose?"

"What about her?" Rachel gives him a pointed stare. "You still think we're having an affair? I haven't spoken to her in like six months! We finished the production we were working on around the time of my birthday last year."

Hmmm… "Okay."

"You should know that I'm not a womaniser, Rachel. That's Ejike's territory. I've just been doing all I can to get my label going."

"And how is it going?"

Doug bobs his head and shrugs. "It's okay. It can be better, but I'm pushing."

Rachel smiles. She feels a little better now. Some of her anxieties have been cleared.

"So, we good?" Doug asks.

She nods. She'll have to be. He said he hasn't been unfaithful, so she has to trust him. "Yeah." She swallows. "And again, I'm sorry. I behaved badly."

Doug hugs his wife. "Thank you."

Rachel relaxes and leans into her husband. Time for a second chance.

***

The next day, Rachel decides to visit Rochelle and Ekene at home. It's the weekend before Valentine's week. Rochelle arrived last week from the States with little baby Justin. Rachel's seen the pictures, but she's yet to behold the child in the flesh. Unfortunately, Doug's working, so he won't be able to accompany her.

"Congratulations!!!" Rachel says at the door, when Ekene opens up. She hands him her gift, and they hug briefly.

"Hi, Rachel! Thank you."

Rochelle's breastfeeding the little darling on the sofa. She smiles up at Rachel. "Hi, Rache!" Rachel gives her a kiss on the cheek, then sits down.

"Oh, Rochelle, he's so cute!" she gushes over the infant, watching as he sucks on his mother's breast, his eyes shut with delight. "He has so much hair!"

"I know, right! I think he gets it from mom. That her Hausa blood is strong!" Rochelle laughs.

"Can I get you anything, Rachel?" Ekene asks.

"Water will be fine. Don't worry, I'll get it myself."

Ekene sits down and picks up his newspaper. Rachel helps herself to a cup of water from the dispenser, then returns to sit and chat with the grownups while Jen and Ezi play.

***

On her way out, Rachel sees Ejike driving into the compound. If she knows what's good for her, she'll hurry up and get out of there. She walks briskly to her car and straps Ezekiel in his car seat. The normally easy, hassle-free task is now met with confusion and stress, as she fumbles for the straps and struggles with the clips. Finally, it clicks shut.

She turns around to enter the driver seat and make her exit, but Ejike has already parked and is now walking in her direction. It would be rude to ignore him. Casually, she lingers to say hi.

"Hi," he replies. He also seems hesitant. "How are you?"

"I'm fine. And you?"

He nods. "I'm fine too. Take care of yourself, Rachel." And then he walks into the house without so much as a glance back.

To think that less than 48 hours ago, they'd been professing undying love to each other. Rachel enters her car and reverses out of her spot. *I guess he can live without me after all…*

***

"Hey, Rache. How are you doing? It's been a while. I just thought I should check up on you 😊*"*

Rachel smiles on receiving this message from Ihotu. She must be in the spirit because Rachel's looking for someone to talk to and was just about to reach out too.

"Hey, dear. I'm fine. How are you?"

"I'm alright. How's the family?"

"We're good. Things are better, actually."

"For real? That's great! What's new 😊*?"*

"It's a long story…"

"Should I call?"

"Sure…"

Rachel picks on the first ring.

"So, what have I missed?"

Rachel lies on the sofa as she recounts the life changing developments of the last few days. Ihotu listens attentively, as usual, and is careful not to pass judgement. She shares her thoughts after hearing Rachel's account.

"I think it's really good that you and Doug are giving yourselves a second chance. He's pretty cool to have forgiven you so quickly. That must have been tough. As much as you can, do give him the benefit of the doubt. It's great that you are now able to see things from his perspective too. I really hope you guys grow closer through what has happened."

Rachel sighs. "Yeah…"

"So, have you guys, ummm, *reconciled* yet?" Ihotu giggles.

Rachel chuckles. "Not yet. We're planning to do something on Valentine's Day. We're going to get tested first, though, just so we can be truly trusting and feel safe with each other again."

"That sounds wise. Good luck with it!"

"Thanks, dear!"

Rachel sighs after her call with Ihotu. If she's being honest, she's nervous about Valentine's Day. She knows better than to have high expectations, though. In truth, she's more nervous about her part in the act.

CHAPTER THIRTY

Rachel's at work early to deal with the extra demand for services on Valentine's Day. She and Doug have agreed to go out tonight to celebrate. There's a special play showing at Terra Kulture in Victoria Island, and Doug thought it would be interesting. Then it's just a short stroll to Rachel's favourite Chinese restaurant across the street. They also have the option of eating at the Terra Kulture restaurant, in any case.

They already exchanged gifts this morning. For her, he bought a gift bag containing a card, a box of her favourite chocolates, a small bottle of Baileys, and his printed results from his medical screening yesterday. She actually loved everything, especially seeing that his results confirmed that she is not at risk of contracting HIV, hepatitis, gonorrhoea, nor syphilis from him. Granted, it didn't cover all bases, like the more common chlamydia or herpes, but his willingness to test was encouraging. She'd produced her test results on Monday, and they were just as reassuring.

For him, Rachel bought a card, a set of boxers and a pack of condoms. She hopes the condoms are suggestive, expressing her interest for sex, protection, and contraception. Even though he's never been a fan of the rubber, she chose a special kind that promised heightened pleasure for the man. He seemed to appreciate them when they exchanged gifts before leaving for work. Hopefully, they will be sufficient so she doesn't have to go back on the pill. Having another baby is the last thing she wants to do right now.

With a few days of practice, she's getting better at keeping Ejike out of her mind. But today's not a good day for that, with all the reminders of love, romance, and happiness. It's one of the reasons she's eager to leave the office, actually. Lolu has shown sufficient competence to be left in charge, so Rachel isn't worried about that.

On her way home, Rachel gets a call from Doug. He doesn't think he can make it in time to pick her up for their romantic evening as planned. If they are going to catch the play, then she should meet him at Terra Kulture. That also means she will be driving herself home, and they might end up not leaving together, as is often the case whenever they go places separately. Rachel's sad because she'd been counting on them spending as much time together as possible.

"No problem, dear," she says, changing her route. "I'll meet you there."

***

It is a lovely night out for Rachel and Doug. Even though she isn't a fan of stage plays, Rachel is impressed by the performances tonight. Instead of walking or driving to the Chinese restaurant, they settle for the in-house café and restaurant. The food is tasty and filling.

The conversation, however, is on the stale side. They talk about the ambience, the play, the food, and a bit about work. Standard things, but the silences in-between feel long and painful.

Rachel can't understand it. They used to have so much fun together when they were dating. Even if they didn't say anything, they were comfortable in each other's presence. But here they are, after going months without talking, still having nothing to say to each other. She is happy when, rather than extend their outing, they agree to head home.

Rachel arrives home before Doug. He'd been driving behind her, but deviated along the way. She assumed he wanted to branch somewhere or maybe he knew of a better route.

He arrives 20 minutes later. Apparently, he'd stopped at a supermarket to get a few things. Rachel makes a hot chocolate and Baileys beverage for them, as they prepare for the main event. When she returns with the drinks, they sip them as they begin foreplay with kisses.

With their beverages finished, they decide to retire upstairs.

***

That was different... Rachel thinks, as she lies down on the bed after the act. *Where did he learn to do that? He seems way more experienced than the last time we did this... Hmmm...*

She watches as Doug goes to clean himself up. She also needs to clean up as the condoms she'd bought had failed to satisfy and had been roughly discarded in irritation. Now, she's going to have to get the morning-after pill!

And even though he claims to have been faithful, he has definitely picked up some new tricks from somewhere, or someone. She swallows. Maybe she needs to get tested again, after all.

One thing hasn't changed, however. Their intimacy. It's as dead as the last time they did this. Rachel knows that it will take work...and time...and trust. But somehow, she doesn't see that happening, especially in the absence of honesty. She's more convinced than ever that her husband is a cheater and a liar.

***

May 20th, 2017
Dear Diary,
Three months ago, my world fell apart. The man I love walked away from me because our love is forbidden.

My husband caught us making out in my office and reported to my parents, who decided to sit us down to resolve the issue. Doug stated his case and made it look like we've been having a long-time affair, even though we were just friends harbouring feelings of love for each other, for the most part.

After he said he'd forgive my betrayal and that he was sorry for making me feel unloved, I felt like I could give my marriage a second chance. And even though nothing has changed between us since, I've tried to abide and remain faithful to Doug by forsaking Ejike. I've also tried to be a better wife while juggling motherhood and a growing business.

Doug wants me to be a traditional wife, who stays home, cooks and cleans, gives him sex and babies, and looks after them too, while he is left with the responsibility to provide for us...even if it means he never gets to be at home, with us. I don't want that. We live in a modern world, and besides technological advancements, there are social initiatives and revolutions that allow women to live more well-rounded, fulfilling lives.

I mean, that's what Haven for Moms is all about! I can work and have my child/ren looked-after in a safe, child-friendly environment and not feel guilty about having a life that isn't centred around the fact that I'm a mother or a wife. Before those titles, I am a woman! A human being!

So, we still don't agree, but I'm trying to be more accommodating by coming home early to cook. Thankfully, he doesn't mind that we have a maid who does the cleaning, though he tried to fight me on keeping a nanny. He said, because I have the crèche at H4M, that I don't need to pay for a full-time nanny at home.

Well, I was fine not having a full-time nanny with my job at the radio station, which was pretty much part-time. But I'm actually running a company now, and a profitable one at that. Our first quarter accounts were super impressive, and we've been getting even more business this quarter. So, he didn't win that one.

Doug's studio business is doing well too. After the meeting at my parents', they gave him the funds he needed to expand it. I guess he got in their good graces by being such a "loving, forgiving, and gracious husband…"

But I still don't believe him. I wanted to, but after we had sex again, and it felt like I was sleeping with a completely different person, I can't believe he hasn't been sleeping around in the 14 months he refused to touch me. I just can't.

After Valentine's Day, I got tested again. Thankfully, I had nothing serious. Just a urinary tract infection. I'm so scared of catching something every time we have sex, since he keeps rejecting the use of condoms. Needless to say, we don't have sex often.

Anyway, I feel like I've finally accepted that this is my life… It's not like it's uncommon. There are a lot of people who stay married for their kids, or for money, or even so they aren't alone. It could be worse. At least, he isn't beating me, not that I'd ever stand for that, mind you.

Right now, what keeps me sane is my work and my baby. They both need me, and I love them madly. I think I could be content without romantic love in my life…with God helping me.

It's Ezekiel's birthday next week. I'm organising a party for him at the spa. It will be the first time we're having a children's party at H4M, so I can't wait! It is actually for the kids only, much like a playdate. Lolu's concept :) I hope it brings us more business.

Aight… I want to see if I can nap now Ezekiel's sleeping. Later!

***

"Wow, Rachel! This is amazing! I can't wait to do Jenny's 3rd birthday here," Rochelle gushes, taking in the party decor of Event Hall A, the venue for Ezekiel's party.

The hall is big enough to be spacious and small enough to

be cosy. Rochelle likes The Lion King theme Rachel chose this year. And she really likes the Pride Rock set-up, an arrangement of beanbags and teddies to replicate a scene from the Disney movie.

The sign at the entrance says only nannies and event planners are allowed inside the hall. Moms can stay and make use of the spa, or go out or home to rest. Rochelle has booked a spa treatment, like a few of the other moms invited. After that, she plans to go shopping and come back for Jen and Justin at 6pm, when the party would be over.

Turning to Rachel, after handing Justin over to his nanny, Rochelle adds, "You've really done an incredible job with this place, Rachel. I'm so proud of you."

Rachel hugs her sister. "That means so much, Rochelle. Thanks!"

"So, how's Doug? I thought he'd be here," Rochelle asks.

"He can't today. He made his contribution, sha," Rachel says, implying the cheque she'd collected to settle the caterers of the event. It was enough to get a really fancy Simba cake made too.

"Does he have a choice?!" Rochelle giggles.

Rachel takes a deep breath. *You'd think so…* Getting money from Doug is like pulling teeth, even though his purse strings should be looser these days. She's never known someone who has been given so much to be so tight-fisted. It's something they often argue about.

As Rachel escorts Rochelle to the main spa upstairs, she asks, "How's Ekene? How are you guys coping with the new addition?"

"He's good. We're great, actually. The kids are a handful but a real blessing too."

Rachel coughs. "How about Ejike? Is he alright?"

Even though they've never really talked about it, Rachel knows everyone in her immediate family is now aware of her affair with Ejike. For the most part, she's kept her head down and tried to avoid the topic altogether. But it's been a long time, and she is curious to know how he's doing.

Rochelle gives Rachel a closed smile. "He's fine. He comes around once in a while. He seems to be taking his break-up well."

"Break-up?"

"Yes, he and Ifeoma broke up. Didn't you know?"

Rachel shakes her head.

"They've been separated since February. Ifeoma's back at her parents'."

"Wow. *Hmmm.*"

"Yup... It's sad, *sha*... I keep hearing about young couples breaking up, but I never thought it'd be so close to home. Anyway..." Rochelle sighs. They are at the door to the changing room leading to the spa. "You and Doug okay?"

"Yeah, we're fine," Rachel says, choosing to hold her tongue. "I'll let them know you're ready. I have to get back to the event hall."

"Sure. Later."

Rachel sighs as she goes back down. Ejike's separated? Is it because of her? Should she reach out? She swallows.

In the hallway leading to Event Hall A, Rachel is approached by one of the mothers, whose child is attending the party, a regular at the crèche. "Hi, Rachel. I really like what you did in there. I have my niece's 5th birthday coming up next month. Would we be able to use the hall?"

"Yeah, sure. The hall is available for birthday parties for children up to five years old."

"Okay, cool. I'll reach out to you tomorrow with more details. Any chance we can get a discount?"

"Members have 10% discount on the use of our halls. Would that be okay?"

"It's awesome! Thanks! And congrats on Ezi's birthday too."

"Thanks, Yejide."

That was fortunate, Rachel thinks. Her mind soon returns to Ejike. The feeling of loss is not as overwhelming as it had been. She knows if she contacts him now, she'll just reopen old wounds. It's best for everyone if they just move forward, she concludes.

CHAPTER THIRTY-ONE

It's a short drive from their home to the Oriental Hotel in Victoria Island, where some of her family and a few friends are meeting to celebrate Rachel's birthday. The black, off-the-shoulder, high-front, cocktail dress Rachel bought about a month ago, in preparation for her special day, now feels a little tight. After going back on the pill, she's put on a little more weight, but she's actively working to counter it. She'll have to watch what she eats tonight.

Doug is looking handsome in a pair of blue jeans and a dark purple shirt. His eyes are fixed on the road as he conversates via a Bluetooth headset. He's been on his call since she came down the stairs to leave for their outing.

Rachel smoothens her dress. She's feeling great about herself today and looking forward to hanging with her family and friends. She looks out of the window at the night lights as they cross from Lekki to Victoria Island via the toll gate. It is indeed a beautiful night.

At the hotel, they take the elevators to the Oriental Garden restaurant. There, they meet the rest of their party. Rachel receives and gives hugs and kisses to her friends and siblings and their spouses. Only the youths are out tonight.

Doug ends his call and greets everyone, before they take their seats. He kicks off the night with, "Thanks everyone for coming out tonight to celebrate my queen."

Rachel beams at her friends and family, who are all smiling back at her.

***

The double portion of prawn dumplings Rachel ordered have arrived. Rachel's been dreaming of them since she learnt they'd be dining at this restaurant. She picks a dumpling with a tooth-pick and takes a bite. *Hmmm… Awful!* She spits it into a napkin.

"Is it me or is something foul with these dumplings?" she asks Rochelle, who's sitting next to her.

Rochelle picks one and pops it in her mouth. "Hmmm… Yummy! It's seems fine to me."

Rachel puts the rest of her cut dumpling to her nose and withdraws it. She can't stomach the smell. *Oh, no!* She loves dumplings, especially prawn dumplings. She pushes her plate aside, shaking her head. "You can have it if you want…"

Rochelle collects another one. "Are you sure you don't want any?"

Rachel shakes her head and looks for something else to eat from among the spread. She settles for the white rice and chicken and broccoli sauce.

Ekene takes one of the dumplings. "These are delicious, Rachel!" In a lowered voice, he adds, "Are you sure you're not pregnant?" He remembers how Rochelle seemed to develop a sensitive nose and new taste buds with her pregnancies.

Rachel begins to laugh it off and stops mid-laughter. She has been feeling nauseous lately…and her breast have been a bit tender. She just thought it was her period coming. *Oh, no! God, no!*

***

The next day, a visit to her gynaecologist confirms that Rachel's ten weeks pregnant, which sounds about right. The last time they'd had sex would have been the night of Doug's birthday in July. She'd been on the pill, but remembers missing one about that time, and since she was on her period, she thought she'd be safe and didn't take the morning-after pill. *Oh, crap!*

That afternoon, Rachel gets a call from Doug when she's back home. He'd been eager for her to go and confirm the pregnancy, as he's keen on another child, particularly a girl.

"I'm pregnant," she says.

"Praise God! Is it a girl?"

Rachel raises her brow, even though she's aware he can't see. "We won't know until the 20th week or so. I'm 10 weeks."

"Okay, cool. Get some rest. I'll see you later."

"Okay. Bye."

Another baby... Another reason to endure and hope for a turnaround in her marriage. *God, You know best. Help me to make a loving home for this baby...*

***

Rachel's in her second trimester. She now sports a noticeable bump and dresses to show it off. She loves the attention and assistance her delicate condition affords her, at least from strangers. She's quite surprised that rather than show more care, Doug has been as disinterested in her as ever, not even offering to help with her new medical expenses.

However, she's been taking advantage of the classes and therapies at Haven for Moms, and she's feeling so much better about having the baby. She may not be happily married, but she's a happily pregnant mommy. In fact, with the way she's glowing, she could be the poster-mom for Haven for Moms. No longer camera-shy, she's started posing for more photos and is excited about her pre-delivery shoot in her third trimester.

Today, she went in for an ultrasound at the hospital. Her baby is growing fine, though the gynae said her pregnancy is high-risk due to her age. He advised that she takes things easy and cuts down on stressful activities. So, instead of going back to the office, Rachel decides to go home.

There's a strange lady entering her compound just as Rachel turns into her street. Rachel enquires from the security guard after she's driven in and parked her car.

"Na Oga's sister, Ma."

"Oga's sister? When did she come?"

"It has been long, Ma… Since October."

"Okay, thanks."

Rather than go into her home, Rachel goes to the boys' quarters to meet this 'sister'. Why didn't Doug tell her his sister was around? Why would his sister even want to hide her presence from Rachel?

Rachel knocks on the door to the external studio apartment attached to their home. The person seems to be bidding their time or pretending to be asleep. Rachel knocks again, louder, shouting, "I know you are there! Can you open this door?!"

The door swings open, and the young lady shows her face. She must be in her early 20s, but she doesn't show any respect to the older woman before her.

"Who are you?" Rachel demands to know. "What are you doing in my house?!"

"Mr Dog said I can stay…"

Mr Who? OMG! Dodging the comedic moment, Rachel continues her inquisition, "What's your name, and who is Mr Doug to you?"

"Susan. He is my brother's friend."

"How long have you been staying here?"

"A few weeks…"

Rachel wants to ask more questions but decides it's best she saves them for her husband. She turns around and leaves the woman standing in the doorway. How can Doug have a strange woman staying in their house and not tell her?! What exactly is his relationship to Susan?

***

Doug's phone is giving a busy signal now. It rang the first two times she called, but he didn't pick. Rachel sighs deeply. She really doesn't want to have this conversation over WhatsApp, and she has no idea when Doug will be home.

Now she has been discovered, the girl is freely walking about the compound and even chatting and laughing with the security guard. Rachel can hear them through the kitchen window. Unfortunately, she can't tell what they're saying because they're speaking Yoruba, a local tongue but foreign to Rachel, who's from the south. However, she can't but wonder if she's the butt of their jokes.

When it's late, and it doesn't look like Doug will be home tonight, Rachel decides to send him a message.

"Hi, Doug. There's a woman in the boys' quarters. She said you put her there... Why?"

Thirty minutes later, a response comes. *"She's renting it."*

Rachel tries to call but the line is cut again. Doug sends another message. *"I can't talk now. What is it?"*

"Why didn't you tell me you're renting out our boys' quarter? I just found out that she's been there for weeks!"

"Look, I'm busy. We'll talk later."

Rachel flings the phone across the bed in her frustration. Is this how people treat their wives? Do they all make decisions that concern them without involving them? And why the secrecy for God's sake?!

Also, something isn't adding up. If Susan's a tenant, why did Abdul say she is "Oga's sister," unless Doug told him that? What exactly is going on here?

***

Rachel's still up when Doug returns home at 1am. She waits for the sound of the front door opening, but no such thing happens. Where is he?

She can hardly sleep thinking of where he might have gone and what he could be doing. Her gut is telling her he has

246

gone to meet Susan, and perhaps that's why she's been secretly residing in their house. Should she go down and investigate...? *God, why would he do a thing like that?*

Brimming with pent-up frustration, Rachel's body shakes. She's so mad at Doug! It's one thing for him to be messing around outside, but to bring the disgrace to her home?! And while she's carrying his baby?

She wants to go downstairs and lock the front door. Lock him out of the house! Wherever he's gone to, he can stay there all night for all she cares.

Sitting up in bed, she slips her feet into a pair of slippers. It is then that she hears the front door unlock, open, and shut. Checking her phone, she confirms that it is 1:25 in the morning. She decides to go down anyway.

"Where have you been? You've been home for like 20 minutes!" Rachel confronts him.

"Go back to sleep," he says, going to the sofa to make himself comfortable.

Maddened by his response, she shouts, "Who is Susan?!"

"I already told you she's a tenant. I'm exhausted, okay? Go to sleep!"

"I will when I know what you've been doing for the last 20 minutes..."

Doug huffs. "With all the fine women outside, it's this one you're worried about. I was just checking the generator, okay?"

Rachel pauses. That's plausible, but she's not convinced. Regardless, it will have to suffice. Her chest feels tight from all the pain and anger she's bottling in. All she wanted was someone to love and care for, who would do the same for her. *What the hell is this?!*

***

Am I doing the right thing?

This is Rachel's constant thought, especially since she found out that she's pregnant again. Why would she want to bring another baby into her unhappy home? Her instincts are telling her that she's in for a major crash, the way things are going with Doug. Why is she still trying to hold it together when he obviously doesn't give a damn?!

Whenever she sees Doug acting so normal, in company, and pretending that he treats her right, Rachel feels such anger...and hatred for the liar she knows him to be. She really feels like she's bidding time, postponing the inevitable. Her depression over her marriage is beginning to overflow into other areas of her life, and the thought keeps coming to her – *it's not worth it. I don't want to live...*

Rachel wipes her tears with tissues from a box on her desk. She's got a lot of work to do, and she needs to focus. With Christmas just days away, the spa is abuzz with activities. Tomorrow, the crèche is hosting a Christmas party for their members' children. The moms are supposed to buy one present for another child, as part of the Secret Santa exchange programme. Extra gifts will be donated to Rachel's chosen orphanage.

Rachel presses the buzzer for Lolu to come to her office. A few seconds later, Lolu opens the door.

"Yes, Ma?"

"Have all the parents brought their gifts?"

"Yes, Ma. They're all under the Christmas tree."

Rachel nods. "How many extras do we have?"

"There are about...eighty...*five*? I'll confirm," Lolu says. "By the way, there's a lady here to see you."

"You didn't get her name?"

"She refused to say, Ma. She's with a baby..."

"Oh, okay. Let her come in."

***

Rachel's surprised to see Bose standing in her doorway, carrying an infant in her arms. Bose doesn't look like herself. She looks exhausted, thin, and haggard. What happened to her?

Concern overtakes anger, causing Rachel to rise and go to her friend. "Bose, are you okay?"

Bose shakes her head as she lets the tears flow. "Rachel, I'm so sorry. I'm so sorry for how I treated you. Please forgive me."

"I forgive you," Rachel says. Leading Bose to sit on the sofa, Rachel carries her baby from her. "Can I give this to one of the nannies?"

Bose nods, and Rachel steps out with the little one. When she returns, she sits across from Bose and asks, "What happened? Whose baby is that?"

Bose looks up at her friend, and their eyes meet. "You know whose." Rachel swallows. She feels the shakes starting but resists. "I'm sorry, Rachel. I didn't want to hurt you, but I've been so lonely, and I've been jealous of you. Doug told me all sorts of things about you, how you behaved like a spoilt rich girl, were disrespectful, and even withheld sex from him. I thought you didn't value what you had..."

"You were my friend, why didn't you come to me?"

"I don't know why. I guess I wanted to believe him... I've sort of always had a crush on him," Bose swallows. "But I know better now."

Rachel looks on as Bose wipes her tears. She rises up to get the box of tissues, and Bose takes a couple. Rachel waits patiently for Bose to resume her tale.

"Before I got pregnant, I lent Doug some money he said he needed for his studio. He promised to pay back with interest, and I really believed in what he was doing. I gave him most of my savings. When I found out I was pregnant, I told him and asked him for some money. It was then I saw his true colour."

Rachel's shaking her head. She swallows.

"He refused and denied that the baby was is. He accused me of being a whore and sleeping with his talents. I couldn't even believe it. *Last last*, I thought he would just give me my money back, but *lie lie*! He said he doesn't have it, that he has invested it, and I'll get it when he makes a profit. Since then, he doesn't even answer my calls or anything, and they won't let me in his studio."

"Oh, my God," Rachel breathes. The shakes have now taken over her hands. Rachel fights to stay calm, even as tears burn the back of her eyes.

"I even tried to get the police involved, but since there was no proof of the money I gave him, they said I have no case."

"You paid *cash*?!"

Bose nods. "N500,000. I had been saving that money for three years. I stored it in my house because of all these ATM scammers."

"Oh, Bose…"

"I know. I was stupid. But I need your help, please! Things have been impossible since I got pregnant. I haven't been able to get back to work. My parents are struggling, so they haven't even been able to help me either. They gave me all they could when I gave birth in April. I've just been getting by with help from Church since. Please, you have to help me, Rachel! I can't make rent."

Rachel nods, tears streaming down her face. *Oh, Jesus! What have I gotten myself into?*

TO BE CONTINUED…

ACKNOWLEDGEMENTS

To my Father in Heaven; for being my muse, my counsellor, and my strength. To my father on Earth; for doing your very best for me. To my mom; for your sacrifices and unconditional love. To my heart; for your sincerity and perseverance. To Ijeoma and Chioma; for your editorial input and advice on this project. To my readers; for your feedback, encouragement, and prayers!

THANK YOU!

ABOUT THE AUTHOR

Hi, I am Ufuomaee. I am a writer, blogger, and Christian fiction author. I tell stories to help young people make the right choice before marriage and deal with challenges that often arise during and after. I also use parables and poetry to teach about God's love. When I'm not writing or working, I love to watch action movies and romcoms on Netflix. I also love reading romantic and inspiring books by other amazing authors, which I review on my blog, www.ufuomaee.blog.

CONNECT WITH ME

BECOME A PATRON: www.patreon.com/ufuomaee
AUTHOR PAGE: www.amazon.com/author/ufuomaee
FOLLOW ON FACEBOOK: @ufuomaeedotcom
TWITTER: @UfuomaeeB
INSTAGRAM: @ufuomaee
WEBSITE: www.ufuomaee.org
BLOG: blog.ufuomaee.org
EMAIL: me@ufuomaee.com

Check out my full catalogue of books at
books.ufuomaee.org

Printed in Great Britain
by Amazon

64855244R00154